SAFE WORLD GONE

SAFE WORLD GONE

Short stories by women from Wales

Edited by

Patricia Duncker & Janet Thomas

HONNO MODERN FICTION

Published by Honno
'Ailsa Craig', Heol y Cawl, Dinas Powys
South Glamorgan, Wales, CF6 4AH

A catalogue record for this book is available from The British Library.

ISBN 1 870206 770
EAN 978 1870206 778

The publisher gratefully acknowledges the financial support of the
Welsh Books Council

Cover design & typesetting: Nicola Schumacher
Cover image: Ryan McVay, Photodisc Blue, Getty Images

Printed in Wales by Gomer

Contents

Introduction i

King Arthur is Dead
Dahlian Kirby 1

The Cry of Bairns
Patricia Ace 9

Making Perfume
Laura Morris 17

Last Tango in Sketty
Barbara McGaughey 23

Fleeced
Sue Coffey 31

The Cactus Man
Vanessa Gebbie 39

Me, Daphne Dupree and the Bible of Decisions
Nicola Daly 49

Knitting with Kate Moss
Penny Simpson 55

One for Rose Cottage
S A Tillotson 63

The Use of a Mother
Ruth Joseph 69

Early One Morning
Angela Rigby 77

A Journey to Berlin 1964
Linda Baxter 83

Lemon Mousse Surprise
Melanie Mauthner 95

Charlie
Jenny Sullivan 103

Tossed
Lesley Coburn ... 111

The Accident
Imogen Rhia Herrad ... 115

Across the Downs
Carolyn Lewis ... 121

Rash
Janet Thomas ... 133

Flora
Sarah Todd Taylor ... 139

Unwrapped
Lara Clough ... 145

Swimming
Sarah Jackman ... 151

Son and Lover
Lesley Phillips ... 161

How to Murder your Mother
Patricia Duncker ... 169

The Red Dress
Brenda Curtis ... 177

One Little Room
Sue Morgan ... 183

Gasping
Jo Verity ... 189

The Essence of Kasyapa
Alexandra North ... 195

The Cat's Real Name
Cal Walters ... 205

Biographical Notes ... 211

Introduction

What is a short story, and how short is short? Some short fictions can be as little as three hundred words, some run for over forty pages. We would argue that the definition of a short story depends on its relationship to the reader: a short story is written to be read in one sitting. A novel and its characters may accompany a reader through a period of their life, but a good piece of short fiction should work like a firecracker or a depth charge. Its aftermath, even when the explosion is subtle, muted and works slowly, should be far-reaching, lasting, like an echo endlessly repeated. It is this element of shock which accounts for very passionate or hostile responses to the form. A good short story should be a disturbing rather than a comforting experience. A good short story should make you think.

The theme for the 2007 short fiction anthology was 'the turning point'. Every work of short fiction has a turning point of some kind, which usually signals a moment of no return, of transformation. In asking for stories that focussed on this moment of change, we wanted to encourage writers to explore the form's potential to shock and resonate. The short story is an experimental, unsafe form, and therefore perfect for expressing experiences of disturbance and risk.

The title *Safe World Gone* comes from Dahlian Kirby's story *King Arthur is Dead*, which expresses this double meaning of change as danger and liberation. How would you feel if you believed that 'the safe world was gone'? Thrilled or afraid? This divided reaction echoes throughout the collection. Many of the stories demonstrate a turning point as positive, as liberation and possibility, including *King Arthur is Dead*, Janet Thomas's *Rash* and Ruth Joseph's *The Use of a Mother*. The moment of change can be a tiny shift in perspective, for example Sarah Jackman's beautifully observed *Swimming*, where the teenage narrator simply comes to understand the power balance between her and her friend in a new way. It can mean finally facing up to what you know about yourself, in Penny Simpson's honestly drawn *Knitting with Kate Moss*. Or it can be a massive decision, the beginning of a new adventure, like the moment where Imogen Rhia Herrad's heroine thrillingly takes off into the unknown in *The Accident*. These stories capture the longing we all have to reinvent ourselves, confront the limitations in our lives, and take the chance to start on a clean page.

Several stories exuberantly celebrate adventure. In Barbara McGaughey's vibrant *Last Tango in Sketty* magic breaks down the dull barriers of normal life. In Nicola Daly's *Me, Daphne Dupree and the Bible of Decisions*, it's not a love potion, but a self-help book that enables the contained heroine to expand her choices. In Lesley Philips' *Son and Lover* self-expression begins with a blackboard. In *Son and Lover*, the risk taken is not all triumphant, the magic does not last, but this story makes the point that change is positive even when it is not long lasting, that an 'almost and nearly' experience is also worthwhile.

Sometimes escape from a problem can simply mean looking it in the eye. In Linda Baxter's *A Journey to Berlin 1964*, the narrator thinks she is dealing with a clear choice, only to find there are other options. In Jenny Sullivan's *Charlie*, with Sullivan's typical energy and life, a curse has to be faced to be outwitted. In *Lemon Mousse Surprise* by Melanie Mauthner a revelation the narrator is dreading turns out not to be such a dilemma after all.

But these changes are not without risk. In Lara Clough's *Unwrapped* the possibility of rescue is ambivalent. It is also temptation. In Patricia Duncker's *How to Murder Your Mother* one member of a family's freedom is won, deliberately, at the expense of another. This story acknowledges that the longing to escape is mixed with anger, frustration and a longing for revenge. Brenda Curtis's *The Red Dress* is clearly a story of liberation, but where the vulnerability of the person trying to change is deeply felt. He is reliant on the understanding of others. In Sue Morgan's *One Little Room*, a tale that plays cleverly on our modern ambivalent attitudes to close relationships between teachers and pupils, a moment that shows the narrator the widening possibilities in life is also laced with suspicion. Lines are being crossed, in a way that feels both positive and dangerous.

Change does not always mean liberation. In Leslie Coburn's unsettling *Tossed*, new knowledge is a prison, trapping the narrator. Another teenage woman, the heroine of Angela Rigby's *Early One Morning*, comes to realise too late the risks she has been taking, that force on her a further terrible choice. And in Laura Morris's *Making Perfume* the child heroine is not able to fight the change coming in her life, because she is not yet able to understand or express her own feelings. *Making Perfume* is a clever, delicate story where the real moment of realisation is in the reader, as our perspective on the relationship we are being shown changes.

Change is not necessarily chosen – Jo Verity's *Gasping* is a true depth-charge story, but where a new knowledge of reality has pulled the ground from under the character's feet, not enriched her. In Sue Coffey's sharp, vivid *Fleeced*, the narrator has to lose her innocence in order to learn that she can fight back. Patricia Ace's *The Cry of Bairns* also contains a loss of innocence. Here the turning point is the realisation that evil is lurking in the community, because it cannot be defeated until it is recognised. In Vanessa Gebbie's *The Cactus Man*, it is the evil inside the narrator's own character that has to be faced before it can be resisted.

And change is not necessarily wanted. These stories look too at characters who refuse to change. Carolyn Lewis's *Across the Downs* makes a powerful contrast to *King Arthur is Dead*, where the narrator instinctively resists the new friendship offered to her and stays as she is. Sarah Todd Taylor's *Flora* depicts the central character's extreme battle to resist aging and change, an absolute refusal to face how change is part of life. In Stephanie Tillotson's fierce *One for Rose Cottage* a woman's attempt to stay in the safe world, to 'behave', breaks her spirit completely. These stories demonstrate that resistance to change and risk is a refusal of life, and can be impossible. The safe world is a trap – and closed off resistance is another kind of temptation. The choice between staying closed off or opening yourself up to feeling also forms the basis of Alexandra North's haunting *The Essence of Kasyapa*, where whether the narrator has changed or not, whether there is hope or not, is left to the reader. There is no safe world. We end the collection with Cal Walters' *The Cat's Real Name*, a moving, resonant tale about the stories and lies we tell ourselves in order to survive.

We had far more male narrators in the stories submitted for this collection than usual, which perhaps expresses a willingness in our writers to try new voices, to tell fresh stories, to change. We also had far more stories submitted for this collection than our previous anthologies, demonstrating perhaps the way change and choices are so central to all fiction writing. We thank all the writers who have submitted work and Honno for all their support of the collection – and for their support of women's writing both from the past and by women now.

Patricia Duncker and Janet Thomas

King Arthur is Dead

Dahlian Kirby

I used to change trains at Liverpool Street Station. It was before they did it up and it still reminded you of scenes from *The Elephant Man*. Even without steam trains, it was just that kind of place. I worked in Ilford and lived in Hackney, a dreadful place to get in and out of. I had everything worked out precisely. If I got on the farthest carriage at Ilford, if I walked briskly across the bridge at Liverpool Street and if there were no more than three people queuing, I had time to buy a carton of freshly squeezed orange juice and a croissant then get into the first carriage before the train to Clapton left. Once on the train I had eleven minutes to consume my goodies before we pulled into Clapton Station. That way, if Richard was waiting for me at the station, he wouldn't know I'd been eating. Richard would probably not have considered my daily snack a sin, just an unnecessary indulgence. Besides, it's supposed to be good to have a little mystery in a marriage.

On that particular day, the first time, I'd queued patiently behind a woman buying a large coffee and a Danish pastry. She fumbled with her change. I began to grow impatient and wonder if I should forgo my repast in favour of a dignified stroll to the train. Then she fainted. Sort of crumpled at the knees and sank slowly and gracefully to the ground. I went to inform a porter whilst numerous less formal people loosened her clothing. I missed my train.

I waited till the fuss had died down then purchased a large fresh orange juice and a mushroom croissant. I felt a little anxious: what if Richard waited for my train? What if he worried? I watched the board for details of the next train. I considered a cab. But Richard wouldn't approve of that. Not the expense of a cab. I could take the cab to Clapton Station and then walk home. But he could be waiting for me at the station, see me getting out of the cab.

If you have been involved in an extramarital affair my problem must seem a little tame. Well, Richard and I, we were a little tame. It's not that he dominated, it was just easier for me to fall in with his ways. I sat on the platform and read the now flashing notice informing me that due to a derailment, there would be a delay in trains to Hackney. *A tramp sat down beside me.*

I turned away from the imagined stench of the dirty down-and-out, moved none-too subtly to the end of the bench and stared into space. He shuffled nearer and bent forward, looking at my face. Chin in air, determined to avoid any action which could be misinterpreted as encouragement, I sat rigidly in a way that only a British woman in a London station could. I denied that he was there.

Minutes passed. He laid a hand gently on my arm; from the corner of my eye I could see his profile. Large hooked nose, long wispy pale-coloured hair. I sighed and moved my body further away. I was now twisted into an impossibly uncomfortable position. He sighed and mirrored my action. I turned to him and gave him a long look of disapproval. He did the same back. I could feel my neck and face redden. I was embarrassed, but also angry. I made a determined effort to relax my shoulders and drank from my large polystyrene cup. This was wrong. I usually drank the orange on the train. I bit into the now cold and greasy croissant. From the folds of his brown robe the tramp brought a quarter bottle of scotch. He drank from it. When he spoke his voice was surprisingly light and cultured.

'Could you possibly spare a drop of your orange juice? It would make this rather rough whisky a little more palatable.'

I, of course, ignored him. I turned my attention to the board in front of me. It informed me that there wouldn't be a train for another fifty-five minutes. It would have to be a taxi then. I stood and walked towards an exit. He rose and followed me. I felt uncomfortable and turned around to look for the protection of fellow travellers, who all rushed past, presumably in order to buy their fresh orange juice and be home in time for their spouses. I joined the taxi queue, he stood beside me. I turned and boldly handed him the orange juice. I couldn't take it into the taxi and there were no bins around.

His hand shot out from the robe and took the juice. He tipped half of his whisky into the cup and held it out to me. 'Share it with me,' he suggested.

The queue turned and watched us. I looked to the nearest man for help. He looked at his feet. I tried to catch the attention of two women standing next to me, two women whom I recognised from many journeys between Liverpool Street and Clapton. They quickly turned to each other and started up a vital conversation about the evening's TV viewing. The long bony arm was still stretched towards me. I looked at him, a final attempt to shrivel him with my respectability. He smiled, lips curved and eyes merry with amusement. I took the bottle from him and sipped the whisky and orange. My life changed.

If I left work seven minutes early, if the Ilford to Liverpool Street train was on time, if I took a cab, I was able to have thirty-five minutes in the company of King Arthur. That was who he introduced himself to me as. He would wait for me on the bench next to the orange juice stall, reading a paper or gazing into space. I would purchase a large fresh orange juice and two croissants. I would stroll to the bench, he would move up for me. We would eat the croissants and drink the juice, occasionally laced with whisky or rum. How much sweeter the juice tasted, how much tastier the mushrooms, when I shared them with King Arthur at a leisurely pace. Some days we would talk, some days not.

He was very knowledgeable about history, particularly English history. He would scoff at the theories of where he'd been buried. I must admit at first our meetings made me feel self-conscious. Sitting on a bench with a loony who thinks he's King Arthur drinking whisky and orange whilst commuters hurried past was not part of my usual life. Richard and I didn't believe in drink. Richard and I were angry at the suggestions that there were some people in England who were homeless. We believed that such people were parasites on tax payers. We believed that they had fallen through their own immoral behaviour. We felt they were tainted, had diseases that others would catch if they sat too closely. Diseases of the mind as well as the body.

King Arthur knew all the others – the papers called them homeless people, Arthur called them tramps. They often stopped to inquire after his health. Sometimes one of them would ask me how I was, and offer a sip from their cider bottle, which I always politely refused. Sometimes I would fetch a coffee for myself, Arthur and some of his friends from the orange juice stall. Each time I stepped off the Ilford train and Arthur wasn't there, I felt a sense of loss. Each time he was, I felt elated and rather afraid. I had broken the rules of decency and would surely fall from grace.

Richard suspected nothing. How could he? I continued to be what he wanted me to be. As far as he knew I was a good wife and excellent housekeeper, working in a very respectable office till we had saved enough money to buy a house. Richard and I didn't think you should bring children into the world if you didn't have a garden.

King Arthur hated the police with a passion that I found embarrassing. After all, I was married to one of them. Every time he saw a policeman he would start to shake and wave a long bony finger at him. Curses would be muttered, then he'd get to his feet and walk away without even saying goodbye to me. This was in contrast to Arthur's usual impeccable manners.

One July afternoon, as we sat sucking orange lollies, I heard Arthur groan, and as his spare hand appeared from under his robe, and a long bony finger waved, I noticed two policemen approaching a tramp. She was banging on a cigarette machine and swearing at it. Arthur started to shake and utter his curses. I was cross and tired after work and wanted to enjoy my lolly before the airless journey home.

'Arthur!' I said. 'For goodness' sake calm down, eat your lolly. It's too hot to get all worked up.'

He ignored me, and rising to his feet, began to condemn the two officers of the law to eternal damnation. They, not noting his royal fury, had reached the old woman and were standing very close to her, watching as she hammered on the machine. The policemen started to laugh at the woman. She turned round and looked them up and down.

'Hello gorgeous,' said one, and both roared at the joke.

Arthur moved forward, I grabbed his hand and pulled him firmly back onto the bench. He turned and snarled at me.

'Arthur,' I said, 'she is breaking the law.'

I knew I sounded pompous, but I thought the woman was bringing trouble on herself.

The second policeman grabbed the woman's arm and pushed her backwards, away from the machine. She fell and we all got a viewing of her knickerless parts. She lay there, subdued, like a sick animal on its back, unable to struggle back into life. The policeman laughed, the first made a mime of being sick. The commuters hurried back to their spouses and their safety. Arthur pulled away from me and walked proudly towards the policemen. They had by now moved away from the woman, perhaps she was already forgotten. Arthur stood in front of them. He looked at them; they were forced to stop, if only to negotiate a route round him. The woman lay on the ground. I walked over to her and offered her some assistance.

'You'll never do it on your own,' she said practically. 'I weigh fourteen stone.'

I turned to see what kind of trouble Arthur was getting into, just in time to see one of the policemen take him by the shoulder and march him towards the nearest exit. The other followed behind, looking rather embarrassed, to give him his due. Arthur screamed and cursed. The commuters, heads down, hurried by. Only a lone youth, distracted from picking a pocket, stared at the policemen and the King.

'Leave the poor old bugger alone!' he shouted after them. 'Fascist pigs!' he yelled. Then followed them at a safe distance to see what might happen.

I pushed past him and tried to catch up with the rapidly disappearing trio. 'Nick your purse, did he?' the boy asked as I passed him. 'Poor old bugger was probably hungry. Care in the fucking community!'

The policemen were trying to fold Arthur up and put him in a police car when I caught up with them. 'Tell them who I am,' he said to me softly.

'King Arthur,' I said without pause. Because that was what he had told me. That was indeed his name.

'Where did you get that briefcase?' said the second policeman to me.

'Debenhams,' I said. 'Now let Arthur go, he hasn't harmed you.'

I confess to feeling more than a little out of my depth. Should I call a solicitor? Or the Citizens Advice Bureau? Arthur demanded more practical assistance.

'Get these nutters off me. They intend to do me harm.'

I pulled at Arthur's arm, the policeman pulled at the other. His friend radioed for assistance. Then, as the tug-of-war over King Arthur heated up, Arthur accidentally backed into the policeman with the radio, who fell into the gutter. Arthur looked at me – I took my chance and hit the other policeman on the side of the head with my over-stuffed briefcase. We fled.

For an older gentleman, Arthur had some stamina. He took my hand and we ran down a series of back alleys then out on to a main road. We stopped for breath as a bus pulled up, and Arthur pushed me up on to its platform. The bus pulled away, leaving Arthur waving to me from the pavement.

I never saw King Arthur again.

Next day I skipped work and went looking for Arthur. Not a sign. I asked a couple of familiar dossers but they just shook their heads. I took a fortnight off work and searched the day shelters and hostels. I told Richard I was sick. And truly I was. After returning to work I continued to look out for the King, always hoping he'd be there, sitting on the bench by the orange juice stall, waving a quarter bottle of whisky at me.

On this particular Friday evening, my train was delayed due to another derailment. I was sitting on our bench drinking orange juice when an old lady limped across the station in front of me. She turned slowly and looked at me, then painfully hobbled towards me. She sat as Arthur had done that very first time, and tried to make eye contact. I turned to her.

'King Arthur is dead,' she said.

'You don't have a bottle, do you?' I asked.

'No, I don't, but there's a pub out there.'

I helped her to her feet and we left the station, crossing the road to a pub with the name Dirty Dick's. It was dark and gloomy inside, the floor and walls covered with a thick layer of dust. The tables and chairs were made from old beer barrels. I fetched us both a pint of bitter. We sipped it in silence. When we had drained our glasses, I glanced at my watch.

'Someone waiting at home?' she asked.

I shook my head and took our glasses back to the bar for a re-fill. The youth at the bar turned and looked at me.

'Here's to the King,' said the old lady. We raised our glasses. I started to feel a bit tipsy. It was a wonderful feeling. But I wanted to cry, because Arthur was dead and I was about to go home and tell my husband that I wanted a divorce. The safe world was crumbling.

The youth placed two pints of bitter on the barrel in front of us. 'I'm

Ross,' he said. 'I was there when you rescued King Arthur.'

'I'm Karen,' I said and picked up the pint of beer. 'And this is…'

'Guinevere,' said my drinking partner.

The safe world was gone.

The Cry of Bairns

Patricia Ace

A house without the cry of bairns is like
a farm without kye or sheep – Gaelic saying

We were wakened in the middle of the night by a knocking on the door. At first it was barely discernible through the noise of the wind which roared round our four walls like an angry father, but soon enough the urgent rapping penetrated our dreams and we stirred in our cots, swimming through soup into consciousness. Aunt Rachel reached the door as I sat up in my cot. A blast of icy air gusted into the room, making my scalp prickle, as the shadowy form in the doorway grabbed Aunt Rachel by the wrist.

'Rachel. It's time.'

The room brightened slowly in the moonlight and then darkened again as the wind blew ragged clouds across the moon. We scrabbled in the blackness for our clothes and equipment, then banged the cottage door behind us as we headed out into the night. The ground beneath my feet felt solid and dense, but all around was chaos. We kept close to the line of cottages as we made our way along the street. I glanced out from the plaid that swathed my head to the bay where the moon hung full and pregnant above the lashing waves. The jagged peaks of Dun met my gaze from across the water like a sleeping dragon, the moonlit white breakers surrounding the island with fire. A few doors along, Neil Gillies ducked down to his doorway. Aunt Rachel and I followed and came at once upon our business.

Ann Gillies was leaning on the table in the middle of the room, swaying and murmuring. Her prayer was almost inaudible above the wind which rattled under the eaves of the tin roof. From a cot in the corner, two small children, a boy and a girl, stared sleepily at their mother as she stood braced at the table, offering her song to God.

'Here's Rachel now,' the man said to his wife, 'and Lizzy McDonald to help her.' He nodded in my direction.

'I'll take the children to Mother's, Annie, and come back when the sun's up. Callum, Jane, come kiss your mother,' he said.

The children shuffled forward out of the gloom and offered their pale faces up for their mother's kisses.

'Be good for your father,' Ann told them.

'God bless you, Annie,' said the man as he stumbled out into the dark.

Aunt Rachel has been midwife on the island since she was my age, nineteen. Her mother had done it before her and Aunt Rachel had been along to help since she was twelve or thirteen years of age, so you could say it came naturally to her. She was used to seeing the women in their great pain and suffering. She made teas from herbs that would hasten a birth or slow one up if it came on too quickly. She knew what to do if a child was coming the wrong way or if two came at once or if one arrived blue-grey and limp, as sometimes they did. She would put her finger in its mouth to clear it, pat it on the back and rub its floppy limbs with her brisk, nimble fingers until its skin started to glow a soft pink. Then she wrapped them in a plaid and laid them by the small fire to keep warm. Some were born almost black and for those there was nothing even Aunt Rachel could do. That was just Nature and God's way. But others uttered their first cry before their bodies had been fully born. As soon as their heads were out, Aunt Rachel hooked the cord with her finger and lifted it free of the child, so often the cord was round the child's neck, and the child would cry out and take its first gulp of air and then the body would follow all in a rush, slippery as a fish, into the safe guiding hands of my Aunt. I'd seen it happen so a score of times since I had been helping Aunt Rachel. I secretly hoped she would never ask me to catch one. I felt sure I should drop it on its head if she did. Aunt Rachel was a miracle worker. There was no doubt she had saved many babies from the horrors of their own births and also many mothers. Whatever it was that she did with her herbs and her ointments, her needle and her scissors, it was universally acknowledged as a good thing and the women of the island were grateful for it. That meant that we were never short of birds to eat or hand-knitted stockings, even in hard times and there were plenty of those. Aunt Rachel herself had never had children, had never been married in fact. She told me she had no interest in men and as for childbirth, she'd seen enough of that to know it wasn't for her. My mother always said it wasn't natural for a young girl to attend confinements as Aunt Rachel had and it was no surprise that Aunt Rachel had been 'put off' men because of it. But my mother never understood the way certain things were done on the island, being an outsider herself.

Ann Gillies' boy arrived before sunrise, in the eye of the storm. After the high winds, a strange sort of calm had descended so that the baby's first cries sounded eerily loud in the sudden stillness. The oil in the lamp was getting low but our eyes had adjusted to the semi-darkness and the birth was straightforward. He was Ann's sixth child, her body understood what was required of it. I'd been at the birth of her last child, another boy, but he hadn't lived ten days. The two who'd been born before him also perished of the eight-day sickness. For no matter how many babies my Aunt managed to drag kicking and screaming into this life, there were few who survived beyond their first month. There was some sort of curse on the children of the island. Of those born sound more than half fell victim to this hateful disease. The first sign came on the fourth or fifth day after birth when the child gave up sucking at the breast. By the seventh day their gums became so clenched together that there was no way to feed them or even give them water. Soon after this they became convulsed with muscle spasm and stiffness, arching their little backs and drawing down their chins in tormented fits. By this their strength was exhausted and soon they died.

There is no way of knowing what causes this blight on our children. The Minister blames Sin, although a more God-fearing people than those inhabiting this isle would be hard to find. My mother said it was the custom of intermarriage, for it is difficult not to marry your cousin with less than twenty families in the village. My mother herself was different, of course, a rarity, having come from Lochinver, in Sutherland, to serve the Minister. She could speak English, read music, sing and sew, which marked her out from the other local women. But what use was her singing and sewing, reading and writing, when she went to her watery grave before her time? If she had not been so energetic, so smart and talkative and gay, perhaps she would not have gone with the men, with my father and brother and the others, on that fateful journey to the

Long Island. Twelve years I have lived with my Aunt Rachel, my father's sister. Twelve years since I held my Grandmother's hand and waved my family off in that boat with its cargo of cloth and salt-fish and precious lives. I can still hear my mother's last words carried on the brisk breeze from the sea, 'Don't cry, Lizzy! I'll bring you back a doll, my darling!'

Instead she left me a legacy of coldness. The cold care of my Aunt, who'd never wanted a child. And the cold, stiff bodies of week-old babies buried in the hard ground.

'Girl, cease yer dreamin'…there's work to be done.'

Aunt Rachel shuffled towards me, the scrap of a child held out in her hands.

'Here, take this boy and fix his wound. You have the oil about you?'

I nodded dumbly, feeling tired and disoriented by the sleepless night and my own bitter thoughts.

'I'm out for a breath.' Aunt Rachel went out of the cottage, digging in her apron for her pipe.

I took a deep lungful of the smoky black air which hung in the room like a pall. The tang of the birth smell caught in my throat making me cough. The mother lay in her cot in the corner shivering slightly under a thin blanket.

'Mrs Gillies, don't you want to see the bairn?'

'Plenty of time for that,' she sniffed, 'if he lives.'

I patted my pockets for the bottle of fulmar oil which I needed to anoint the wound left by the cord. It wasn't there. I'd forgotten to bring it with me in my haste to leave our cottage. I opened the cloth in which the child was wrapped and gazed at the place where he had been anchored to his mother inside. It looked raw, like a sheep's intestine. I heard Aunt Rachel coughing and spluttering over her pipe outside, shifting from foot to foot on the stones to ease her lumbago. I heard the dawn chorus of the birds starting up from the cliffs and knew that soon the village would be up and about and in to see the new boy born to Ann Gillies. I heard the footsteps of this boy's father approaching down the street in the early grey light. I ran to the shelf and reached down the bottle of spirits which was kept in each home for medicinal purposes. I opened the bottle and soaked a small rag in the amber liquid. Then I rubbed some over the wound on the tiny belly, wrapped a clean cloth around it and swaddled the child up in its plaid. The child's face puckered and it started to cry, lusty and loud.

'You've a son, Mr Gillies, and a fine proper bairn at that,' I heard Aunt Rachel say from outside the cottage. 'Annie's no worse for wear either, thank the Lord.'

'Mrs Gillies,' I whispered, pushing the howling infant towards his mother's punctured form on the cot, 'Mrs Gillies, I think the boy is hungry!'

For the few days after this birth I battled with my conscience. I had no appetite for food or exercise and gave up my walks on the hill, preferring to stay close to the cottage. I felt sure that the child would soon die and that I would be to blame for cleaning its wound with spirits rather than the oil of the fulmar. I lay on my cot, longing for sleep but when finally it came it was fitful and anguished and my dreams were cruel. I saw the corpses of bairns bobbing in the waves, my mother holding a bundle out to me and saying, 'Here's a doll for you, Lizzie, all the way from Harris. Isn't she pretty?' But when I unravelled the cloth that covered its face, the skewered grimace of a dead child met my gaze and my mother threw her head back and laughed, in that way that she did, and I woke in a sweat, rigid with terror. Then I heard the snores of my Aunt and I knew that she would beat me if she ever found out I had disobeyed her and I felt ashamed that I hadn't the courage to tell her. So I suffered in silence and swallowed my guilt and my shame because I knew I was bad, bad to the core, and that was why I had no kin to call my own and that was why everything I loved was taken away from me. I went with Aunt Rachel to attend to Ann Gillies and the new boy, who she called Neil for his father, and I watched that boy like a hawk, waiting for the first signs of the sickness to appear. The Minister called round and baptised the babe, it had to be done quickly before the sickness set in and took the wee children off to the Devil, and he said that Ann should be proud of such a fine, strong bairn and she said that she hoped he would remain so, God willing. The fourth day came, and the fifth, and Wee Neil continued to suckle with ardour and Ann stared down at his tiny face as he lay at her breast with hopc in her eyes. And sometimes a tear would shine from her velvet cheek as she remembered the others who had been there before and now were gone.

After the second week had past and Wee Neil had not succumbed, I began to sleep easier. I ate my porridge and potatoes, some eggs and mutton and I picked up my weaving again. The days passed more quickly and my dreams were less troubled. I sat at my spindle and tried to make sense of it, how had Wee Neil survived my mistake? Surely no good could come from my disobedience and dishonesty? But here he was, a full eight weeks on and perfect as the day he was born. It puzzled me.

In the early spring the dog caught his foot on a rock. He came to me as I sat outside the cottage, milking. The blue-white liquid hissed in the pot, the slap of waves at the shore keeping a steady rhythm. My neighbour called over from her spinning, 'The dog's lame, Lizzy, look!' And sure enough he limped up the street looking downcast. So I took him inside and looked at the wound and before I knew what I was doing I had got the bottle of spirits from the shelf and set about the gash as I had done at the birth of Wee Neil. The dog yelped but I held him fast until it was done and he hobbled off to the corner in disgust.

Aunt Rachel and I attended several other women that spring and early summer and we fell into a familiar pattern with our work. Once the child had been safely delivered, Aunt Rachel would step outside with her pipe and I would be left to clean up the bairn and see that the woman was made clean and comfortable. On these occasions I did not forget to bring my small canister, as I had done the night of Wee Neil's arrival, but instead of the pinkish fishy oil of the fulmar, it now contained the clear yellow fluid of strong liquor. My heart always beat hard in my chest as I did it, one ear cocked to the door as I listened for my Aunt's return, but with each child that thrived I grew in confidence and stealth and I knew that I couldn't be wrong. It must have been Aunt Rachel. Aunt Rachel, who'd never wanted any children of her own. Aunt Rachel, who didn't like children, who saw children as a drain on precious resources, an annoyance, an encumbrance, an evil. The knowledge dawned in my mind as the nights lengthened out, slowly, inexorably, inevitably. Aunt Rachel had brought the eight-day sickness to the children of Hirta and I was the only one who knew it. And then I understood what I must do.

By luck, it wasn't long before an opportunity presented itself. Unlike myself, Aunt Rachel was large and strong, a striking tall woman who had

had her fair share of suitors in the days of her youth. Being physically robust she often joined with the other younger, fitter women who carried turf from the other side of the island or went to tend the sheep on Soay and did other demanding work. She had recently returned from such a jaunt to Boreray where the women, with the help of their dogs, had been hunting sea-parrots and collecting their eggs, staying at night at an old hut on the islet. But Aunt Rachel was the oldest in the group and she had slipped while climbing the cliffs in search of the birds and had got herself a vicious cut over her shoulder and down her back. By the time she had reached the village after some nights away, the wound was angry red and festering. The same could be said of Aunt Rachel herself. She was cross as a horse in the middle of summer. She pulled off her shirt and got me to look at the sore.

'Clean it up, girl,' she instructed me, and I smiled at the familiar phrase. It was what she always said to me when she handed over a newborn.

'Yes, Aunt Rachel,' I said, going to the shelf where the bottles and jars were kept. My hand hovered between the two containers sitting side-by-side on the wooden ledge. One contained the greasy oil extracted from the stomach of a fulmar, the other held the water of life.

'Hurry up! I'll catch my death of cold,' barked Aunt Rachel.

I soaked the rag in oil and pressed it hard into the laceration.

Making Perfume

Laura Morris

We've been making perfume, Lucy and me. Lucy's my cousin. She has strap marks on her back from where she's been wearing her bikini. You wouldn't know that today because her vest covers them, but I know it.

The smell isn't very strong but I reckon if we leave it for a bit then it will get better. We thought that we could sell it to the old ladies who live in my street. Mrs Clarke might like some. She looks like the kind of lady who wears perfume. So, after we have ridden around the block a few times, and I have timed Lucy and Lucy has timed me, we decide to go to Mrs Clarke's house. Simon from next door is out in the street kicking a ball up against Mr Jones's garage door. Mr Jones doesn't mind because he is deaf.

'Where are you two going?' he says, staring at Lucy.

'We're going to Mrs Clarke's house,' I say, 'to sell her some perfume we made.' I unzip the bag on the back of my bike to show him.

'I heard she killed her husband,' he says, 'and buried him in the garden.' I don't take any notice of him, but before we knock on Mrs Clarke's door I say to Lucy that we should have a look in the garden just to check that there's no sign of any funny business going on. We put the stands down on our bikes and balance on the pedals so we can look over the wall. Only we're still not tall enough to look over it. So we come down and lean our bikes up against a tree and I take two bottles of perfume out of my bag and follow Lucy up the path. I notice how good she walks, like someone off the television. When we get to the front door we have to push each other to knock because neither of us wants to, but neither of us wants to say that we don't want to. In the end, after Lucy says that Mrs Clarke is my neighbour not hers, it's me that steps forward. I knock the door, quite quietly, but it's a knock. We wait. Nobody comes. I peep through the window to see if I can see anybody. *Countdown* is on the television and there are three or four cats crawling around. Maybe she fell over or something. After all, she is a very old lady and I know that my grandmother fell down the stairs once. I go to knock the door again, but stop because I hear somebody coming. I turn around and see Mrs Clarke walking towards me. I've never seen her this close up before. Although I'm trying to be polite and look at her face, something on her hands makes me want to look at them. I look down: her hands are old and thin like the tissue paper we wrapped the perfume in and they're covered in earth.

'Why were you looking over my wall?' she asks me. Then she turns to Lucy. 'What were you hoping to see?'

I think carefully about my answer, but decide it's better to go with the truth. 'Simon told me that you killed your husband and that you might have buried him in the garden.'

She raises her eyebrows at me and blinks slowly. 'Did he now? And how on earth would Simon know that? Perhaps you should come and have a look in my garden.'

I look at Lucy: she doesn't move, breathe, anything.

'Come along,' says Mrs Clarke.

I fiddle with my shorts, leaving dirty marks on the turn-ups. Then I take a long, hard look back at our bikes. She must notice because she says, 'You can bring your bikes with you.'

Without speaking, we get our bikes and push them up the path and follow her round to the garden. When I see her garden, I swear to God, I almost stop breathing. There is just a long, green lawn and some pathetic flowers. I am gutted.

'You can leave your bikes here and come in for a cup of tea,' she says.

Her house smells of cats, like the way my Aunt Mary's house smells, and everything looks a bit yellow, like the old films that my mother lets me watch when she's doing the ironing and my father's in the office and I can't sleep. She says that I shouldn't tell my father or anyone that she lets me watch these films. Mrs Clarke looks a bit yellow herself. She takes us into the living room and tells us to make ourselves comfortable while she washes her hands and makes some tea. I feel funny, but Lucy looks okay. She brings the tea in on a silver tray, with a jug full of milk and sugar in a bowl like they have in the restaurant in Debenhams when I go and have dinner with my mother. I sip it, trying not to make a noise, because my father often tells me that I eat and drink far too noisily. It tastes a bit funny and I think for a minute that she must have poisoned it. But then I realise that the tea that she's drinking came from the same teapot as ours, so she couldn't have, otherwise she must have poisoned herself as well.

She shows us a picture of her husband meeting Prince Charles. She points at the scarf that he is wearing and says that she knitted it for him. Then she takes a cigarette out of the packet on the table and offers us one. I say no because I wouldn't know what to do with it, but Lucy takes one, although she doesn't smoke it, she just sits there turning it through her fingers. Mrs Clarke tells us that her husband died. She says that he used to be a teacher and asks us what we want to be when we're older.

'An actress,' says Lucy straight away. She always says actress. I always say different things, depending on how I feel.

'An actress?' Mrs Clarke looks at Lucy for a long time. Then she tells us to sit still while she goes upstairs. While she's away I ask Lucy for a go on the cigarette, but she won't let me, so I don't talk to her and we sit and watch *Countdown* in silence. I'm making words in my head. I don't know what Lucy's doing and then I hear Mrs Clarke coming back down the stairs. She walks very slowly, like the way Lucy's mother walks. I run up and down the stairs unless I'm trying to be quiet. The nights I come down to watch films with my mother and eat bread and butter and drink tea on the settee, I walk very, very slowly and carefully so I don't make a noise and my father doesn't hear me. I have to open the living room door really quietly or he'll hear.

Mrs Clarke comes into the room with her arms full with bags and a vanity case. She takes a purple shawl out of the bag, looks at it and sighs. It's got lots of beads and sequins on it. She wraps the shawl around Lucy and ties it at the front. She stands and looks at her for a moment, like she is thinking about something. She opens the vanity case. There's loads of stuff in it, much more than my mum has got, and all different colours in tubes and jars and bottles. She puts pink lipstick on Lucy's lips and some blue stuff on her eyes. Lucy looks at me. She doesn't look embarrassed or anything. In fact, she looks lovely. Mrs Clarke is enjoying herself too. She tells us about the first time that she met her husband. His name was Alan. She says that they had been at different schools. She was at the girls' school and he was at the boys' school. Every Christmas, she says, the two schools joined together and had a dance, and that's where she met Alan.

'When I first met him, I didn't really like him. I thought that he was cheeky. But then I saw him smile and…' She stops, remembering it. I try and catch eyes with Lucy but she isn't looking at me.

'I was wearing my hair like this,' says Mrs Clarke. She scoops up Lucy's hair and twists it in close to her head, holding it there with hairgrips. 'Yes, just like this. I had long hair once,' she says, 'just like yours. You must never cut your hair short.' I feel my hair, and wish that it was long like Lucy's.

She asks if we've got boyfriends. Lucy says yes and tells her about Will, a boy that she met on holiday while she was in France with her father. She told me about him before, but I don't like listening. She knows that I don't like it. I hum a tune in my head, a tune I made up myself.

Mrs Clarke gets up and goes over to her record player. She flicks through her records, deciding which one to play. She says that she'll teach us to dance. She shows me how to hold Lucy. I have to put one hand on her shoulder, then one on her waist. She comes behind me and shows me how to move my feet. She tells us to take our sandals off. We dance barefoot on her carpet. The carpet is really thick, and feels nice and warm under my feet. I think about how funny it would look if someone was spying on us through the window now and saw us dancing there in her living room, and I think that it is possible someone is watching us right now. But I'd feel bad if I stopped dancing. Mrs Clarke is having such a good time. Once we get the hang of it Mrs Clarke sits down on the settee and watches us dance. She sings to the music and claps along. Then there is a slow song and Lucy's face goes all serious and she is concentrating. I look at Mrs Clarke and see that she has stopped singing. Her eyes have gone still and she's staring and whispering sorry over and over again. She starts crying. It's horrible. I've never seen such an old lady crying before. She says sorry, but she misses Alan and that he shouldn't have died when he did. She says that she has enjoyed us being at her house, but that it's late now and is time for us to go home. 'You must come back and see me though, any time you like.'

Lucy gives back the shawl and the hair-grips, and we leave her house. When we come outside it's like we have come back into a new street. It's quiet and still. The other children have gone in. When we get in, my mother doesn't even mention Lucy's make-up, or ask us where we've been, but she says that the hospital phoned and that she has some good news: Lucy's mother is nearly well enough to come home and soon Lucy will be able to go home.

I can't look at Lucy. I go into the kitchen. I feel hot, like I want to cry. I take my nightie from the pile of ironing next to the fridge and change into it. I don't even care if anyone walks in. I know it's wrong to think it, but I didn't want Lucy's mother to get better. I thought that Lucy could just live with me in my room.

I take off my shorts and then remember about the perfume in my pocket. What with Mrs Clarke scaring me, and the lawn and drinking tea and dancing I'd completely forgotten why we had knocked at her door at all. I unwrap the tissue paper and ribbon and have a look at the perfume. I hold it up to the light. The water is beginning to go brown and sludgy. I take the lid off and sniff it. It doesn't even smell that nice any more. It all seems like such a waste of time.

I kiss my mother goodnight and run upstairs to bed. I call goodnight to my father through the keyhole of his office door then rush back to my room thinking that it'll be too late, but it's okay because Lucy is still in her shorts and vest. I can hardly bear to watch as she undresses and slips into her satin pyjamas.

I close my curtains and notice that the light is still on in Mrs Clarke's house. I click my lamp on and turn the big light off. It doesn't make much of a difference because it's still light outside, although I know that it will start to get dark again soon. I close my bedroom door and get into bed with Lucy. She lies face down on the mattress. I push up her pyjama top and stroke her back with the tip of my nail until she falls asleep. I won't be asleep for a long time yet.

I think about things. I think about Mrs Clarke, and realise that I too will soon be alone. I think about my mother, my bike and going back to school in September, and then Lucy. I think about Lucy. As I'm about to sleep, I hear my father opening his office door and the sound of his footsteps as he crosses the landing.

Last Tango in Sketty

Barbara McGaughey

Mrs Eunice Protheroe, retired teacher and widow, placed the brown phial on the kitchen windowsill as gently as if it was an unexploded bomb. It had arrived by post that morning, modestly wrapped in brown paper and sooner than she had expected. The wrappings now lay in the kitchen sink where they had fallen when she had sawed through them with the bread knife. Mrs Protheroe, heart thumping and face flushed with excitement, looked much younger than her sixty-two years. The respite between sending for the bottle and receiving it was over; now she had to use the stuff. Her hands trembled as she picked up the little bottle, then, curiosity overcoming fear, she uncorked it and sniffed. There was no smell; she placed her forefinger over the top and tipped the phial slightly, so that a tiny smear of liquid was left on her finger. It looked exactly like water.

God, she thought, half in panic and half in relief, I've spent all that money for nothing!

For what Mrs Protheroe held was a love potion, which claimed to make her irresistible to the opposite sex. That was something she had never been, even in her youth; something she had never hankered to be until now, when she had fallen in lust with an ex-Regimental Sergeant Major of the Welsh Guards.

The revelation of physical desirability in a man over sixty had shaken Mrs Protheroe. Since the death of her husband six years earlier she hadn't given a thought to the men around her. She was not one of that breed of elderly people who, having lost a partner, are not content until they have grabbed a new one. She looked around for things with which to fill her life, and one of them was The Fifty Plus Exercise Morning held at the Leisure Centre, where you could take part in all sorts of activities, from bowls to yoga.

Unlike most of the older women, Mrs Protheroe liked using the exercise machines. She had taken to walking fast for twenty minutes at a time on the treadmill in the Gym. It was there one morning that she saw this beautiful man, tall, tanned and still muscular, with a close-cropped head of grey hair and an air of relaxed authority. The air around him seemed to pulse with testosterone. Everything inside Mrs Protheroe flipped. Pole-axed with desire, she stared at this glistening, sweaty wonder. He became aware of her.

'Hi,' he said cheerfully, patting his curly chest hair with a towel and straddling the rowing machine in a way that made her feel faint.

Years of self-control reasserted themselves in Mrs Protheroe. 'Hi,' she said, and scuttled away to the water fountain to cool herself off.

This had happened three months earlier, and they had never progressed beyond that friendly greeting, but within Mrs Protheroe there now seethed and bubbled half-forgotten desires. She could settle to nothing, she lost her appetite and woke several times a night, sweating from erotic dreams, the details of which made her blush to remember. In a charity shop she found a much-thumbed copy of a paperback called *The Joy of Sex*. Even a look at the illustrations made long-unused muscles in her lower abdomen jerk.

Of course she tried to find out more about the ex-Regimental Sergeant Major, but, even in her state of turmoil, she was naturally discreet, so this took time. Bit by bit she pieced together what she needed to know: his name was James Jones, he had been a regular soldier for most of his life, then a security guard. He had been married twice, once widowed, once divorced, and was not thought to have a partner at the moment. Obviously, looking as he did, it was not only Mrs Protheroe who fancied him. She saw with disgust how other women, less reserved, threw themselves in his path. Female attendance in the gym trebled in weeks, so that the air-conditioning had to deal with musky perfume as well as healthy sweat. As far as the watchful Mrs Protheroe could see he had singled no one out. He was polite and cheerful with everyone and that was that. Mrs Protheroe was heartsick. She could no longer keep to the sensible, elderly routine she had set for herself. Resignation was gone; for a moment she had glimpsed a poster-bright world, full of emotion and excitement, and she could not bear to sink gradually into old age, illness and death.

And then she saw the advert. It was in the back of one of those silly magazines that she only read while waiting her turn at the hairdresser's. THE ELIXIR OF LOVE. Mrs Protheroe got out her glasses to read the small print underneath.

A secret, until recently known only to the Mormons, this odourless liquid, distilled from concentrated female pheromones by Dr. F. Pandarus Quilp of Salt Lake City, Utah, is guaranteed to make any female wearing it instantly attractive to males. Don't delay! Limited stocks available at a bargain price of £50 a bottle. Full refund if not completely satisfied. Send cheque to Aphrodite Products Ltd., St. Agnes House, Jude Street, Deptford, London E23. We accept all major debit or credit cards. Phone us on … She read no further.

Hope and excitement surged through Mrs Protheroe. Surreptitiously she tore the advert out of the paper. Hair still dripping, she marched straight across the road to the Post Office, wrote out a cheque and sent it off to Deptford without giving herself time to think. Then she went back to the hairdresser and had her hair set.

The bottle had arrived on a Wednesday, the day of the Fifty Plus session, so it was now or never. She placed it gently in the middle of the roll made by her bathing costume and towel and caught the bus into town. In the queue for tickets at the Leisure Centre, she hugged her gym bag in case some thoughtless idiot knocked it out of her hands. She saw the tall manly figure of the RSM at the head of the queue, and quivered with fear and anticipation.

She doused her passion in the cold water of the swimming pool, doing her set six lengths of breaststroke, carefully keeping her neat, permed hair dry. In the changing room afterwards, mopping off most of the water, she bravely stared at her image in the full-length mirror. The full frontal view didn't look too bad for her age: plump, but not fat. Men liked plump women, they always had. You only had to visit an art gallery to know that! She turned sideways and quickly turned back, dismayed by the flab and sag. Still, thought Mrs Protheroe, wrapping her towel firmly around her damp body, I'd rather be a fat old woman than a scrawny one. She opened her locker and carefully lifted out her trainers. The sight of the elixir bottle, wrapped tenderly in her socks and placed upright in the heel of the left shoe, frightened her. The next thing she had to do was smear herself with the stuff and go to the Gym. I can't do it, she said to her reflection. She wasn't sure if it was her cowardice or credulity that shamed her most. And then she remembered something.

Next to the pool was an area called The Neptune Suite; here she lowered herself gratefully into the bubbles of the Jacuzzi. Not many people used this place and today she had it all to herself. After all, she thought, I don't *have* to use it today. Next week will do just as well, when I'm more used to the idea. She sat relaxed, her body slapped gently by the moving water. Then she jerked upright, her heart hammering. The RSM, naked except for boxer shorts, came into the suite and went straight into the steam room.

The sudden shock of seeing so much of his splendid body galvanised Mrs Protheroe. All doubt disappeared and she moved with a speed that would have done credit to a fit twenty-year-old. Back in the locker room she grabbed the precious little bottle and patted a small amount of the elixir behind her ears and, after a second's thought, behind her knees as well. Then, having carefully locked it away again, she took a deep breath and stepped into the steam room.

She had never been in one before. Blinded by steam, she sat down gingerly as near the door as possible, and gasped as the hot steam entered her lungs. In a moment or two she could dimly make out three large shapes sitting in a row on the bench opposite, two lumpen ones and the third – obviously the RSM. They resumed the cheerful conversation that had been interrupted by her entrance.

Minutes passed and sweat began to run out of every pore in Mrs Protheroe's body; it dripped from her eyebrows, it ran down her back and collected in pools on the stone seat. She felt sick and ill. She began counting in sixties as a way of estimating how long she had been in this wet hell. Part of her mind became aware that the men had stopped talking; they were shifting on their bench as if they were in some discomfort, and then they were peering through the steam in her direction, but she was past caring. After counting to sixty twice more she knew she must get out or die. She rose and staggered into the ice-cold shower next door.

I hope I've got a strong heart, she thought, as the stinging water smashed into her. Surely it would wash away any traces of the elixir of love not already sweated out in the steam room. Shutting herself into a cubicle in the changing room she slurped off her bathing suit and saw with horror what the steam had done to her hair. She considered pouring what was left of the love potion down the drain, but prudence prevailed and she put it carelessly back in her bag. After all, it didn't work. She wondered if she could get her money back.

Loud men's voices and the banging of cubicle doors made her race to get dry and escape. She peered under the partitions on either side and saw large wet feet. The men must have dried and dressed at the double, for by the time she had emptied her locker they had all emerged, a bit damp and ruffled. It was, of course, the RSM and his steam room cronies. Close up, the RSM was even more handsome than she had thought, with a craggy, interesting face and steel-grey blue eyes. His friends were big, cheerful, pot-bellied men, and they all beamed at her.

'Well, hello there,' said Pot Belly Number One. 'We wondered where you'd rushed off to.'

'We thought we might have frightened you away and that's the last thing we wanted, ' said Pot Belly Number Two. 'Do you come here often?'

'Could we buy you a cup of coffee?' asked the RSM; then, seeing her discomfort, 'though we don't want to impose.'

Oh, help! thought Mrs Protheroe. I'm being chatted up!

She gave them a frightened smile and scurried away down the corridor.

They followed politely but determinedly, calling her back to come and have some coffee, but by now she was quite unable to think straight. She dived into the exercise hall and saw with relief that a class was about to begin. It was the one called 'Bums and Tums' and few men had the cheek to attend that. Mrs Protheroe breathed more easily and joined a queue for floor mats. For some reason these were always in short supply. In front of Mrs Protheroe was a large, athletic-looking woman with bulging calf muscles. She picked up the last available mat, but as Mrs Protheroe moved away, the woman turned, stared hard at her and then presented her with the mat.

'You have it,' she said tenderly, and patted Mrs Protheroe's arm. 'Shall I carry it for you?'

Oh, help! thought Mrs Protheroe. It's still working. *She* fancies me now!

She mumbled some sort of thanks and bolted back to a place as far away from Bulging Calves as possible. She flopped onto the floor and at once, as from nowhere, the two Pot Bellies came and lay down, one on either side of her. She sat up again, fright turning to temper. 'Men don't usually come to this class,' she hissed at them.

They grinned back affectionately. 'We couldn't bear to lose you, honey,' the fatter of the two murmured.

'I'm not your honey!' said Mrs Protheroe loudly, and then realised that people around them were listening.

She measured the distance to the door and the number of recumbent bodies she would have to climb over to get out, and subsided. They couldn't do much to her with all these people around and all she had to do was go through the motions until this class ended, then leave in a smokescreen of other women. Once she got home she'd have a good long soak in the bath; surely that would get rid of these damn pheromones. As the exercise class continued peace returned to Mrs Protheroe, and with it a niggling regret that the RSM himself hadn't seen fit to pursue her further. Perhaps, she thought, hope rising, he would be waiting outside.

Almost the last floor exercise was one called the Pelvic Tilt. This entailed legs apart, knees bent and a slow rhythmic raising and lowering of the lower body. Up until then the two Pot Bellies had joined in all the exercises, but as she lowered and raised her hips Mrs Protheroe became aware that they had stopped and were sitting up looking at her with undisguised lust.

It was too much! She lowered her hips convulsively, kicked the nearest Pot Belly in the guts and rushed out of the hall, leaving him writhing on the floor, the class and the instructor staring after her. She had just enough sense to retrieve her gym bag before rushing out into the street. A fine rain was falling and it mingled on her cheeks with tears of fury, mostly at herself, as she rushed towards the bus stop and home.

I'll never be able to face any of those people again. Perhaps Pot Belly will sue me for assault.

Still trembling, she stood at the bus stop between a really old lady with a shopping basket on wheels and a splendid young man whose lips, eyebrows and nose all had silver rings in them and whose hair was a spiked coxcomb of shocking pink. Despite her distress Mrs Protheroe found him startling enough to glance at a second time, and as she did so he gave her what could only be described as a lascivious wink. Oh, dear God, is there no end to this? She turned away from the bus stop and began to walk home.

'I thought it was you,' said a voice quite close to her. Through her tears she saw the RSM at the wheel of an old but shiny blue Volvo. 'Can I give you a lift home?'

At that moment he was her saviour; she forgot that it was his sexiness that had caused all this trouble. What she needed now was to get home and hide her shame; he and his car were a means of doing just that.

'Thanks very much,' she said and got into the passenger seat.

He drove carefully through the town centre, following her directions, and within minutes she was home. He didn't make a pass at her, but when they arrived he came round to her side of the car to let her out. 'Home safe,' he said cheerfully. There was a pause – and then Mrs Protheroe crossed the Rubicon.

'Would you like to come in for a cup of tea?'

He looked very big in her neat little sitting room, but he behaved beautifully, admiring the view and talking about the weather. As she put the tea-things together in her kitchenette, Mrs Protheroe, recovering fast, found that she was both disappointed and irritated by the RSM. He was behaving more like the vicar than a man consumed with desire. She dug in her gym bag, found the little phial again and dabbed a minute amount of the potion behind her ears. At once her cat Napoleon, who had been asleep in his basket, awoke and stretched, and, purring loudly, began to wind himself sinuously around her legs in a figure of eight.

'Well, really,' said Mrs Protheroe, very embarrassed. 'Go back to sleep, you old fool!'

But Napoleon only purred louder, and rubbed himself against her calves.

It was because of Napoleon that Mrs Protheroe, trying to carry the tray carefully into the sitting room, fell headlong into the RSM's arms. Cat and tea-things scattered, but were ignored. She was swept off her feet and crushed against a rough sweater. Kisses rained down upon her face and neck and large knowledgeable hands ran over every nook and cranny of her body.

'Oh, darling, darling,' moaned the RSM, 'I never thought this would happen to me again!'

In the last sensible corner of her mind, Mrs Protheroe wondered how many more doses of the elixir were in the bottle – then her body melted in a rich, warm honey-glow.

'Oh, yes, please,' she gasped.

Fleeced

Sue Coffey

'Eurgh! What's this?'

'Hmmm?' On her knees with dustpan and brush, Kay's mind was far away. She was wondering if, now that both Mam and Dad had gone, they would fetch up together again. Perhaps in their version of a perfect eternity – mid-terrace, Heaven Street, a chapel at one end and a club at the other.

She looked up to see the little packet being winkled out from behind the pipes at the back of the now empty airing cupboard. Her daughter was treating it with all the curiosity of a juror examining Exhibit A.

'Shit. It looks like a piece of … skin! And who's the hippy?'

She got up, recognising it immediately, resisting the temptation to snatch it away. Years had passed, decades even, since she'd slipped the passport photograph of Jason and a piece of his pelt inside the plastic pouch. When had she hidden it? It must have been during a visit home from the University invariably referred to in this house as being: 'the wrong side of the bridge.'

'Let me see. Some old rubbish from my student days, I suppose.' She pretended to inspect the package before dropping it casually into the black sack that crackled with the discarded history of two much more innocent people. 'Yeah, nothing important.' Knotting the handles, she relegated the grubby residue of Jason to the darkness again. It was where he existed for her – always would.

She didn't want any more questions. 'This is full, take it downstairs. I'll join you in a minute. I've almost finished up here.'

The gruesome discovery had summoned up ghosts of her former self. They shimmered in the shadowy corners of the bedrooms, beyond the reach of the vacuum cleaner. A happy child, a restless teenager and a brittle young woman planning escape, believing that village-forged armour would keep her safe. It was strange that she'd hung onto the evidence instead of destroying it immediately. Or perhaps not. It's quite a big deal whichever way you look at it: peeling a man.

God, it had felt good too: hack, snip, clip. Like Delilah giving it rock all with the shears when she had the chance. Why, why, why, Delilah? It was obvious, wasn't it? Her man had it coming too. Poor, old Samson nothing. He got what he wanted by charm and fame and was economical with the truth when it suited. That's what men like him and Jason were good at. Lying and laying. None so blind as those who won't see, as Mam used to say. Though, back then, of course, it was Kay Harris who was the blind one.

'Oi, woolly-back, you got shares in the brewery or what? C'mon, fill it up.' He was in most nights yelling at her over pulsating Black Sabbath and holding his glass aloft over the bar. As if she didn't have a name, just a persona – another grass-green fresh-out-of-the-valleys joke.

'You've drunk some,' she'd say. Stating the bleeding obvious.

'No, I haven't, love.' His come-to-bed-and-be-fucked-senseless eyes were all smutty innocence. But the creamy coating to his Sergeant Pepper moustache told a different story.

'If you don't like the measures here stick to the Farmers Union.' Routinely dismissive she might have been, but her antennae quivered in his presence. Even when she was apparently focussing on the sea of student bodies demanding her attention. Lots of facial hair there too, but Jace-the-Face, as she privately thought of him, was different. Different as in older, bolder – golder, somehow. Tawny locks curled over the collar of his butternut Afghan coat (genuine article, so rumour had it, not a pale replica from some market stall). Honey-brown eyes of a jungle cat. A medallion, bright as daffodils, winking an invitation from luxuriant chest hair via the strobe lighting. Here in the sticky, spliffy student bar he was the Alpha Male and everyone knew it.

She could have told you what time he came in, where he stood, what time he left and with whom. He was spoiled for choice and it was rarely the same girl twice. They were usually the trophy ones, like middle-class, confident Helen, who lived in the same Halls of Residence as herself. They'd lean in close, frowning under the onslaught of the deafening music, sinking fingers into velvety sleeves while bringing eager ears close to that prickling mouth. She felt the sensation across the fuggy distance by osmosis. And wanted his hop-breath on her skin so bad she felt desire tweaking hard between her jutting hip bones.

It went on like that for weeks – him giving her the glad eye, fancying his chances all right, but too lazy to make a play for someone not a sure fire bet. Her not playing hard to get so much as not playing at all. And then one night he arrived early, almost as soon as the doors were open.

She had come out from back, balancing a couple of ice buckets and there he was. Lone wolf in a forest of stained tables. It was quiet. All they'd ever done before was shout at each other over an insistent bass line. She caught her breath.

He smiled, easy and sure of himself. 'Hi, Kay.' His natural speaking voice was soft as warmed wax. West Country.

'Oh, it's you.' She turned away and clattered her burden down. The optics-obscured mirror showed the treacherous flush spreading from bony collarbone to coal-black hairline. Her hands were suddenly damp with perspiration and the ice stuck to them as she brought unnecessary order to the slithery cubes. In the warped glass she saw herself being sized up by knowing, hooded eyes.

He licked his lips as if it was necessary to lubricate them before sliding the words out from under his saffron whiskers. 'Thursday's your night off, isn't it? Come out with me.'

It was less a question more a requisitioning, a taking by right. Cheeky bastard! As if she was just going to roll over saying yes, yes, yes. As if.

'No. I can't. I've got essays to write.'

'Essays!'

'It's okay for rich boys whose Daddies send them fat cheques from the farm so they don't need to work. Some of us have to boost our grants and pass exams.'

Silence.

Fuck. Her heart sank. She'd overplayed her hand. Too late now to take back the hard words and prissy tone. While she wiped the bar with measured movements, her mind plucked urgently at his: You see how it is – I can't lose face and make it easy. Don't give up. Don't go.

He stiffened, gnawed on a knuckle while calculating his next move. She half-expected him to tell her to 'piss off'. But, instead, he relaxed, grinned, apparently prepared to swallow a jibe, even about capitalism, if it meant he got his way. 'Right, so not tomorrow. When then?'

'Who says it's at all?'

'Isn't it?'

Given a second chance she'd been so careful not to blow it. Kept it noncommittal, cool but not unfriendly. 'Next week might be convenient. I'm not sure. I'll think about it and let you know.'

There really had been a couple of essays outstanding. One scripture, the other literature. Calvinism and Romantic poetry: a heady mix of mind and matter, dark and light. But carnal thoughts about Jason, complete with zoom ins and slow mo, intruded into literary considerations. She'd had to keep leaving the library to masturbate wildly on her narrow bed. Urgent fingers burrowed towards gusset-obscured target and cascading relief. Then, lying with thudding heart and breath, she'd watch Jason fade back smugly into the alleyways of her wanton imagination.

Not that she was falling in love, of course. It was obvious she just needed a good shag. It was six months, more, since Mick had dumped her for going away to university. (Why was everyone so bloody surprised when she'd actually gone and carried out her stated intention?) So much for the young promises made on top of the Graig mountain.

And now Mam had written to say that Mick had found someone new, a nice, convenient local girl. 'You missed your chance there,' was the implication. But no, really, it was fine, Kay didn't want him. And if Mick could forget quickly so could she. A girl had to start somewhere so why not a one night stand with someone she fancied the arse off. This Jason fixation was lust, that was all.

By Thursday she was almost shaking with anticipation. Which made the resulting disappointment hard to take. An hour or two of his company was enough to realise that he wasn't any. More of a surprise was the sex turning out to be crap. Not even a proper bang and a whimper, let alone the climax her feverish fantasies had been delivering all week. Only the setting, his flat in student land, was pretty much as expected.

Perhaps it was Brewers Droop or just that he was incapable of living up to the promise of that gorgeous body. All that glitters, etc. And although Cream were playing softly in the background it was all too obvious, the nights in white satin bit. Especially as the sheets were, in reality, greying nylon and there seemed an inordinate number of pubes embedded in the material. As if the mattress was stuffed with them and they were working their way out over time.

His cock kept shrivelling back inside a long, puckered foreskin that reminded her unpleasantly of cavity flaps dangling from the Christmas poultry. Anyway, after she'd done her best to encourage him into a protracted state of arousal, she gave up on the whole idea and settled for a few hours sleep.

'Kay, wake up. Hey, lover.'

Fingers of daylight probing through moth-eaten curtains told her it was morning. She rolled over, hurriedly moistening her dry mouth with a parched tongue, determined to avoid a repeat performance. Only to find that she didn't have to. Jason was standing by the bed with a breakfast tray looking pleased with himself. She would leave as soon as she finished the unappetising-looking Weetabix sprinkled with damp brown sugar.

She really didn't want it but felt a kind of sympathy for him as he went on and on about how great they'd been together. So she shovelled it in, nodding vaguely. If he wanted to brag up the action to save face it was OK by her.

What had he put on the cereal? It spun her into a lurid nightmare. She'd never know how much he'd actually done to her and how much of her memory was hallucination, featuring Che Guevara, who stepped out of a poster wielding a barley wine bottle.

When she came to again, sick and sore, Jason was holding her clothes. 'Ever been had, little black sheep? Best stay clear of us rich farm boys in the future.'

She couldn't think straight, let alone answer back. All the sassiness had bled out of her through the raw slit between her legs. Although she felt the rough difference with shaking fingers she didn't comment on it. Her skin there was swollen, bald as that of a young virgin. One with terrible knowledge; of hurting, ripping, and a soft voice alternately singing *Baa, Baa, Black Sheep* and threatening violence if she told.

Flu was doing the rounds that winter so it was easy to be out of circulation for a few days without exciting attention. Countless hours were spent curled up in the cocoon of her bed, the radio used indiscriminately to drown out insidious sounds and images. When she got up again Helen was the first person she saw. Mainly because she was the one who kept knocking the door until Kay finally dragged herself over to answer it.

'You look awful.' Helen had come in uninvited and bustled about, picking up discarded clothing, clearing surfaces, brewing fresh tea. The brisk ministrations were like the rough soothings of a mother cat and were more than she could bear in her weakened state.

'Please don't cry any more. What's happened to you? Tell me or I can't help.'

Helen didn't look shocked by the sorry tale, only thoughtful. 'Let me show you something.' With as little emotion as stripping off in the changing room at the swimming pool, which always seemed her natural habitat, she unzipped her mini kilt and let it fall. Lacy panties were pulled down matter-of-factly to reveal stubbly blond fuzz.

'Hair by Jason,' she said laconically. 'I was out of it at the time. I kind of went along with things – or guessed I had. It wasn't a bad trip like yours but I felt used afterwards. Not sure how much I'd really agreed to.'

Kay stared at her. 'Jesus. How many other "scalps" has he got, do you think?'

'Too many. But no one's talking. So much for the sisterhood.'

'What are we going to do?'

Jason was taken aback when they'd barged in. But his reactions were swift and it was a struggle to contain him. They'd succeeded only with the combination of Helen's athleticism, and her own growing fury.

He was wild. 'What the fuck are you doing? Get off me you crazy bitches!' He was kicking and shouting fit to rouse the neighbours until Helen managed to stuff a sock into his mouth. The bandana he was wearing came in handy as a gag. A shopping-line cord they'd brought with them to secure him to the bed needed to be reinforced with belts and ties snatched up from around the room. It was in a drawer, ransacked for the purpose, that Kay found his collection. The result of his hunting and gathering. He'd used money bags, little plastic ones from the bank designed for coins but stuffed instead with pubic hair. The packets were labelled according to victim's name and date.

She turned back to him, murder in her eyes, and he bucked and struggled desperately as she pulled the dressmaking scissors from her duffle pocket.

The sound the material made as the blades glided harshly through cheesecloth and denim, slicing, laying bare, was so satisfying that she'd taken her time – folding aside the swathes of cloth lovingly like a master surgeon. Helen provided the soundtrack while carrying out a makeshift haircut and shave. 'You're a rapist, a vampire, a beast of prey. Well, now you know what it's it like not to have control over your body.'

He was naked, spread-eagled, a sheen of terror on his peachy skin. The blades lay open across his navel: a gaping threat. It was mesmerising – that perfect contradiction; clean outer shell and invisible rotten yolk.

'Do it, Kay.'

In a dream-like state she had inserted her thumb and forefinger into the handles of the heavy duty scissors and reached for a flaccid dick that seemed to be getting smaller by the minute. She'd held a fledgling once that had fallen from a nest. This one still fluttered feebly, helplessly, as she felt along its vulnerable length pinching lightly at the root. She aimed her weapon, pistol-like, at his crumpling face before lowering it to the threatened task. That's when he'd started to cry, watery snot clogging his nostrils so that he seemed in some danger of suffocating.

It was enough – almost.

The Afghan coat had been tough but she was persistent and it eventually yielded. Shreds of mossy hide littered the floor by the time they left Jason unbound and unbloodied. They took a piece each, and a photograph. Kay, the passport version she'd found together with the damning packages. Helen's was inside the camera she'd brought along. It was a lot less flattering, and one, he was quick to agree, that he wouldn't want showing around as a result of making any allegations.

That was the end of the incident. The end of Jason's swaggering around campus, or the student bar, where he rarely appeared. They never spoke to each other again. It was the end, too, of a sort of innocence.

The next time she'd come home, many months later, she'd bumped into Mick. He couldn't believe how much university had changed her. She seemed so confident and independent. He wouldn't have known her, he said.

That was probably when she'd done it: disposed of the thing she'd been obsessively carrying around with her for so long like a warning, or a talisman. Because someone qualified to tell the difference recognised that this woolly-back was sporting a new, formidable coat. And had become quite another kind of animal.

The Cactus Man

Vanessa Gebbie

I

Social Workers. 'I'm Angela,' she says.

Open-toed sandals. Hairy ankles. Small talk in the lift. Graffiti on the mirrors, etched like train windows. Smell of civil service dust and stale cigarettes under a No Smoking sign. Then her office. How does she breathe? I want to open the window, let in some air. She pulls out a chair and she's sitting opposite. Our knees are nearly touching.

'Yours is an interesting case.'

Her desk is cluttered, haphazard. Unfinished business. This *chlorophytum* is just by her. Grey as the cabinet it's on, lank as a probation officer's dick. She's fingering one leaf, running her nail up and down.

'You shouldn't do that. They don't like it.'

She jumps as if the leaf is hot. 'The spider plant? Sorry, I didn't know.'

'You know what they do? They absorb toxins from the atmosphere.'

She looks at the *chlorophytum*, as if maybe it's just spoken or something. To me it looks like it's soaked up all the grief that's ever been through this room.

'I was saying how unusual your case is.'

'Can't be doing with too much usual.'

'Sorry?'

'We feed off being unusual, us lot.'

'Oh, I see.'

This Angela, she leans forward at me like she wants to read my small print. She's got brown eyes. She was probably pretty once. Not that she's old. But she just looks tired.

'I need to know why. Why now?'

I'm looking past her. Cacti on the windowsill. Stunted, pots too small.

'Why not? Are those *mammillaria* yours?"

She smiles. 'The cacti? Yes, sorry. I'm not much good with plants.'

'They'd look healthier if you looked after them. That little round one is from Mexico. *Mammillaria bombycina*. It should have babies attached to it by now. Round the base. Try putting it in the sun.'

'OK. I will,' she says, then, gently, 'Spike? Why now? You're twenty-two. You've had four years.'

'If you were called Spike you'd want to know your proper name.'

There's not enough room here for my legs. My knees are starting to ache. I rub them. My hands brush her skirt.

'I'm getting married,' I tell her. 'April. I need a proper name for chapel.'

She turns sideways and crosses her legs. Her foot is pulsing gently up and down.

'That's lovely. Date?'

'The something. Elaine would kill me if she knew I'd forgotten.'

'Elaine?' She's taking notes, using a file to lean on.

'Yes, I've known her since – since my third mam, I think. The nice one, who died. Mam Thomas from Gwilym Terrace. Elaine lived in Gwilym Terrace. We used to play up the tip. We called it "catching ponies". Only we never did. They were way too fast.'

I see Elaine, late, running in to my eighth birthday tea, black with coal dust, hair in her eyes, laughing, her party frock all muddy. She's panting. 'Spike, come and see, fast. There's two foals down by the railway line!'

That's it. We're kicking away our chairs, Mam Thomas is shouting at me to take my coat, I've grabbed a handful of cakes, and we're scorching down to the railway, me scattering crumbs, the two of us laughing like banshees.

'But you did have a name before?'

But I hardly hear Angela.

The ponies, on the patch of wasteland by the tracks. Two foals, still trying to balance, steam in their nostrils. The mother, unmoving, her neck at an odd angle. It's so real, I can't swallow.

Her fingers touch my arm. 'Spike? You had a name before?'

I need air. 'Yes. Ages back, I was called Algernon.' I breathe deeply. 'I was called Algernon for years until I became Spike.'

'Go on.'

'This teacher. Miss Edwards. She had all these cacti on the windowsill in her classroom. She got sick. I took them home to look after them for her, but she never came back. I started collecting them then. It was a joke, Spike. But it stuck.'

'I like it. It suits you.'

I look at her. I go to get up and our knees touch. She's blushing. We both move our hands at the same time. They brush, then fly apart like sparks. 'Sorry,' I say. I go to the window. I stand, look out over the valley, at the black line of the hills against a sky grey as a dove's belly. The light is fading.

'I remember Mam Thomas telling me the coal tips used to glow when the sun hit them. The bits of coal were so small no one could pick them up. They used to catch the light like they were diamonds.' I run my fingers over the sill. 'Now there are whinberries. Black and blue. If you know where to go.'

'You can see my old school from here,' I hear Angela say. Close. 'And the park. It's nice.'

She must have got up. I can feel her standing behind me. She smells of ice cream. 'A nice view. I watch the rugby sometimes. Or the cricket in summer. I prefer the cricket, really. It's more peaceful.'

'Oh, you must have seen me then. Fly-half in winter, slow left hand spin in summer.'

Silly, but I almost expect her hand on my shoulder. It doesn't come. I try to sense her there, but she's sat down again. I turn round. Suddenly, she's busy. Pulls open a drawer, pushes it back. A metallic snap.

She says, 'I don't understand, Spike. What's wrong with being Algernon for chapel, just for one day?'

She reminds me of a teacher now.

'I can't be Algernon. Everything's ever gone wrong, it's always Algernon.'

I look back to the hill opposite. Charcoal fading into a charcoal sky.

'My record is under Algernon, isn't it?'

'Well yes.' And she's flipping a file open. 'Look,' she says, and her eyes are laughing as though she thinks smiling's out. She's holding a small piece of flimsy paper. Pale blue. 'Here's the shoplifting.'

'Shoplifting? I reckon the shop should have been done for cruelty. They'd got this plant – *Saintpaulia* – fallen out of its pot on the floor. Bright blue flowers, black soil everywhere. I took it for Mam Thomas after she got sick and I'd been moved. I took it to take to her in hospital. But I got caught.'

She takes out another sheet, pale green this time.

'What's that?'

She is smiling now. 'Natalie Cummings,' she says.

'Oh Christ, Nightly Cummings. Twice Nightly. We had bets who would do it with her first, because she did it with everyone in the end. I won. Then she tried to say I forced her because I wouldn't do it with her a second time, said I'd, you know, but I hadn't.'

'I know. It's all here.'

'So, you can see what I mean. Algernon's not me any more. Never was.'

I turn to the cacti. 'Know what this one's called?'

Angela shakes her head.

'It's another *Mammillaria*. *Mammillaria zephyranthroides*. Only this one's different. It doesn't grow babies. Stays solitary – that's what the books say.'

She doesn't say anything.

'But this name business – Elaine says my Mam must have called me something. That's why I'm here. Please. For my name.'

She indicates for me to sit back down.

'Know why its called *Mammillaria*?' I don't wait for an answer. 'They're like nipples.'

Angela peers over. Her eyes are heavy again. Exhausted.

'Where's the toilet?' I ask.

When I come back there's this buff folder on her lap. Brand new. She puts one hand on the cover, as though the words inside will come right through to her fingers. There are scratches on the back of her hand. She's moved the chairs a bit, because our knees don't touch now.

'So what's my name then?'

'It's not as simple as that.'

I wait.

'How do you know all this stuff about plants?' she asks. Then she runs her fingers through her hair, as though it used to stay there. It flops back.

I shrug. 'I read it.'

'Tell me, Spike–' She pauses. Her nose is red round the nostrils. Her foot is pulsing up and down again, one-two, one-two. 'Tell me what you know about your birth circumstances.'

I get up. Back to the window. It's shit out there. I strain to see the hill. 'It's all there, isn't it? In the file, I mean. Some girl in Cardiff.' I think I can make out the hill, but the colours merge. They flow together, and I can't separate them. 'My Dad must have been a rugby player. Got it all over me, don't you think?'

She doesn't answer. I look back at her but she is looking so hard at the file, like her eyes are glass in the sun and it'll burn to ash. I sit down again, and she says, 'Were you told that?'

'No. I just – I just think she was little, like Elaine, but like me, too, a bit chippy. I must be a bit like her, mustn't I? Probably had a giggle like Elaine's, one that makes you want to laugh too. Eyes that sort of look up at you.' I stop for a second. 'But I suppose that's just me, isn't it?'

'I think so. But everyone needs to have a picture in their heads, don't they?'

I'm thinking. Yes we do. Pictures. That's all we have. Not real ones. Just pictures in our heads. 'Elaine says I could find out. Find out who she is. My Mam.'

It's spilling out now. I reach up for the *chlorophytum*. Dusty leaves. I start to stroke it gently, leaf by leaf. 'Elaine says we could ask her to the wedding. It'll be so good for her to see I'm OK. Elaine wants to show me off a bit.'

Angela's smiling again. 'Tell me what Elaine would say.'

'Oh, she'd say things like – Spike has a proper job now. Apprentice down the garage with Mr Evans. Doing well. And I think my Mam would be proud if she knew I had a job. I'd tell her that I'm learning all sorts of things with Mr Evans. He says I'm going to be really good.'

I'm following the shape of one grey leaf with my finger. It was greener once, but it's tired, like Angela. Sunk into itself.

'Mam might tell me I've got brothers. That'd be great.'

This time I see us, me, a Jimmy, a Craig, arms round, walking away to the pub, heads down, talking, going to the match. I look up smiling at Angela, but she's watching me and she's not smiling.

'I'm wrong, aren't I? Why didn't you stop me? She's nothing like that, is she?'

Angela's hands are palms up. Like she's praying, but not in my country. They are very pale, the palms. The fingers are long, narrow.

'So she was a fat old biddy with warts, was she? It was in the dark, down some stinking alley for a fiver?'

Angela shifts in her seat.

The leaf I'm holding is thin. Like its job is over. Needs water.

'I need to know. I need to know what she called me.'

Angela leans forward again. Her hair is dyed. It's not really that colour. It's grey and old. 'I'm afraid you were not named at birth, Spike.'

'You should give that water.'

Then she's talking fast and I'm looking at the wall. 'There's no name here. As I said, most unusual.' She stops, puts both hands on the file flat. I shift in my seat. The leaf breaks away in my fingers. I tear little pieces off it, onto the carpet.

'It happens,' Angela says, then her voice goes so low I'm leaning forward to catch it. 'I'd leave it now. Go to Elaine. Get married. Just do it.'

I screw up the leaf and drop it.

'What are you saying?' I haven't heard my voice like this before. 'Leave it? That's me – my fucking life – in that folder.'

Angela looks hurt and glances at the door. We both go quiet. There's a hush like a funeral. When I speak again, quieter, I'm shaking my head slowly.

'That's my story. Not someone else's. My file. My right, isn't it?'

She looks at my hands. They're shaking and I hadn't noticed. I make fists. She waits. I count to five in my head.

And then she says, quietly, 'You have a right. No question.' She's leaning forward again, and she's circled my two fists with her hands. They're cold. 'You don't need to do this.'

I just look at her.

Spider plants. Why do we call them that? Most people don't even like the bloody things. In the wild, they have to be in the warm, where the sun filters through the trees, and you can just hear the sea. Angela's voice, soft, 'Most birth mothers give their baby a name, even though they know it will be changed. A parting gift. I have seen a few cases like this, normally in specific circumstances.' Her voice tails off. There's a hole in the air waiting for my words to fill it.

'What circumstances?'

Now I am thinking what's Angela holding back? It's like a film in my head, going so fast, hard to keep up with it. First there's me getting born. My real Mam dies. A pretty pale face on a hospital pillow. Then a big mix-up at the hospital. A kidnap. Faster and faster it goes. Night-time on the ward, there's a man, hunched over, a white bundle under his coat. No alarm. But I can't stop Angela's voice. 'Two possible scenarios you must be aware of are incest and rape.' Her voice doesn't change. She rattles out incest and rape as though she's saying Welshcakes and tea. I get back up and go to the window again. It's darker, dust grey.

'Over there,' I say, 'the old railway tunnel to Tredegar. That's where I went with Natalie.'

'Can I get you a glass of water?' she says.

'No thanks, not for me, but the plants could do with some.'

She eases out of the office, comes back with a jug. She waters the plants, smiles at me. I breathe in. I rest a finger on the longest spine of one of the cacti, and press down. I feel the skin begin to give.

'OK. Tell me then.'

And then she says, very, very slowly, 'Spike, I'm so sorry. Your mother was attacked. On the way home from work. She–'

'Why don't you just say it?'

'Raped. Your mother was raped.'

The cactus spine breaks through the skin. It must be near the bone, but I'm holding my finger steady as a rock.

I don't remember what she says after that. I've tried but it won't come. I think I sit with her for ages, and we don't say much at all. Except I tell her how to look after her cacti properly. They're special. Just need a bit more care and they'll be fine. Probably better at home, sunny. A while later, I get up to go. When she takes her hand off my file to say goodbye, she leaves four dark fingerprints. I leave her office holding the *chlorophytum*. She walks with me to the lift. I turn to say thanks, and she kisses me. A dry whisper-kiss that just misses my mouth.

'It's OK,' I say. 'At least I know what my name is.'

She smiles.

I try to smile back. 'I'll stay with Spike.'

She touches my shoulder with her hand, and I step into the lift.

II

I'm walking away towards the high street in the damp. It's been drizzling, but it's stopped. The street lights are on. The road shines, orange coal. I turn and look back at the office block. Lights in reception, a couple of higher windows. I can't see Angela's room, but I can see her in my head, drawing a line under, tidying me away, back into the drawer. I need a drink. I'm holding the *chlorophytum*. This damp air's good for it. I brush at the leaves to get the air under them, then hold it, almost like a baby. I'm not meeting Elaine until seven. When I walk in The Crown, a few faces look up. It's smoky, warm. I go to the bar for one, just to settle things. I put the *chlorophytum* down. The barmaid, smudged eyes says, 'One for your friend?' looking at the plant. She leans on the bar and smiles. Christ.

A few pints later I hear my voice, 'Mine shafts.'

She's drinking with me, 'What?'

'We dig our shafts, they go parallel, straight down.' My laugh is too loud. 'This guy's was OK. Started off rubbish, but, hey, now it's fine.'

She's looking into my eyes. I look away, at the bottles behind her.

'Sometimes, these shafts, they get too close to each other. Doesn't matter how far down you are, how much you think it's just you, your shaft, the walls between can give. Wham! Your life is mixed with someone else's. The walls are gone, the earth falls in, and what was yours gets mixed up with what was theirs.'

She's stroking the back of my hand with her finger. I look down, then look at her face. She's smiling, but only with her mouth. 'Of course it does,' she says.

I pull my hand away. I look at the clock. It's gone seven.

'I've got to go.'

When I get outside, the air hits me like a fist. I run to The Crawshay, I don't stop. I just run to Elaine. It's freezing, but she's waiting outside, sitting on a low brick wall, chewing a strand of her hair. She sees me coming and gets up, a smile so wide. She runs towards me, her heels clicking on the pavement. Her hug nearly knocks me off my feet. Her curls have tightened in the damp. She's put eye shadow on.

'What's that?' she says, looking at the *chlorophytum*, her hands under my jacket. I don't know why I don't answer. She digs her chin into my chest and looks up into my face. I can feel her body through her coat. 'You've been drinking,' she says.

'Just the one.' I put my arm round her and we go inside.

'So who am I marrying then?' she says when we sit down.

'Me,' I say, thinking, me, the bloke you were with this afternoon.

'Ah, go on, daft thing. What was the social worker like? What did she tell you? Can we ask your Mam to the wedding?'

'Look. It's not as easy as that.'

I push my fingers into the hard earth round the *chlorophytum*, breaking it up. She's looking at me, waiting.

'I wasn't called anything. Nothing at all.'

I'm expecting a pause, Elaine to go quiet. But it's only a second. 'So she didn't call you anything? There's funny.'

'No.'

'Well, I still love you,' she says. Then she says it again as if it will make it twice as real. 'I love you.'

'I need another pint,' I tell her.

Later, we're walking home. We've got past the shops, the cinema. We cross the playing fields and we're by where the Tredegar line was, by the tunnel. It's dark down there. It's cold. Elaine pulls me in for a kiss, leaning close against the wall. My shoes squeak on cinders as I bend to her mouth. She's warm, soft. Her tongue baits mine. She catches my lip between her teeth, nips at it, giggling. I can taste her, smell lemonade. I'm breathing faster.

'Look it's not–' I get out, because it's not fair. Elaine wants to wait for the wedding. This sort of thing winds me up. But her hands are everywhere. Her fingers are playing me, stroking me. She moves her hips slowly against me.

'Fair,' I say, and then there's something. Black flashes, like someone has pushed between us. I drop the *chlorophytum* and now it's like there's someone else here, not me. This other person's here, his tongue in Elaine's ear, his hands on her, rougher than before. He's rubbing Elaine's breasts with one hand, his other hand moving downwards. She's making small muffled noises like a cat in a sack. She twists her head away, says, 'Spike, no.' But she doesn't mean it. I know she doesn't. We're getting married, and it was her started this, wasn't it? She was all over me. She got me like this. I'm kissing her so hard, lifting her up, my hand under her skirt, pulling.

'No, please,' Elaine says again.

It'll be so easy, just there, so easy, so easy. Nothing would be said. Please what?

'Please, Spike, please. I want to wait.'

But I don't.

I am lifting her up. We can do it here.

Then I hear him, he's grunting uh, uh, uh, but it's not him, it's me, and the small noise, the little whimpers, they're Elaine, they're Elaine, and she is trusting me to stop, she always trusted me.

And I stop.

I don't know how long I just hold her, but I just hold her. There's a dim light from the footpath and I can just see the *chlorophytum* and the broken pot on the floor. We are together, and now I can smell the damp and the piss of the tunnel and I'm so, so sorry. We've been crying, both of us, quietly, calming down, but it's then that Elaine says she wants to do it. We can do it now, here in the tunnel, she says. My foot is touching the *chlorophytum*'s broken pot.

'No way,' I say. I manage a little chuckle as I call her a hussy, kiss the top of her head. Then I ask her, say what we always said.

'We were going to make it special?'

'Yes,' I say and I feel her pull into me tighter than ever. I just hold her as tight as I can. I can still hear my heart thudding in my ears. Like a clock, ticking.

We work together, pick up the spider plant, take it home.

Me, Daphne Dupree and the Bible of Decisions

Nicola Daly

It was George, Daphne Dupree and the young girl with the pin through her nose who sculpts vacuum cleaner parts into angels that helped me make up my mind to become a sparkling personality. When I say Daphne Dupree, I am talking, of course, about her self-help book *Decision Making for the Dizzy*. I have never been described as dizzy, but I'm not known for being decisive. I suppose that the rat, George, has played a small part in my decision to live life to the full.

I should start at the beginning: last summer my husband George informed me, rather casually, that he was leaving me for Flip-flops. Obviously that is not her name. That is what I call her, largely because she wears flip-flops even on the coldest days in Cardiff. Her actual name is Joyce Price. An insignificant little name, I know, but it makes me feel physically sick. I was not only ashamed, and so mortified that I had to spend several days being weaned on to solids by my neighbour Meredith Scott, I was shocked. I had always presumed that George was happy. However, it seems I was boring and he feels more complete living with a woman in flip-flops with scuffed nail varnish on her toenails. I failed to see how living in the squalor of the Mountbatten estate with a burnt-out caravan and two old sofas in your garden can make you feel complete. I thought living with three dogs, a parrot, two hens, her ex-mother-in-law and a brood of delinquents would eventually force George to come crawling back to me. Oddly enough he seems happy and according to friends he has no intention of ever returning.

At first, obviously, I was humiliated and desperately upset. I did all the clichéd things people do in my position:

1. Burnt his piano in the backyard.
2. Had a make-over.
3. Sent his remaining golf clubs to Oxfam.
4. Cut down the apple tree he planted in 1972.
5. Joined an arts and crafts class.

6. Rang up people I hadn't spoken to for years, plus people I hardly know, to slag George off. I rang the children daily, but the boys sided with George and my daughter wanted to stay neutral.
7. Hired a solicitor who looked at my financial situation and advised I took a part-time job. He also thought I should get a cat for company.
8. Bought myself a self-help book.
9. Analysed myself endlessly. Wondered if I was boring. Is it boring to do crosswords, iron pyjamas, visit art galleries?
10. Began to ask myself why I had let George make all the decisions for me.

Overall, with the help of Daphnee Dupree's book, I came to the conclusion that I had let George push me around. Apparently this was because I am not a born decision-maker. George is. When he makes a decision he sticks to it. I waver, change my mind, and then have to ask somebody else to decide for me. Daphne Dupree suggests that people like me unconsciously allow others to make the decisions for them because with decisions comes responsibility. I don't really agree. I let George make all the decisions because it was easier. If I had argued with him every time he ordered me fish instead of steak, put all our money into some doomed investment scheme or booked us a holiday without asking me, I would have spent every day arguing with him. As I am sure Flip-flops is finding out, George is childish. If he doesn't get his own way, he sulks and makes a horrendous fuss.

The book, which became like a bible for me, asked you questions, such as, 'When did you last make a decision?' I got mine down to 1967, when I decided to defy my mother and go on a cycling holiday with George. It was the worst decision I've ever made, as it resulted in pregnancy and our marriage, because it was 1967.

So those two very important decisions were taken out of my hands by what Julian, my night class tutor, would call fate. He is a great believer in fate. I can remember the expression on his face when my self-help book dropped out of my bag at his feet. He picked it up and flicked through it. He is not the type to wait to be asked. He just gives you his opinion, even if you don't want it. 'Decisions make themselves,' he said. In some respects he is right, but I can't take somebody seriously when they are wearing a cravat and cigarette-burned charity shop clothes. But if he hadn't spoken to me that day, I would never have decided to model for his class.

It was what Daphne Dupree would call a '4am decision', a decision that one makes rather flippantly in between reality and dreams. There are several different types of decisions and different types of people who make them. I tried to explain all this to my daughter, but she didn't seem interested. All she wanted to know was why I had burned her father's piano and cut down the apple tree she climbed as a child. In fact she got quite nasty. 'You are obsessed with making decisions!'

'Nonsense,' I said. 'I fail to see what is wrong in taking an interest in the decision-making process.'

At which point she made the hasty decision never to speak to me again.

The girl who sat next to me in art class, Siobhan, a vibrant little thing, made me realise that I might have been a very different person if I hadn't met George. I always wondered if I could have been one of those women who went to Greenham Common or did around the world yacht races. I don't mean to sound bigheaded but the book tells you to say a mantra every day about what a spectacular person you will become.

Siobhan has a real passion for art. Sometimes I think it is the only thing she cares about. She was the one who said my name when the regular model failed to show up for our life drawing class. I would never have put myself forward like that. I would never have considered sitting there naked as a frozen fish finger being torn to pieces by a room full of eyes. Only Siobhan reckoned I had an 'interesting shape' and Julian agreed. He said he was tired of unreliable stick insects who didn't turn up. Every argument I came up with for not doing it, he came up with a better reason why I would be perfect.

'Just think of the sacrifice you are making for art,' Siobhan said and Julian nodded and muttered that I'd be saving the class because without a model he couldn't see how they could carry on.

I liked the idea of doing something different and irritating George. I was sure he wouldn't like the thought of me and my stretch-marks being displayed. I told everyone I knew in the hope it would get back to him, and he would come storming back, like something out of a soap opera. But George was not even remotely interested. According to friends, he was too busy enjoying life. I suppose that made me even more determined. I wanted to prove, to the world and to myself, that I could be lively and compelling. That there was more to me than knitting and *Countdown*.

The modelling itself was not really how you would imagine. I was more than a bit nervous. In fact, I don't think I would have got there without the two double vodkas and Julian. He found me fretting on the college front steps and ushered me in.

'Just remember we are only looking at you as a subject.' Julian handed me a dressing gown that smelt of stale sweat and mothballs. There was a brown stain on the pocket that looked like curry. He then directed me behind this screen in the corner of the classroom, where I slowly undressed.

I was OK at first, but as I heard people arriving I became panicky. I stood there in my underwear and tights listening to people talk about garlic presses, Cocker Spaniels and the price of charcoal sticks. For a moment I debated if I should take my tights off. Putting my coat back on and heading for the door seemed a better option. I probably wouldn't have come out at all, if Julian hadn't got my name wrong.

'Let's be having you, Cheryl,' he shouted.

It always annoys me when people forget my name. But it didn't seem the time to shout back I was Olivia. And Cheryl had a certain ring to it that suited a woman who was about to show her all to a room full of amateur artists. I gingerly walked towards the chair in the centre of the room. Minutes felt like hours as I tried to undo the knotted belt of the dressing gown. The room was silent apart from the odd person rummaging in their bag for a HB pencil or a mint. As I slowly disrobed, I felt clammy. It reminded me of that wrapped processed cheese as you slide it out of its plastic wrapper. Every muscle in my body was rigid with fear as I stood there naked, not quite knowing what to do. My heart was pounding so loudly I thought it might explode. I only realised as I fell back into an accidental pose on the chair that George was the only man to have seen me naked. Apart from my GP, and I don't suppose that counts.

When you've sat there for a while, you forget that you are naked.

Your mind starts thinking about all those little jobs you need to do, like defrosting the freezer and driving to the bottle bank. Gradually you realise that the sea of heads drawing you aren't interested in your sagging breasts or scars. They are just drawing a figure. Many of the end products don't even look human.

I kept my eye on the clock, willing the hands round to 7.30, when we usually had a coffee break. My nerves had stopped twitching, but I was tense. As soon as Julian clapped his hands and the crowd dispersed, I slid back into the dressing gown and sat behind the screen. I thought about getting dressed and fleeing. It was overhearing Siobhan and a male member of the group that made me stay. They were completely unaware I was hidden away gulping Evian straight from the bottle.

'I think the model is fantastic. I wouldn't have the guts to do that. I feel really positive about what I've done today. Usually when I get home the first thing I do is throw my work in the bin or simply sit down and cry because I'm so frustrated, do you know what I mean?'

The other voice said he knew what she meant, but that didn't stop him wishing the Swedish girl was still doing it.

I have been sitting for them every week since. Not bad for a woman who spent years caravanning in the Lake District and has only just started trying recipes including butternut squash. Just the other night, when I was reviewing the year without George, I decided to write a list of the decisions I had made by myself:

1. Model for the class
2. Never eat a sensible meal again.
3. Paint the living room gold.
4. Take in stray cats.
5. Exhibit some of my artwork.
6. Rent my back bedroom to a man who collects beermats.
7. Grow tulips in my front garden.
8. Travel to Australia.
9. Learn Japanese
10. Do a course in Chinese Medicine.

All these things seem tiny to some people, I am sure. However, when you have never made decisions before, they feel huge.

Knitting with Kate Moss

Penny Simpson

The young glue-sniffer was back in the dock. He was a regular before the magistrates and the reporters' bench where Sîan sat out far too many of her working days for her liking. The addict was called Rhys Gruffudd. She had first seen him eighteen months ago when she had joined the *Echo*. In those days, he had been a curly-haired teenager, invariably dressed in trainers and trackie top, but in recent months his appearance had undergone a shocking alteration. His face had turned into a wolf's muzzle, the cheeks collapsed in on themselves and the nostrils unnaturally distorted. He had put Sîan in mind of a comic book's wolf-man, sort-of-human but not really quite there. He certainly wasn't with them that morning, still visibly dazed from whatever chemicals he had been inhaling prior to his latest arrest.

She checked the charge sheet. Nothing much had changed since they had last met: Rhys was still seventeen years old and of no fixed abode. This week, he had been charged with theft, to be precise he had lifted a cheese and onion pasty and a Mr Men toothbrush from Sainsbury's in Colchester Avenue. His brief was as skinny as Rhys, but in slightly more acceptable clothing. Pinstripes (too big on the shoulder, Sîan noted) and buckled patent leather shoes. She slipped a note to Darren, who wrote for the *Western Mail*. Sîan could never remember names, but Darren was a walking address book.

'Macnamee,' he hissed back in a loud stage whisper which caught the ear of the magistrates' clerk. 'Just opened his place in Canton. On the bus route for the heroin addicts from Ely.'

'Nice line in marketing,' she whispered back.

Then Rhys suddenly stood up. The court fell silent, apprehensive as to what might happen next. The policeman who had been sitting beside Rhys struggled up on his feet. He'd obviously got pins and needles and was finding it hard to stay balanced. Rhys was still as a rock, his eyes vacant. It was a few minutes before Sîan realised they were focused on her.

'Fucking witch woman,' he shouted out.

Things moved very quickly after the delivery of his impromptu verdict. Rhys was bundled back down to the cells, whilst the prosecution and defence started to bicker over the correct procedure to follow in this detour from the usual proceedings. Sîan took her opportunity to slip out of court, breaking into a run once she had left the building. She headed for the nearest Starbucks. Witch woman needed caffeine badly. True, she was dressed (as usual) in black, so Rhys Gruffudd might well have mistaken her for a supernatural character in his glue-muddled imagination. She ordered a skinny lemon muffin and a cappaccino and took a seat by the window, which looked out over the tag end of Queen Street. If she really was a witch, she would make spells, she thought, and if she made spells, she would magic away the world she lived in. Sîan bit into her muffin. She had only a few hours to come up with The Excuse to fob off her husband – again. She wondered if this was how Rhys felt whenever he was confronted with a theft charge: the pressure to come up with a story that would magically reverse the endless mistakes of a life lived in the wrong lane. Her mobile rang, as her reflections reached their usual conclusion. It was Howell.

'He did what?'

'Said I was a witch. It was like something out of Salem.'

'Shall I come over?' Howell demanded rather than suggested.

'He was a saddo addict, not the Inquistion,' Sîan began, before he cut in again.

'But it's more of the same, isn't it? That job should carry a health warning.'

She snapped her mobile shut. She couldn't face any more of Howell's verdicts on the unsuitability of a reporter's lifestyle for a woman on the verge of conception. Nor could she stomach any more of the skinny muffin. She abandoned it halfway through and headed back for the office. As she walked, she ran through her mental inventory of Rhys Gruffudd's short and so far rather pointless life. She had first come across him when she'd been writing a feature on the homeless who slept out by St David's Market. He was fifteen at the time, but small for his age. The bed he had been lying in had been conjured up out of old fruit boxes.

'Not a bad kip,' he had argued, as if she had just complained about the lack of en-suite facilities. 'And they gives you the stuff they can't sell.'

Rhys had always claimed he had no family and maybe it was true, or maybe he just hadn't wanted to make any claims on them. Sîan understood that point of view only too well. The demands of her nearest and dearest had long since defeated what she had always believed to be a conciliatory nature. Shortly after meeting Rhys – a lost boy with his stomach full of out-of-date fruit – it had seemed obscene to arrive home and find Howell exploring the different paternity rights extant in the countries of the European Union.

'You think we should still go through with it?' she had asked, petulant, with an emotion she couldn't really express, but was somehow mixed up with Rhys and his pathetic alfresco bedroom. 'I mean, there's kids sleeping rough down behind Debenhams with no one looking out for them. They must have had parents once. Where are they now?'

'Your point?'

Howell had sat poised on the re-upholstered Edwardian chaise longue waiting on her answer. Sîan had blushed. She tried to look him in the eye and say what was spilling out of her heart, but she couldn't. Silenced again.

'Sîan, it's hardly rocket science,' Howell had persisted. 'You're thirty-four. You've made headway at the paper, you can afford to take some time out.'

Howell's theme tune: having-the-baby-blues. He was twelve years older than her, scared his body clock was running on empty, but she couldn't reach out to him. It had something to do with Rhys Gruffudd and his solitary box-bed, and a lot more besides which she couldn't reckon up even with the help of a homeless drug addict.

'I want to do my bit, darling. You can still work. We can get someone in to do the ironing and so on.'

Ah, the clinching factor: a lady that does, so she didn't have to, except she wanted desperately to do anything other than this, confronting her now in her park-side home. How it had reached this perilous state, she hardly dared consider.

Returning to her office desk from Starbucks, she found it submerged under a heap of dead flies.

'Strip light came down and the buggers were inside that,' explained Don Black, Politics Editor and Tea Club Manager, who sat opposite her. '50p in the tin, Sîan, or no fig rolls.'

'I don't like fig rolls.'

'Not much you do like, is there?'

Sîan took a sharp intake of breath, even though she realised it was just casual office banter. She felt her doubts must be pock-marking her body, like a rash. Don had twin boys and existed in a state of permanent exhaustion. He had once come in to work with a half-eaten rusk stuck unnoticed on the top of his head. Sîan fed her security code into her computer. If she wrote something, it would stop her thinking. She flicked through the photocopied court list she had by some miracle remembered to take with her in her flight from court earlier. And there he was again: Rhys Gruffudd. She rang Ed for an update. Ed was an ex-serviceman turned court usher and a mine of information for the journalists on the press bench whom he always referred to as 'the Fourth Estate'.

'Call me old-fashioned, Sîan, but a spade is a spade,' he boomed down the phone, as she swept the flies from her desk with her free hand. 'A no-hope bastard like that and they've just bound him over. Should have suggested a bath, an' all. Thing is, he'll go back out there and rob again. Might be an old lady next time, or you, or me. What you gonna write then?'

Sîan made some quick notes on the back of an envelope, as Ed ranted on. In between his calls for the return of the cane – 'Never did me no harm, did it, and I was one of eight' – she struggled to remember what else Rhys had confided in her when she had interviewed him at the market. Eventually, after thanking Ed profusely, she banged the phone down and began writing up a series of court nibs for a fractious news editor. She summed Rhys's case up in one paragraph. The feature she planned to write on him and the other rough sleepers would have to wait.

Arriving home – late again – she found Howell in the kitchen on his hands and knees. He had been about to cook a lobster, but it had escaped. Sîan joined him in his search, but secretly she hoped the lobster was a marathon contender. Howell had spent a lifetime cooking things from the sea, ever since staying with a crab fishing family in Fiji as part of his backpacking days. Sîan had never liked eating lobsters, or crabs for that matter, not after discovering they were cheated into death by being cooked whilst they were still asleep. She was the first to give up on the hunt for runaway crustaceans, preferring to guzzle a glass of red wine.

'Phyllida's here,' Howell announced from under the kitchen table.

Sîan's day had started badly, but now it went into a tailspin. Phyllida had no doubt been summoned to lend weight to Howell's arguments over the baby. She was his mother, after all.

'She's here right now?'

'Upstairs in the bath.'

Sîan took another slug of wine. She badly wanted a cigarette, but Phyllida had asthma and Howell disapproved.

'Rhys was up before the magistrates again,' Sîan said, in a bid to rid herself of the idea of smoking. 'He's looking really poorly now.'

'I expect he does. Glue, isn't it?'

'Whatever he can get his hands on.'

Howell emerged from under the other side of the table. A dark wing of hair drooped over his left eye. He pushed it back and smiled up at Sîan. 'Looks like I need a plan B.'

Sîan smiled back. Howell, widely regarded as the country's leading writer on food and nutrition, would have a Plan Z organised if necessary. She always fell back on a tin opener. She felt on the verge of tears suddenly, but knew she couldn't weep in front of her mother-in-law. Phyllida was like Ghengis Khan re-incarnated, albeit one who was quoted on matters pertaining to natural childbirth rather than military strategy. She had turned her life as a single parent into a game of winner takes all and quite simply couldn't understand how failure had entered her family through the back door. When Sîan had had a breakdown shortly after qualifying as a journalist, Phyllida had taken it as a personal affront and then as a challenge.

'I have a colleague who runs self-assertion courses,' she had offered. 'He'll soon get you to shape up.'

But the shaping up hadn't gone to plan. Sîan had stayed too thin and she tired easily, neither qualities likely to ready her for childbirth. This was a potential catastrophe as Phyllida wanted a grandchild and Phyllida shared another characteristic with the legendary warrior: she took no prisoners either. Later that evening, she displayed great restraint towards her dysfunctional daughter-in-law, but Sîan knew it was just the charm before the storm.

'It's so zeitgeist,' Phyllida gushed, after emptying a bottle of Spanish brandy along with a pot of Fair Trade coffee. 'All the famous models are combining motherhood with the catwalk these days. It's not about being mumsy anymore. Oh, no. These women are setting new benchmarks. And, would you believe it, even Kate Moss knits!'

Sîan's heart sank down to the newly sanded floorboards. Phyllida wanted physical perfection on all fronts and Sîan knew she was far from a prime specimen. Her gym membership had lapsed after six months, in which time she had managed just one solitary visit to the organic Juice Bar. Howell tried to rescue her. He put his arm round her shoulders and told Phyllida a visit to the doctor was on the cards. They would (apparently) be looking into things. Sîan's misery flooded through her, like an anaesthetic.

'Oh, my good God!' Phyllida suddenly interrupted her son. 'Down there. By the video.'

It was a lobster's claw, waving not drowning. Sîan surprised herself for the first time that evening by volunteering to lure the lobster out using a draught excluder as bait. The lobster bashed away fruitlessly at the fabric sausage roll, before Howell succeeded in tying its claws up with a pair of Sîan's tights. Phyllida laughed her big, magnificent laugh.

'We can have a midnight feast now. Won't that be fun.'

Howell and Sîan exchanged looks. 'Fun' was not registered on either of their features.

The day after the lobster hunt, Sîan made a trip back to court. Ed had more news for her, but it was not good: Rhys had been taken to hospital shortly after leaving the dock and had died in the night, thanks to a heart seizure 'brought on by substance misuse'. The technical term disturbed Sîan. The heart of Rhys Gruffudd had died long before he began sniffing lighter fuel. Next, she made her way down to St David's Market, a snake-thin enterprise which thrived just a stone's throw from the city centre.

'Get your gums around me plums!' yelled a thickset man in a Welsh Rugby Union shirt, as she walked in from the Charles Street entrance.

Plum Man claimed 'the dossers' had left months back. A small woman selling plastic bags full of root vegetables was less sure.

'They're still here, lovely, but they comes down late. I never seen them myself.'

Sîan bought a bag of wrinkled looking turnips, even though she had no idea how to cook them. Her mobile rang. It was Howell reminding her she was supposed to be home in time to go to the doctor's. Standing still in the middle of the market, wedged in between shopping bags and potato sacks, she finally found the words which had long been eluding her.

'I don't want to go,' she said, shutting off her mobile quickly, before he could answer.

Back at the office she requested her colleagues didn't pass on her husband's calls. They assumed she had given him a row, or he had given her a row, and best not meddle. By mid-afternoon, she had interviewed a man who had been cheated out of his life insurance by a dodgy colleague, an award-winning cake maker with learning difficulties, and a hip hop poet with an impenetrable West Walian accent. Filing the last of her stories, Sîan made the call she had really wanted to make all day. She phoned a police contact and asked him more about Rhys' background.

'The lad's not got anyone interested in him, Sîan. We've certainly never been able to trace anyone. His social worker tells me the funeral's next week. You'd best buy a hat.'

Sîan remembered Rhys staring up at her from his fruit box bed, his strange grey eyes made stranger still by his wired state. Rhys had found his hell on earth a long time since. And now he would be buried without a fuss, or a do, just a social worker and a vicar in attendance. No music, no cuddly toys, or flowers garlanding his coffin – and certainly no grieving mother. Sîan wondered if she was still alive and when might she have given up fighting for her son? The truth, which had been waiting to hit her for months, hit her now and hard: she couldn't face being a mother at this point in time. This is what she had to tell Howell, pure and simple.

Sîan made her way home by bus. She watched the streets around the *Echo* flow away behind her. Next stop would be – where exactly? She had no idea, but she did know that she would write Rhys Gruffudd's obituary. A tribute to a young man who had crossed her path for a reason, and it wasn't anything to do with honing her skills as a crime reporter. Sîan sat back and closed her eyes. Howell was supposed to be finally cooking the runaway lobster for a celebratory meal. She realised what she was about to tell him would probably mean a life could be saved, after all – even it was only a lobster's.

One for Rose Cottage

S A Tillotson

There was no moon that night. Beyond the window panes the snow twisted and turned in a void of black. The ward was quiet except for Bobby, moaning gently, rhythmically and low. Diane sat at her desk in a shroud of orange electric lamplight. It was gone midnight when the telephone rang. Bobby shuffled past the nurses' station in his slippers, a paper trail of hard, knobbly, golf ball-sized faeces falling from his trouser leg. Reaching for her yellow stickies, Diane made a mental note to speak to someone about Bobby – his medication was obviously far too strong.

'12b?' A calm, confident, familiar voice. 'It's the other side.'

'Maggie. How are you this evening?'

'You know. All quiet?'

'Fairly.' Diane rolled her newly sharpened pencil towards her across the surface of the desk.

'Listen. They've got a girl they're sending up from Casualty and we just haven't got a bed for her. Can you take her?'

'Yes, we can take her.'

'She's been an out-patient over here for six months but it seems she took an overdose last night. They've pumped her out, but Dr Shar will need to see her. Pain in the fucking arse, she is. They'll all be at it now. Just to get some attention.'

'Send her up.'

'Good, 'cos she's on the way.'

'Name?'

'Phoebe Kane.'

As Diane pressed into the paper with the lead of her pencil it snapped with a loud ping. She reached for another, equally sharp.

Diane carefully inserted the pencil into her special, tortoise-shaped sharpener. The wood rested reassuringly against the blade. She twisted one against the other and blew the shavings away. Carefully she replaced the pencil in the container, tip pointing into the air, a sharp cluster of wooden stakes angled like a longbowman's barricade slammed into the ground to keep the bastards out. Phoebe Kane, she wrote in a small, neat, rather beautiful script, even as the lift doors concertinaed open and a tall, blond, ringleted yet ugly young man pushed an occupied bed before him onto the ward. She couldn't see the prone patient over the top of the desk so she stood up. Diane found herself looking down on a lump in the bedclothes and a sweat-plastered head of short, brown hair on the pillow. The young man paused, folded at the waist and resting his forearms along the bedrail, ankles crossed, his chin on his thumbs. He glanced at Diane from under heavy lidded eyes before letting his attention return to the body on the bed.

'She's twenty-nine. Took sixty-odd paracetemol, washed down with a variety of alcopops and several joints of quite good blow, if the lump she's got left in her pocket is anything to go by. Waste, eh?'

'The girl or the blow?' asked Diane, steadying the clipboard against her midriff.

'Both! Where do you want me to put her?'

An attempt had been made to clean her up; just a few snail-slime trails of vomit remained in her hair and behind her ears. She was going to need a bath in the morning. The acrid smell from the carrier bag that the porter had left at the bottom of her bed, suggested that her clothes too would need a trip to the washing machine. Diane stood over the girl, looking down at the elfin creature sleeping, then bent to place Phoebe's shoes next to her locker. Half leaning on the edge of the bed, Diane pushed a strand of damp, dark hair away from the girl's eyes. A raindrop of sweat ran down her nose.

Bobby shuffled back, bringing with him a strong stink of cigarette smoke. He moaned gently, rhythmically and low. He would be doing this all night – every half an hour he would scuff himself along like a large, wooden wardrobe, down to the day room where he would juggle and twirl wafer thin paper and strands of sharp tobacco. He would sit for half an hour and then push his wardrobe back to bed.

Diane emptied her handbag out onto her desk top, just as she did later for the duty sergeant. She loved cleaning out her handbag. She lined up the contents and held her bag upside down over the wastepaper bin. A gratifying wisp of fluff floated down among the pencil shavings. A lipstick from Boots, a key-ring from Australia with a koala bear and her name burnt into the leather, a present from her niece who lived in Adelaide. Diane often made plans to visit Australia. She would never go now. Two keys hung from her key ring, her front door key and her car key. She always kept her purse locked inside her car when she was on duty, which is why she didn't have any money when she reached the police station. Automatically she checked to make sure that the key to the medicine cabinet was in its right place. Yes, there it was. All's well! The long hand of the clock crashed down towards the half hour. Bobby began his slow removal back to the day room.

Here was a clean, white, freshly ironed handkerchief, scalloped around the edges and with a dark, blue 'D' embroidered in the corner. A clean, white handkerchief every morning since that stinging shame of being six and having to stand on her chair in Mrs Hopkins' class for forgetting her clean, white handkerchief. An unopened tube of polo mints, a puzzle book and a blue biro which Diane dropped into the holder on the desk and replaced with a sharp, pointed pencil. And a postcard from Graham, showing the high street in Swaffham. She turned over the card, *Darling*, he had written, *skies still endless in Norfolk. It is like walking towards the edge of the world.*

She didn't hear the girl leaving her bed.

Diane carefully replaced the contents of her handbag, everything in its place. Time for a nice cup of tea. She rose from her chair, smoothing down her dark blue uniform. She had always been very aware of the power of authority: policemen, teachers, doctors, people to be obeyed. She always did as she was told, paid with the exact change when she could, and always paid the price on the label. If what she wanted was too dear, she left it for another day. Later, when the young man opened the car door and helped her out, she thought, that's the thing about authority, it's for your own good. She caught the sound of her long dead mother rasping at the snow with her outdoor brush. Old and bent like a comma, she would jab at the stone steps.

'Can we have chips for tea, Mam?'

'No! Anything else you want to know?'

Jab, jab went the outdoor, sweeping brush.

'Have you seen Yvonne?' Diane placed the chair back under her desk and swung her reassuringly-full handbag onto her shoulder.

'She's down in the day room having a ciggie.' Bobby ceased shuffling, ready for a conversation.

'Right ho! When she gets back, will you tell her I've gone to put the kettle on? You want one?'

'Where's that girl?'

'What girl?'

'She should be in that bed. The one the Dutch student brought up.'

'Christ!'

'She's taken her shoes too. Maybe she's planning a trip.'

'Christ Almighty!'

'Shall I get Yvonne?'

'Go back to bed, Bobby.'

Diane dumped her handbag and walked swiftly towards the toilet door.

'Phoebe, are you in there, love? You all right, love?' Silly tart, she thought as she knocked on the cubicle door, which shuddered open beneath her fist. Yes, the girl was here, hanging from the waste pipe, her shoe laces tied tightly round her neck.

'Fucking stupid cow! If I fall down this toilet, it's your fucking fault!' Diane screamed as she climbed onto the toilet seat, scrambling for her scissors. Please let them reach, she implored, pulling on the chain that attached the scissors and the medicine cabinet key to her waist. One snip and the hanging girl fell onto the tiles in a dump of body, her leg bent and caught around the toilet pan.

'Oh God! Oh God!' moaned Diane, dragging the girl out of the cubicle and bending over to feel for a pulse in her neck. But she was alive still, and began coughing loudly into Diane's face.

'Stupid bitch! Stupid bitch!' Diane screamed at the contorting girl who was drowning on fresh air. 'We'd all like to fucking die, wouldn't we? It's not dying that's bastard hard.'

The girl opened her eyes and stared at the woman's shrieking mouth, only two inches away from her own trout-like gaze. That shut Diane up. For several seconds they stared into each other's eyes. There was nothing there, nothing. Then, suddenly, Diane grabbed the girl's ankle and hauled her along the toilet floor and out into the ward, dragging her back towards the bed. The hospital gown rucked up further and further, until it caught under the girl's armpits. Instinctively, Phoebe Kane reached down to cover her pubic hair, the flesh of her bottom slithering and sucking on the ceramic floor tiles.

'Yvonne, help me get this little madam into the bed, will you?' hissed Diane.

'I can get in myself.' One ankle still firmly in Diane's grasp, Phoebe attempted to stand, hopping as she struggled to pull down the hospital gown. She scrambled onto the bed, Diane tugging at her leg.

'Oh no, you don't! If you want to be treated like a pathetic invalid, we'll treat you like one. We will! Get off the bed! I said, get off the bed and let us lift you in.' Diane pulled at the girl, catching her off balance so that she fell heavily onto the floor. The girl began to cry.

'What on earth are you doing? Leave Phoebe to me. Stop it, Diane! Stop it! Now go away and put the kettle on and try and calm down, will you?'

'She thinks she has the right to choose,' screamed Diane. 'Lucky her, eh? Some of us don't get the choice!' The girl began to sob, her hands over her face, her legs sprawled across the floor. Other patients were stirring in the dim ward.

'Diane, go away.'

Diane responded to the tone of authority in her colleague's voice. Quietly, calmly, she walked back to her desk, pulled out the chair and breathed out through her nostrils, a barely audible sound. It was then that she decided what she was going to do.

The rest of the night shift was fairly quiet, until the consultant psychiatrist arrived and made that telephone call to say there was 'one for rose cottage'. Yvonne had gone looking for him leaving her instructions, not to move; but in the darkness of the night ward Diane put her plan into action. It was for the girl's own good. This would keep her safe. But the girl panicked and began vomiting again.

'Good girl,' Diane said, 'that'll get all that nasty muck out of your system.'

By the time that Yvonne returned with Dr Shar, Phoebe Kane had choked on a plug of her own puke. Coughing and screaming, pulling at her leashes, poor Phoebe finally slipped into oblivion, whilst Bobby shuffled back down to the day room.

Diane watched the snow twisting and turning through the window of the police car. It was a grey snow, and a suffocating, grey, grey morning. Somewhere the sun was shining on the other side of the winter sky. At the junction, the police constable bent both his arms to rest them on the steering wheel. Beside the pavement a hedgehog died tidily, only his bristles showing. Diane felt the young man watching her and caught his stare in the rear view mirror – only his eyes, his cold eyes, not caring that she was aware of his glance. She wanted to reach out and peel back the clean, white shirt from his sinewy forearms. She wanted to see his strong, hard, apricot flesh, knowing what it would come to. She knew the sag, the putty texture, the desiccated, dry, autumnal snap of bones. She knew the fall from grace; she knew where it would end.

'Would you like a cup of tea, Diane? You don't mind if I call you Diane, do you? Nice cup of tea for Mrs Wetherall, please.'

'She was her own worst enemy, Sergeant. I had to keep her safe, out of harm's way. I knew what was best for her. I had to make sure she was safe.'

'I see.'

'I had to restrain her, for her own good. That's why I tied her to the bed.'

The Use of a Mother

Ruth Joseph

It was difficult to ascertain how old Leticia Ryan was, although many in the common-room played the game.

'Look, she's got to be forty because there's that kid in year five, whose sister was taught by her and she's left Uni. And practising at least ten years…'

'Doesn't mean anything at all,' snapped Veronica Strange, Physics, slithering deftly into *her* chair before that damned PE lout they called a gym teacher could claim it as his own and clamp his filthy trainers on its worn moquette.

'Well, I think she's got to be at least fifty,' said Endaf Perkins, Welsh, not bothering to raise his eyes and far too preoccupied with the new Plaid manifesto which had plunged into the dark of his empty hallway that morning and was just released from its buff-coloured envelope.

'And that briefcase, you'd think she was carrying the crown jewels!'

'Most probably it's her rolling-pin,' muttered Veronica Strange, exploding into laughter. Proud of her own joke, she turned her face to invoke the staffroom's amusement.

'No, no, but it could be a limited edition bag of flour,' chuckled Edwards, Maths, whilst thumbing the new *Sudoku Compendium* and wondering when he could possibly start it without the students noticing.

The subject of this controversy had already been up for hours, working at home. There was so much to organise with the students' GCSEs. The school now divided her curriculum into modules and it was no longer called 'Home Economics', as she preferred, thinking that it gave the subject status, or even 'cookery' as it had been called in her childhood. She remembered her cookery days and the delicious anticipation of taking her large biscuit tin to school with the pictures of Huntley and Palmers emblazoned on the outside.

Her mother regarded that tin as a treasure and often told the tale of the Christmas just after the war when Uncle Gerald arrived with it tucked under his arm. 'Well, it was such a surprise,' she'd said, 'so posh – a whole tin. We were used to buying a few broken biscuits from our local Argyll stores. The shop had a lovely warm buttery vanilla smell. You remember, they kept the biscuits under a wooden counter, Mrs Everett, the shop owner, would scoop them out from those large tins, like massive building blocks with hinged flaps and then I'd only buy the custard creams or the rich tea. Well, I'd make the rest.'

And, as a teenager, Leticia walked to school with that tin full of the ingredients for cheese scones, or choux pastry, ready weighed and wrapped in greaseproof paper, and it made her feel important. Afterwards, while her baking was cooking and the others were talking about last-night's disco, she'd be concentrating on her oven, checking her watch, wondering how her mixture had melded together, and buzzing with an extraordinary thrill when it rose, golden brown, to sit on a cooling tray, often to be given top marks.

After completing her schedules and study notes, she placed all the documents in a large black briefcase, which had been her father's and travelled everywhere with her, drove to school, and parked her ancient Micra into the last space reserved for staff. She usually took that space although there was a heavy growth of nettles and hawthorn which scraped her woollies or lisle tights. It was autumn, her favourite time of the year, when the cooking apples were British and her thoughts turned to rich-crusted apple pies with dustings of sparkling sugar and maybe a session of plum jam-making with the interested ones from the fifth form.

She pushed open the door to the staffroom. At this time, just before assembly, there was a shortage of chairs. But she was used to that and produced a faded green cardigan out of the briefcase, found herself a corner, and sat on the floor on the cardigan.

'OK, Leticia?' said Mr Harris, aware of the closeness of her folded body below him. He felt the same when he refused the *Big Issue* lads in town. 'You must not give in to them,' he told his wife, Emily, as she scampered to catch his six-foot gait.

'Oh, I'm quite happy down here, it's good for my back. Plenty of room after assembly, then I have a free for the first half of the morning. It'll give me more time for preparation.'

'A few more biscuits to revise for?' breathed Miss Strange under her breath. A quiet titter reverberated around the room.

Leticia felt a blush – well, a flush, she was that age – it burned through her body. 'Well, whatever,' she murmured.

She heard her mother's voice, youthful, vigorous. 'If a dog pees on you, it doesn't know, it's a dog. Ignorant people are the same,' It was the voice she'd used to console Leticia when she had been teased in the past.

And look at Mother now, poor love, did she feel pain, lying in the care home bed? Did she know anything? Don't get maudlin, Leticia, you know you couldn't manage any more. The last straw had been Mother taking the iron to the bath, thinking it was the radio, and it fell in, fortunately before she had dipped a bluish toe. There had been so many incidents before – her gardening wellies in the fridge, and the carton of milk above the boiler. Finally, the social worker had sat down with Leticia after another close shave when Leticia reported her mother missing somewhere in the dark outside in her nightie.

'You've got to let her go, to a place where she'll be watched all the time and cared for: it's for her own good.'

Leticia had agonised for nights, twisting in bed, checking the time, 2.30, 3.30, then turning the polished brass knob of her mother's bedroom-door, padding over the creaking floorboards and hovering over the sleeping lady. She had watched as the soft familiar folds of her mother's mouth quivered with each breath, then sat at her bedside.

'Mum, Mother, love. Am I being a witch to send you away? Do you understand why? I know they all say, "Oh it's for the best," but will you understand, and will they know that you like a dash of cold milk in your hot chocolate so you don't burn, and that you like butter on your toast, not marge? And that you hate your toes tucked in at night like the evening nurse does when she pops in?'

Her life became more insular the worse her mother became. But that was the other facet of her life – the side that had prevented Leticia from meeting 'Mr Right' as she called him. Opportunities became less and less frequent the more difficult circumstances became at home and Leticia did not like to call on the neighbours. Contact dwindled with awkwardness: Leticia feeling more embarrassed, and others crossing the street, afraid of uncomfortable discussions.

Eventually, when Mother was settled in Fair-well Homes, Leticia found the lack of presence in the evening – even that lumpen sleeping body upstairs – lonely.

Then one break, she was talking to Edwards, Lower School Head, who was treating himself to a new fancy Dell. He waved the coloured brochure under her nose, and said to Leticia, 'You should get one of these.'

She looked down, past the serviceable corduroy skirt and lisle tights and shrugged angular shoulders. 'It's not possible. I can just about manage with the money I earn and now I'm going to have to pay for my mother's specialist care.'

'You can have my old computer,' said Edwards, thinking it would be easier to drop it into her house than all that third world stuff his wife had arranged without his agreement. 'Yes, yes, that's decided then. Call it a perk of the job.'

So, every evening after she had visited her mother and dabbed the Ovaltine moustache from the twisted mouth, she came home with glorious anticipation, for the first time in years.

She surfed different websites. One night she gazed in awe at the Waldorf Astoria's website in New York and read the history of the film stars that had danced through chandeliered deco rooms, past silver-mirrored corridors and potted palms. Another night she read discussions from apiarists in Michigan and Utah, absorbing their interest and worries about the loss of the Cyprus bee-keeping industry.

But her main passion was cookery and its origins. Night after night she would research different recipes, pursuing her ultimate fascination – the use of a 'mother' as a means of fermentation in bread-making, vinegars and fizzy drinks, such as ginger beer.

A 'mother' is a small amount of the mixture that has been previously prepared and allowed to ferment. The following day it is added to a larger amount of the raw mixture and thus a natural fermentation occurs. Then a little of that mixture is reserved for the next day's batch. But when she chatted on line with traditional bakers in Sweden, Denmark, Finland, the Ukraine and Ireland, she found that a reliable fermentation was a far more technical business than she had ever imagined; and that a mixture of flour, water, raisins and yoghurt produced the most successful 'mother'. Apparently the raisins produced the most amount of yeast, and the yoghurt to a lesser extent, while the flour produced only bacterial colonies. Some of the 'mothers' took six days to produce the most successful ferment. And each country had its own speciality 'mother' and method of manufacture. Nothing went to waste. In the Ukraine, they used the whey left from cheese-making to form part of the liquid, while the sharp vinegary juice that was created from pickling cucumbers in dill and garlic formed the basis for very treasured savoury 'mother'. And some of the leaven mixtures they cherished were one hundred years old! Her studies developed. She began to collate the letters and emails from Ivan and Stephan, Fergus, Giuseppe and Maria.

Almost two years later on a dark chilly evening when her breath blew before her in icy puffs, Leticia was taken to one side by the visiting consultant at her mother's home. 'You should congratulate yourself on your exemplary daughterly devotion. No one could have done more. But I'm afraid… your mother has taken a turn for the worse… the end, I'm sorry, is pretty near.'

The words ricocheted around the room, peppering the flowery bed-screens, and hitting Leticia as if they were bullets. She drove home unaware of the roads, the traffic or her own driving signals. She walked into the echoing house, switched on all the lights to make it feel as if there was someone else present, shook some dried food into the cat-bowl and changed into her dressing-gown. Then came downstairs and made herself a poached egg on toast, crying as she cut up the crisp browned bread, thinking how many times in her childhood her mother had prepared that very same dish for her. Then, searching for her accustomed comfort, she switched on her PC. It sat on her makeshift desk, fashioned out of a piece of MDF in an inglenook. Piles of recipes of breads, loaf-cakes, savoury and sweet, vinegars and ginger beers all with their unique and necessary 'mother' lay in stacks on either side in different colour-coded plastics, like a fragrant layer cake.

Still in shock, shivering now, she looked at her PC, her source of comfort, and typed in the word 'mother'. A book by Bertold Brecht and another on Mother Teresa along with herbs, supplements and baby-wear images, flooded the screen.

She looked from them to her piles of notes then stared back at the word. 'Why not!' she said, out loud. 'Why not indeed!' and suddenly smiled, hunching her body then touching her lips with a hesitant finger. The stream of tears that had swollen her face ebbed away. She began to work, the hours racing with the swift movement of her fingers. The dark faded into dawn and she was surprised to hear one sharp birdsong piercing the silence, cutting through the indigo velvet.

It's 7.30, time to get up, she thought. Make porridge, feed the cat (who had abandoned the idea of canvassing the night worker for more food at three, and sourced her favourite velour cushion instead). Leticia rose from her desk and stretched her stiffened, cold limbs.

'Break the rules, have a bath, Letty, love, not good to get cold,' she heard her mother say. She was always there for her, wasn't she? She ran a bath and let the warmth of the water soothe her tired body, then jumped out quickly and slipped into yesterday's clothes that still held her shape and were flung over a chair from the night before. Glancing at her watch, she picked up her briefcase and ran out of the semi.

It was a few months later, almost Christmas, on a Friday morning when the week had been long and tiring. That day, many of 5C had forgotten their ingredients for a mid-term test. It meant she had to drive quickly to the supermarket and push through a throng of harassed Christmas shoppers for a few items; and then the whole day ran late. When she arrived home, she hung up her mother's old best wool coat, which she had adopted as hers, enjoying its comfort, and pushed the computer button, staring at the screen. An email fell into her intray. She stared at it, reading it over and over. Then she hugged herself, laughing, ran a quick bath, came down in her dressing-gown, made another poached egg on toast and ate it quickly. Then re-read the email, savouring each word: *Yes ... maybe ... but there's still a lot of work to do.*

All over the Christmas break she sat at the computer. Days and nights passed and Leticia remained welded to her seat.

The following February, the 28th, an unusually bright day with a few clouds hanging like puffed grey cities in the sky, Leticia approached the school. She opened her briefcase, glanced at the contents and then smiled, closing the heavy lock with a satisfying click.

Inside the staff-room, the lack of seating situation had not improved.

As usual, Leticia sat on her green woolly in the corner. Miss Strange had been coming earlier and earlier to ensure that *her* chair was hers. And Mr Harris still watched as Leticia pretended that she was comfortable in that situation. But something had changed. Leticia was able that morning to rise above any jibes. She was strong, capable, and intelligent even. For, sitting in her briefcase was a letter typed on thick, good quality paper, with a contract, detailing an offer to publish *The Use of a Mother* with a substantial advance.

and say I had been out with Sheila.

Early One Morning

Angela Rigby

I was seventeen when I met Matt in the Caprice café – a new and exciting place with a machine that made a noise like a steam engine and poured out frothy coffee. There were big plastic tomatoes on the tables, and a jukebox with a metal arm that picked out records with the delicacy of fingers. I chose a Beatles number and Sheila and I twisted together. Matt came across and joined in. He had dark hair and blue eyes and moved wonderfully. After the dance Sheila went home early and Matt and I sat and talked and talked. I was home very late that night.

'I don't want you going to that café again,' Dad said. 'It's full of rockers!'

'No it isn't.'

'I'm not arguing. You've to be in by nine o'clock during the week, and ten at weekends. You've got exams next year and you need to do well.'

I rated Dad as old-fashioned and a bit simple, not unintelligent, but he left school at fifteen and did an apprenticeship as an electrician so his thinking was limited. Mum worked in a shop. They weren't going to understand the sixties.

Matt was at the Caprice the following evening and we worked out a system for keeping in contact. He was a mechanic at a garage on the main road outside town and I could phone him there. His parents' home was in London and he had one room in the next village. He said he could sometimes make it into town at lunchtime if I could get out of school. He had his own banger of a car and we could drive out at evenings and weekends without my parents knowing. I would get home by nine o'clock and say I had been out with Sheila.

So we drove round the lanes with Matt doing seventy and me screaming. We went to a fair on the first Saturday and rode on the merry-go-round. Music jangled and gold horses plunged up and down with bared teeth and wild eyes. The fairground lights and colours spun round us and I couldn't stop laughing. I was madly in love. Inevitably somebody saw me and my parents heard about it.

'Who is he? And how old is he?'

'His name's Matt. He's twenty-three and he's a mechanic.'

'What's a man of that age doing with a girl of seventeen?'

'Why shouldn't he?'

'Because he's too old for you. You know what he's after?

'No, he isn't. You don't know him.'

'I was in the army and I know enough. You've got A-levels to work for and a chance your mother and I never had. You're not throwing it away on rubbish like that.'

I was furious. Dad was such a snob. 'I don't care about A-levels. I love Matt.'

And of course they couldn't stop me. They would have had to stay up all night, fetch me to and from school and lock me in every evening and weekend.

'Don't take any notice of them,' Matt told me. 'Parents are like that. They still think you're a little girl. Don't let them spoil your life.'

I was determined they wouldn't. It was my life – my decision. So we drove out as usual, parked in lay-bys and kissed and cuddled. One evening he was stroking my neck and his hand dropped to my breasts. We had sex on the back seat. There were other times after that, either in the car or in the grass beyond the hedge when the weather got warmer. Long stalks reached up round us pointing at a blue sky where the early swifts were racing and screaming. I closed my eyes and it was fantastic and joyful.

Mum came out with the direct question; the one I had been refusing to ask myself. 'Are you pregnant?'

'What makes you think that?'

'You look it.'

I was as thin as ever and couldn't see how she arrived at the idea. 'No, I'm not.'

But I was, and I told Matt.

'You can't be. I was careful.'

'Yes, I am. Matt, we'll have to get married. My parents will go mad.' I put my head against his shoulder. 'I want to be with you all the time.

This is our baby. You do love me, don't you?'

'Yes of course I do, but it'll take some working out.'

We arranged to meet by the church as usual. The system was that I hid just inside the gate until his car drew up, and then rushed out and got in before anyone saw me. I waited for two hours that evening. I counted the arched windows on the church, examined stone carvings on the porch and got to know that building as I had never known it before. I stared at the tall spire pointing at puffy white clouds moving overhead until the church and I sailed in the opposite direction and I was dizzy. It got cold and I crossed my arms over my chest and pulled my cardigan together. I thought his car must have broken down. The next day I phoned the garage and he'd left. They didn't know where he was. I phoned every evening for a week, until the man at the other end got really angry. On the next Saturday I took the bus into the village where he said he had a room and the landlady told me that he had left. There was no forwarding address. I walked home from the bus stop and went into the kitchen where Mum was cooking. I sat down at the table and cried with my elbows on the table and my head in my hands. Out of the blue I remembered, as a child, standing in a shop sobbing because I wanted a toy that Mum said I couldn't have. Immediately she would bend down to comfort me and I got the toy. It always worked. Suddenly she was in the chair next to me with an arm round my shoulder.

'He's left me,' I said.

'Is that the boy your Dad said you weren't to go out with?' I nodded. 'You've been seeing him all this time?'

I sobbed and sobbed with tears falling on the plastic cover. Her voice came quietly. 'You *are* pregnant, aren't you?'

I nodded and she put her head against mine. When she told Dad he looked as though I had hit him.

Later we had the first of several talks. I was to leave school at the end of term and we would say I had a job to go to. Mum would find out about mother and baby homes, as far away as possible, and I would come back after the baby was born. No one was to know the truth.

'I've worked all my life in this town,' said Dad, 'and I don't want people looking at my daughter as if she's got no morals. Your Gran mustn't know. It would kill her.'

That gave me a cue to be self-righteous at last. 'Is that all you care about?' I wept. 'What people think! It's all about yourselves. It's not about me.'

'It's life,' he said, 'that's what people are like. And if you'd cared one scrap about your mother and me you wouldn't have done this to us.'

'To you!' I exclaimed, 'It's me – me – my baby.'

There was no option on that, of course. The baby would have to be adopted.

'You've got your whole life in front of you,' said Mum. 'You can still do your A-levels and have a proper career. You're bright enough.' She held my hands between hers and rubbed my fingers. I knew she meant that she hadn't had that kind of life.

I left in August; first to stay in lodgings that Dad paid for, and then to be admitted to the mother and baby home six weeks before I was due. I'd hoped all along that Matt would reappear. I jumped inside every time the front doorbell or phone rang in the evenings and weekends. I imagined rushing down the garden path and into his arms as he came through the gate to tell me about the little flat he had gone away to get for us.

It was a journey I chose to do by myself, sitting by the window in the train and watching the houses going backwards and away from me with their ordinary lives inside. I was outside now. There was a kick from inside me and I put my hand against it. The train passed a field with horses galloping and I remembered the merry-go-round with jarring music and wooden animals with vicious eyes. It came to me that I would never ride on one again, and I saw the little things in my life that would always be changed for me: a certain kind of café, a Beatles song, swifts. I saw too that my crusade for freedom had been a rush to a cliff edge with Mum and Dad chasing after me begging me to stop and that, as I was shouting that I had won, I shot over the edge, and hurtled towards the wreckage of my life.

I waited with other girls. A few had boyfriends who visited, but most of the fathers had 'disappeared'.

'It's magic,' said Anna. 'You say, "I'm pregnant," and, Puff! men disappear. It has an effect on male anatomy.'

She was several years older than me, had already parted with one baby and announced her intention of keeping this one.

'Has your new baby got the same father?' I asked.

'No, and I've never seen that one again either.'

'Did you mean to have another baby?'

'No, but I missed the first one so much. I suppose I wanted someone to love and someone to love me. My welfare worker told me a lot of girls who have their babies adopted go straight out and have a second one. It's something to do with maternal instinct. My family don't think I'm doing the right thing this time.'

'What's the right thing?'

'Don't you know? We come here to be made back into virgins. The baby goes and never existed, and we might be able to get married after all, if we're lucky enough to find a decent man who'll take us. What my family means is that if I keep the baby with me I might not get that chance.'

In the nursery, in cots like seed boxes, there were big babies with pink faces, little babies with pale faces, premature babies with strange eyes, babies in crochet bonnets and ribboned jackets, babies waving tiny hands at the world. Puff. They too would disappear.

She started with gentle head butts, pushing towards the light, like a small wave pulsing up the beach and retreating. I pushed with her and we were the same wave, going backwards and forwards. Then there were huge waves and she was battering to escape and we raged together. In the distance there were faces and voices, but they had nothing to do with us.

She was small and wrapped in white towelling. I took her in my arms and looked at the round face with its wondering dark eyes and little bits of spiky hair. She was warm against me and I slept and she slept.

I called her Elizabeth and bathed and fed her for six weeks. My parents wrote and phoned, and sent money for baby clothes and anything else I needed. My mother cried and said they were thinking about me all the time and were missing me very much, but they would not visit me. I guessed she couldn't face seeing the grandchild she would never see again. I understood that my parents loved me, as I had not understood it before. And I knew too that I had never been in love with Matt any more than he had been in love with me. I hadn't even known him. I simply made a selfish boy into the image of a romantic lover because that was what I wanted to do.

I bought pretty little clothes for her and the morning of the adoption travelled towards me. I would have to go to an office and hand her over. I could take a friend with me and a case full of clothes and any toys I had. Her new family might keep them, or might not. I was to take her birth certificate and identify it as hers. I didn't want to do any of it. The matron was not impressed by my doubts.

'You have to put it behind you,' she ordered, 'and forget about her.'

I wondered if Matt ever thought for half a second about what he had done, of his daughter and the life she would live without him, the grief of my parents and the irreparable change in my relationship with them – the shadows over my life. Every morning I would wake up and wonder where she was and how she was. I would look at the eyes of children to see if they were familiar, and later at young adults who might look like me or Matt. I would know the year she first went to school and the year she left. I would know her birthdays and her Christmases. This would be the patchwork of my life and I would live with its tormenting pattern.

Early one morning Anna and I took the train to the office. She carried the case and I held Elizabeth. We were shown into a little room and a social worker came and took the case away. Then she came back with another social worker. The process had to be witnessed to demonstrate that I was handing her over of my own free will. They held out the birth certificate. I put Elizabeth on my lap as I took it in my hands, and she looked up at me. My hands shook so much I couldn't read it. It was like a death certificate. I could have said no. I could have got up and carried her back up the street and into my life. I nodded, and for a moment held her in my arms. One of them took her and she was gone.

Anna had to go off somewhere, so I was alone on my walk to the station, carrying the empty case.

A Journey to Berlin 1964

Linda Baxter

Monday

Dear Richard, You won't believe this. I've missed the coach. Didn't hear the alarm! Anyway, I'm not wasting all my money, I've found a lift like the one I had to London in the Christmas holidays, and will be going tomorrow. I'll still have 4 days in Berlin. I've checked with the hostel, they said I could stay as long as I liked!! Love, Barbara (Hope you like the pic of Professor-Huber-Platz, I'm having a coffee in the Mensa, X marks the spot.)

She looked at her engagement ring. It was pale silver, quite wide. Richard had found it in an antique stall in the Portobello Road. Dear Richard! Barbara had known him for a very long time, they were practically childhood sweethearts. They used to do their homework together in each other's houses, they listened to rock 'n' roll records on Radio Luxembourg, they went to the pictures at the local Rex cinema once a week, sat in the back row. They left their small town to be undergraduates in London, studying Engineering and German. They lived in segregated Halls of Residence, but a rainy afternoon would find them sharing a narrow single bed in Richard's room. They expected to get married as soon as Barbara had finished her year in Germany. Living together was not the done thing in those days.

Barbara found a stamp in her purse and stuck it on the postcard. She went to the counter and bought today's lunch, the one she liked least: boiled potatoes, wishy-washy green salad and a fried egg. Possibly nutritious, and it did cost only one Mark. She planned to go round to Reinhard's digs, a couple of streets away. He was her best friend in Munich. She met him in October, at the beginning of her first semester. He was studying Ancient and Modern History and showed her round the city, explaining many German and Bavarianisms. They spent a lot of time together, in pubs and cafés, in theatres and cinemas, in discotheques, in bed. Barbara felt safe with Reinhard, he was large and protective, though now and then he would have another woman in tow. But Barbara did not get uptight about that, people had to have their own space after all. He had brownish hair and a beard, and wore glasses. He usually wore a big woolly jumper and cord trousers in dark green. He called her '*Du*'. The trip to Berlin was partly a means of getting away from him for a few days, to mull things over.

She changed her mind about visiting Reinhard and bought another postcard.

Montag nachmittag

Lieber Reinhard! Obviously I had too much Gulaschsuppe last night!! Luckily I've got a Mitfahrgelegenheit to Berlin tomorrow. Have a lovely time in your new bubble car, see you on Saturday (i.e. not Friday). Will send a postcard or two! Gruß und Kuß Deine Barbara

She did not need a stamp for this one - she would just put it through his letterbox. The marriage to Richard was looming; she must review her situation.

The next day she did hear the alarm. The driver, Karl-Heinz, lived with his parents in Fuchsstrasse, three stops away on the tram, in the northern part of Schwabing. The house was large and detached, with floor-to-ceiling windows, flowery ironwork and balustrades, and a wooded garden full of lilacs blooming white, pink and purple. Karl-Heinz's friend Stefan arrived, and the two men sat in the front of the car, an old black Volkswagen, with Barbara in the back. It was a short drive to the A9, the motorway from Munich to Berlin. The men talked to each other, more or less ignoring Barbara. She probably looked wrong, no twinset, no pearls, no coiffure, just long, unkempt dark hair, a short skirt, and a suitcase that was not proper leather. Altogether not the *junge Dame* they expected.

They drove past Nuremberg, and after another hour or so they passed Bayreuth and the turning to Hof. Karl-Heinz filled up the tank with petrol, and they came to the border. There was a large *Deutsche Demokratische Republik* emblem, and a guard standing on a podium watching the vehicles arrive through binoculars. He wore the standard uniform: a peaked cap, a belt with a holster over his jacket, trousers rather like jodhpurs and knee-high boots. The frontier control point was a huge stretch of grey concrete and drab huts, overpopulated by sullen guards. To the right, the driver of a West German car and his passenger were standing by as two guards searched the boot and their luggage, to the left, a small van was being examined in detail by several guards, and the driver's documents were being scrutinised. Karl-Heinz drove slowly forward to join the queue approaching the Checkpoint in the covered area. There was a sign saying STOP and *Motor abstellen*. From then on it was a question of waiting, for one guard to saunter round the car doing an exterior check of the vehicle and its occupants, and for another guard behind the window to take his time checking everybody's passports, each one relishing his miserable power.

It felt strange driving through this other Germany. The road was noticeably bumpier. People from the West were allowed to drive on this transit motorway to West Berlin, but they were not allowed to leave it. There was not much traffic, a few scruffy East German cars and trucks, and conspicuously more, much smarter West German cars and lorries. They drove past the turning to Erfurt, Dresden and Gera, past Leipzig, and over the River Elbe, flowing to Hamburg in the West and the North Sea. It was late afternoon when they crossed into West Berlin, into Zehlendorf in the American Sector. Barbara was dropped off at Dreilinden Kleinmachnow, and from here she took the *S-Bahn* to Grunewald. Karl-Heinz and Stefan were driving further towards the centre of West Berlin, to Tiergarten and Charlottenburg, in the British Sector.

Tuesday

Dear Richard, Made it to the hostel at last! X marks approx. where my room is. The lift was in a Beetle, you know, the sort with the engine at the back and the boot in the front. Crossing the border W-E was scary - those Eastern Bloc thrillers aren't that exaggerated! I was starving - had potato soup, then sausages + red cabbage + dumplings. I've met two of the Munich trippers (all from the US of A) - Don and Priscilla. They invited me to their BBQ party the day after tomorrow! Love, Barbara

Dienstag

Lieber Reinhard! There's slightly more room in a Käfer than in an Isetta! The driver and his friend are a pair of stuck-up snobs, and what a hostile reception at the border! Are these real Germans?? This is a classy hostel, in a superior suburb, and the cafeteria food is heaps better than the Mensa fodder. Must be all that American money. I'm looking forward to a Yankee barbecue on Thursday! Gruß und Kuß Deine Barbara

On her first full day in West Berlin Barbara made straight for the Kurfürstendamm. She took the *S-Bahn* to Zoologischer Garten, then the *U-Bahn* to Uhlandstrasse. It was a consumer's paradise. The elegant, exclusive Kempinski Hotel was fronted by a doorman in top hat and tails. There were hoardings of advertisements, and posters for films, including the latest *Nouvelle Vague* film dubbed into German, François Truffaut's *Jules und Jim*. Clothes shops, couture houses, jewellers, leather goods shops, hairdressers, shoe shops, bookshops, florists, bakers, restaurants, snack bars, newsagents, grocers, banks, pubs – you could find everything you wanted on the Ku'damm. Barbara bought two postcards.

You couldn't miss the Café Kranzler: it had a rotunda on top with a red and white striped awning. Barbara was lucky enough to get a seat at a table in the window upstairs. The waitresses wore frilly white blouses and frilly little white aprons over their dark skirts. She had a pot of coffee and a portion of cheesecake. She could see the *Gedächtniskirche*, the bombed remains of a church which had been retained as a bleak reminder of the horror of World War II. Several off-duty British, American and French soldiers were strolling up and down.

Wednesday

Dear Richard, The Ku'damm is something else! It's buzzing with atmosphere. There's so much to see, so much to buy - I could've spent my entire grant in half an hour flat. You can keep Oxford Street! The KaDeWe is a huge department store, and posh and snooty, just like Harrods. I've tired myself out window shopping! When I've recovered I'll go and view the Wall. East Berlin tomorrow! Love, Barbara

Mittwoch

Lieber Reinhard! As you predicted, the Ku'damm is super! Do you know, it's even got a Spar?! And people are friendly. West Berlin is rather more up to date than Munich, and I don't just mean the underground. Some of the renovations are eye-catchingly modern, and there's lots of young trees. Next on the agenda, a walk to the Brandenburg Gate - I'll see it from the other side tomorrow! Gruß und Kuß Deine Barbara

Die Strasse des 17. Juni had been renamed in memory of the victims of a workers' uprising in East Berlin and the GDR in 1953. It was long and straight and wide, and stretched from Ernst-Reuter-Platz to the Brandenburg Gate. Barbara took the *U-Bahn* to Hansaplatz and walked eastwards. This was to be her first view of the wall, a drab, grey, breeze block construction, shoulder-high. The Brandenburg Gate was behind it, in the East Berlin sector, with an East German flag at the very top.

The next day Barbara took the *U-Bahn* to Kochstrasse and walked northwards to Friedrichstrasse and Checkpoint Charlie. YOU ARE LEAVING THE AMERICAN SECTOR read the sign, and again in Russian, and again in French. *Sie verlassen den amerikanischen Sektor* was at the bottom of the sign in small capitals. There were soldiers everywhere, American ones on the West side of the wall, Russian ones on the East side. There were tanks and machine guns too. Theoretically, as a foreigner, Barbara could simply show her passport, first to the Americans, then to the Russians, and enter East Berlin. In practice, she did not think she would feel very safe on her own, so she booked a ticket on a tourist bus that would drive its passengers round some of the important sites in East Berlin.

The coach was very comfortable, with red curtains at the windows. It zigzagged through the Checkpoint. On the East side the East German flag was prominent. There was a delay while the guards checked everybody's passport. Then the coach drove through a wasteland surrounded by barbed wire and punctuated with manned watch towers: the Death Zone. The first houses they saw had 'dead windows'. All windows facing towards the West had been bricked up. The walls were covered in bullet holes. Very little seemed to have been rebuilt. The odd new building was straight up and down, simply functional and constructed from the cheapest materials. There was no *KaDeWe*, in fact, where were the shops? Wherever there was a queue outside. There were no advertisements either, just communist placards. The coach drove along Unter den Linden, past the Russian Embassy, which did look refurbished, to the Brandenburg Gate. They drove round Potsdamer Platz, a stagnating, barren square and the gaunt, desolate Alexanderplatz. The grey, dilapidated blocks of flats only looked suitable for eking out an existence. There was a dearth of ordinary people on the streets, but plenty of soldiers. The few citizens that they did see were pasty-looking and wore dreary old clothes. They did not smile.

It was a relief to return to West Berlin. Barbara bought two postcards of Checkpoint Charlie, but decided to write them later. She put them in her shoulder bag. She considered that the best antidote to the grimness of the morning would be to see the film that she saw advertised yesterday. It might be a French film, but the German film industry was incapable of producing anything worthwhile. She had a vague idea what *Jules et Jim* was about, and thought that it might help her with her dilemma too.

The Filmbühne am Steinplatz was near the University, not far from Bahnhof Zoo. It was a proper art house. There were posters of significant, memorable films in the foyer, *Hiroshima mon Amour, La Dolce Vita, Casablanca*. The auditorium only had about ninety seats. Most of the people there must have been students. There were no advertisements, just a trailer for next week's film, *A Bout de Souffle*. After a while Barbara got used to the dubbing, in fact she had to admit that Eva-Katharina Schultz did a good version of Jeanne Moreau, who played Catherine. Jules and Jim both love Catherine, eventually she marries Jules. The threesome are separated by the First World War, but they get back together again afterwards, and now Catherine wants to have an affair with Jim. When Jim rejects her, she tries to shoot him, and when that fails, she stages a tragic car accident, in which they both die. Jules is left on his own.

Barbara did not exactly approve of Catherine, a capricious siren playing with men, a self-centred woman with no discretion. Modern women, in their relationships with men, had to be very careful. Going to bed with him was all right, so long as you were 'in love' with him, but you did it quietly and discreetly. 'Sleeping around' was not a good idea, as you could be regarded as 'an easy lay', and lose all respectability. Barbara felt that the situation would not have been any different forty years ago. It irritated her that Catherine was immune to all those unspoken rules. She hoped she treated Richard and Reinhard better than Catherine treated Jules and Jim. Perhaps that was why her choice was so difficult, why she kept putting off making a decision – why she was not actually even thinking about it very hard.

Despite her disapproval, Barbara was so bowled over by the film that she decided to watch it again, and in any case she needed to have it firmly in her mind as a basis for the serious reflection that she must make herself do. She could easily get back to the hostel in time for the party.

When she arrived, however, around half past six, the barbecue was already over. The Americans liked to eat early. There were a few snacks left, and a large quantity of Berliner Weisse, the beer that Berliners traditionally drank with raspberry or woodruff syrup. Barbara liked both, and alternated the red with the green. Chubby Checker sang *The Twist* several times, Joey Dee and the Starliters sang *Peppermint Twist*, Little Eva sang *The Loco-Motion*. Barbara danced, or twisted, with Don a couple of times, but was careful not to upset Priscilla. Don said there were a few gatecrashers from the building for full-time students over the quad, but if they brought their own beer, the more the merrier! There was some discussion about *Louie Louie* by the Kingsmen – was it in any way suggestive, did it make your ears tingle, indeed, was it pornographic? Then *Twist And Shout* by the Beatles came on, and Barbara found herself dancing, or twisting, with someone she did not recognise as belonging to the Munich group. He must be from over the quad, she thought.

He said, 'I heard the music and came over.'

She said, 'You do a mean twist.'

'So do you.'

He had floppy brown hair and brown eyes, and was wearing an open-necked red and white checked shirt with the sleeves rolled up to the elbows and khaki trousers. Chubby Chequer sang *Pony Time*, Buddy Holly sang *Brown Eyed Handsome Man*, The Crystals sang *Da Doo Ron Ron*. He kissed her. Caraway and sour cream, she thought, and kissed him back. Oh, Noble Rose paprika! Tokay, just like at Uncle Cyril's ruby wedding!

'I've got some Beatle songs in my room,' he said.

The Beatles sang *Sie liebt Dich*, and *Komm, gib mir deine Hand*. Barbara was wearing a blue sleeveless shift dress with a long zip at the back. He was holding her, kissing her, then he found the zip and pulled it slowly down. Barbara undid the buttons on his shirt. The rest of the clothes came off in a hurry as they stumbled onto the bed.

Barbara looked round the room. There was an overflowing bookcase and heaps of books on the floor, there was a model of a building, a photograph of a distinguished-looking man, a poster of *Casablanca*.

'I don't know your name,' she said. 'I'm Barbara.'

'I like to be known as Rick,' he said.

Bells rang in Barbara's head; she ignored them.

Rick drawled, 'Play it, Sam,' and got up to put *Can't Buy Me Love* on the turntable. Barbara laughed.

'They've only recorded two songs in German so far,' he said.

'You've got a slight accent?'

'Yep! I'm from Hungary. That's my father in the photo. He died in the uprising.'

'Oh, no!'

'My mother, my little brother and I escaped to East Germany.'

Barbara nodded. 'Tell me more.'

'We settled in East Berlin. Mum did all kinds of work so we could eat. My brother and I went to school, of course. That was hard to begin with, learning a new language. About a year before I was going to do the *Abitur* Mum decided to move us to West Berlin. That was just in time – a few months later they built the wall.'

'And now you're studying – Architecture, isn't it?'

'That's right. Now it's your turn. Tell me what you're doing here.'

The kitchen was along the corridor.

'*Buletten*, that's what we need,' said Rick. 'You cut up the onion, quite small, oh, and these bits of green and red pepper, too.'

He rummaged in the fridge and brought out some mince and an egg, and from the larder some breadcrumbs, pepper and salt. He mixed up the ingredients in a bowl. Barbara held him round the waist, put her cheek on his shoulder.

'What talent,' she said.

He fashioned two very tasty beefburgers.

'I've run out of beer,' he said, 'I took my last couple of bottles to the party. I can make some peppermint tea.'

Rick put *Please Please Me* on the turntable, sat beside Barbara on the bed, stroked her hair, kissed her. Kohlrabi and dill, walnuts and marjoram. Barbara looked into the brown eyes. Bells were ringing again, more urgently.

'I think it's probably time for me to go,' she said.

'Oh. You can stay here, you know. I'd like you to stay here.'

'That would be nice. But I think I prefer to go back to my room.'

She stood up.

'I can't persuade you?'

He held her tight and nibbled her ear.

'I've quite made up my mind,' she said, wriggling out of his arms.

'OK. I'll come over the quad with you.'

The quad was eerily still; the party had ended long ago.

'You're here tomorrow, aren't you?' he said.

'Yes.'

'Give me a kiss.' Poppyseeds and honey, juniper and plums. 'Here's looking at you, kid,' he drawled.

In the morning Barbara emerged blearily from the bathroom and found a note pushed under her door.

Kommst Du herüber? (Are you coming over?)

She went to the cafeteria for a roll and a coffee. The hostel was quiet. The Munich trippers had left on their coach some hours before. She thought she would write to Richard, and started to sort out her shoulder bag. Oh dear. There were the two postcards of Checkpoint Charlie. She had forgotten about them. Never mind. It seemed more important to write a proper long letter to Richard first. She could always put his postcard in with the letter. And then she could send Reinhard his postcard, he might receive it before she got back. She put her best pen, the maroon Parker, which she kept in the green leather case that Reinhard had given her, and her best blue-tinged writing paper with the blue tissue-lined envelopes in the shoulder bag, along with the postcards. She hoped the pen would not run out of ink. She put her sensible bathing costume and a towel in a plastic bag, and then took the *S-Bahn* towards the outskirts of the city, to Wannsee.

The lake had a wide, long sandy beach. Barbara felt considerably better after her swim. Further along was a jetty, and she had a lot of fun in a pedalo shaped like a swan. Feeling a bit peckish, she found a shady table overlooking the water at the Wirtshaus Schildhorn. The waitress was wearing a white blouse underneath a dark tunic, a white apron and a white headband shaped like a tiara. Barbara had fish soup with vegetables and saffron, followed by fried fillet of perch with a mustard sauce. She drank green Berliner Weisse, which was served in a goblet with a straw. Then she ordered iced tea and placed the writing paper and fountain pen on the table in front of her. *Wannsee, West Berlin. Friday Dear Richard,* she wrote, and ordered another iced tea.

She thought about *Jules et Jim*. Until yesterday she had had her own *J et J* – well, R and R – and no, R and R weren't friends with each other, they were just her friends – anyway, everything had been absolutely fine – well, not completely hunky-dory, more like all right, not bad, so far so good. Except that on this trip she was supposed to be making a decision between the two. Which one would be her Jules, so to speak? But overnight another R had been added to the equation. Catherine had other lovers, but they were not a Jacques, or a Jérôme, or a Joe, so they did not count. Barbara, unlike Catherine, was not going to turn into a nutcase and do something extreme, but she did have a massive problem now – R and R **and R**.

She began to make lists – on her best writing paper! – comparing Richard and Reinhard and Rick. How long had she known them? What did she particularly like about them? Anything she didn't like? Could she communicate well with them? Did they speak the same language? Were they interested in the same things? Did they have the same beliefs? How sexually attractive were they? Were they considerate? Had they had relationships with other women since she had known them? Did she feel comfortable with them, happy with them, safe with them? How committed did she actually want to be? She thought about her German teacher at school, her favourite best teacher, the inspirational Frau Müller, who was probably to blame for the fact that Barbara was doing this year in Germany, and by extension, whose fault it therefore was, that Barbara had this double dilemma. Frau Müller once said, 'Barbara, you're too cautious!' Actually, 'prudent' was what Barbara would have called herself, or 'wary', maybe 'guarded'.

Barbara bought two postcards of the Wannsee.

Friday

Dear Richard, Greetings from Lake When?...X Barbara

Freitag

Lieber Reinhard! Grüße vom Wann? See...Küßchen von Barbara

Barbara took off her ring and put it in the shoulder bag, along with her writing materials. The Checkpoint Charlie postcards would come in handy as bookmarks. She returned to the hostel, ripped up her lists, and flushed them down the lavatory.

Then she crossed the quad. She went *hinüber*.

Lemon Mousse Surprise

Melanie Mauthner

The scent of Emily, my first lover, stays with me like a sister. Unravelling the purple silk-screened scarf she made me at art college, I scrunch it up and bathe my face in its lilac mauve folds. Ripped at one edge and buried deep in my raincoat pocket it follows me still. The Portsmouth ferry carries me over the dark grey water to the Isle of Wight to say farewell. In the bow, a German Shepherd barking at the shelducks below us, momentarily distracts me from the creeping sadness welling up inside. The autumn chill dries up my tears and numbs my fingers. Emily always used to meet me off the ferry, a dog in tow sniffing at her muddy boots. Eyes stinging, dock approaching, I remove my contact lenses and pack them up in my rucksack. Her fluttering silk scarf wraps itself around my head and neck and I breathe in her long gone smell. The clove and marshmallow moisturiser I rub into my hands and cheeks and lips restores me.

As my feet feel firm land again, Hubert, the man she left me for, rests his broad hand on my shoulder, and walks me up from the water to the car.

'Smooth crossing, Suse?'

'Not a ripple. I sat out on deck and watched the squabbling gulls.'

'Let me take your bag.'

'Emily tied up with the herd then?'

'Gardening. She milks them at dawn, you know, and later at night. You're in time to join in, if you fancy.'

Reassuring Hubert: Gallic charm, olive hue, lanky with mischievous eyes. Emily swapped us around when I wasn't looking. She moved to the Isle of Wight seven years ago when Hubert lured her there to set up a small business with him: cheese and jam-making and bee-keeping. Business partners at first, lovers after six months, she told me. Her rural retreat draws me back like a family ritual: crab-hunting with her girls, island gossip and news of our ex-lovers. Until her girls arrived, Emily crossed the water for a shopping spree twice a year, the only part of urban life she says she misses.

Yellow fields speed by. I swallow hard, fighting back the soft marbles forming in my throat. I blow my nose. Blackberry hedges scrape the silver mirror on my side of the Landrover. When Belinda, my lover, runs her nails up and down between my shoulder blades, I see Emily's shiny crushed-raspberry fingers; when Belinda, spread across my thighs, whispers with her eyelashes, I smell Emily's ebony mane caressing my neck.

As Hubert turns into the lane, Emily saunters down the gravel. She lurches towards me and enfolds me in her arms. Heavy jet hair, a head taller than me, slightly breathless, a touch of make-up around the eyes. She smothers me. 'Susie! Darling! What's happened to your hair? Tell me later. Look what I've done to the garden since last year!' Smokey lavender plumes rise from the bonfire behind the house and waft our way. Feathery kisses split us apart and she leads me along the path around the house. Her lipgloss sticks to my forehead.

Side by side, Hubert and I fall in step behind her. Navy leggings and matching stripy Agnes B. top, ponytail dangling, lapis lazuli earrings. She turns around, pulls me to her, threads her arm through mine and drags me into her garden. Hand on his belt, Hubert lights up a Gauloise and picks up his gardening tools. Bonfire fumes curl up from the back of the girls' treehouse. Then, a brief tug and delicate untangling. Long strides make her disappear into the smoke, shrivelled weeds in her hands. Smoke encircles me and I cough. I step aside out of the billowing shroud and inhale the damp earthy smell of burning leaves.

Racing past the shed, Emily's Irish Setters leap up and lick my face, grunting with pleasure, their tails wagging furiously. Rusty-red with lithe bodies, long snouts and floppy ears, they spring and jump like the wild Emily I knew when we first met. Head high, she waves off the tiny butterfly exploring her fringe. When our eyes meet I look down, smiling wistfully. Our furtive glances, like a copper coil, gently tug us closer and let us go again. The silences between us, like choked kisses trapped beneath my tongue, dry up my mouth. She bends over the fire, mascara running down the corner of her eyes. I walk to the hedge and gaze up at the shearwaters flying over the incoming dusk tide. Sea lovers. A wave of sadness washes over me; a quiver runs down my spine.

Beyond the hedge I spy Emily's mare, gadding about, and further still, her goats grazing in the pale field. 'You two, come away from the hives!' Her dogs race and tumble back towards me. Intoxicated by the rosemary, I slide into the deckchair, next to her resplendent red tree, rowanberries glowing. It's the one I sent her when she moved here.

'Early Grey, darling? Black, no sugar?'

I nod and sink back into the Fauve design material, the sun-drenched colours too bright for me.

'Scone or brownie?' she asks lowering the tray towards me.

'Emily, you shouldn't have bothered. Scone please.'

'Not a patch on yours, Susie! Try the gooseberry jam. Last month's crop.'

I pick at the scone then push it away. Emily's long legs stretch out for the setters to fondle. Closing my eyes to shut out her languorous limbs, Belinda's touch in the small of my back lulls me to her breast and dulls me to the yelping of the dogs. I remember midnight feasts in Emily's minute kitchen, raids to my secret drinks' cabinet and rocking to David Bowie. Her voice calls me back. 'Oh Suse, Suzanne…' Her hand pats my knee and darts of electricity tingle up my black jeans.

Rolling her eyeballs, she looks at me quizzically. 'You OK, Susie? Enough, you two. Come over here. Now!' As she lopes off diagonally to the corner where the weeping willow partially hides her beehives, I slump into the taut canvas. Dog-paw mud-stains down my trouser leg. 'I've let them out into the paddock to run with the mare; but if they get stung, their legs swell up and we have to call the vet. Hassle hassle. You've no idea. What's up, Suse? More tea? So what's your news then?'

It means boiling up fresh water because she knows I like my tea scalding. I watch her step over strewn toys across the grass, marvel at her insouciance. A heron glides by in the afternoon sky. I trace its fleeting path over the fields until it swoops down over the estuary beyond the paddock.

A few minutes later Emily reappears with Victor, her youngest, plonks him into my lap, and turns back towards the house. I know the routine, hold and burp, smooth and stroke. I tend to him absent-mindedly for I never liked babies. The smell of vomit and dog and salt air mingle.

Suddenly, I long for Belinda's Australian lullabies, silk freckled belly and husky drunken lilt. In the fading light tears prickle my eyelids and shards of pleasure bruise me all over. Emily's curt tone startles me.

'So Suse, what's new, babe? How's Belinda?'

'Fine. Good. Yeah, she's OK.' I pluck a cigarette. 'Back in Melbourne, in fact.'

'Don't seem yourself Susie. Not up for a chinwag then?'

'Well, later maybe. Here, something for Victor. Open it.'

'Oh Susie, oooh!' she exclaims at the orange dinosaur armbands for his water-baby class.

I sip the fresh tea and push away my half-eaten scone. Heart racing, my clammy palms grip the red ABCD mug I gave her eldest. I reposition the silk cushion in my nape, breathe in and survey the hilly landscape behind the farm. With dusk descending the air stills and I almost hear the sea tide swirling in. Victor asleep in the crook of my elbow, I crane my neck to glimpse the scampering setters and the horse in the flat field. Hubert ambles past them calling out to the goats. In the deckchair opposite me, eyes closed, I watch Emily's eyelids twitch faintly as she falls into a shallow sleep.

I linger over my cigarette in the deepening light. Hawthorn bramble, dried out nasturtiums and clematis mark out all the segments of Emily's green world. The dogs sprawl over my feet and warm me up in the falling shadows. I offer them leftovers from our tea. Lizard-long tongues nibble up the crumbs from the grass, inviting me to stroke their heads when they come up searching out my hand for more. A low bark shakes Emily from her tranquil pose. She picks Victor up from my arms, walks inside. I catch the last pinky, orange and purple sunset streaks. The dogs snore contentedly while Hubert digs up turnips for supper. Freshly plucked spinach leaves lie on the ground next to him. 'Turnip gratin on the menu,' he confides in hushed tones as he walks past with a tub of goatmilk. 'Get you a drink, Susie? Elderberry wine?' I hate it and ask for whisky, neat, more my drink. Dapper Hubert, tenor voice, trim moustache and cinder sideburns. Solicitous as a brother.

'So Suzanne, how's tricks?' Without waiting for an answer he launches straight in. 'I expect Emily told you about the scan?' I hold his green-grey cat eyes in mine. Wiry chest hairs press through his cotton vest at the neck from under his open linen shirt. 'Twins, you know.'

'Congratulations.'

'From Granny's cousins, you see, on my side.'

Baby machine. All those years together and she never breathed a word about wanting to be a mother.

'Emmie, just updating Suse.' She throws her head back, pats the cream apron wrapped around her middle and chuckles. Victor's wail draws her back inside. Hubert follows hot on her trail with the turnips, spinach and rosemary.

Snug in the deckchair I sling my ash-grey pashmina shawl around my aching back. Emily brought it from her first trip to India as an anniversary gift, before they were in vogue. That's when she first used kohl under her eyes to set off her hair. The sparkly silver thread down the middle reminds me of the flash in her eyes. I wrap it tight to fend off the damp sea air rolling in across the hedgerow. The light fades. I hug the cashmere around my collarbone and shoulders and sit immobile. A family of bats swoop low, I just about detect the hoot of an owl. One dog nuzzles my knee and burrows her head in my lap. Her heat penetrates my stiff body as I stroke her haunches. I feel guilty now about not springing up. Bathtime, nappies, bottles, *Teletubbies* and story time, but a part of me feels distaste for the whole rigmarole. How could she desert me for this? My longing for Belinda's embrace and manicured nails massaging my scalp overwhelms me. I hug myself and squeeze out the air caught beneath my ribcage. I gasp and slump. Basking in the near darkness, stillness swims over me; interrupted by Emily's shrill voice.

'Susie, give me a hand with Victor, will you?'

I light up again, determined to bide my time. That high-pitch sound unnerves me. I snatch another moment outdoors before joining in the domestic activity. I hear the phone ring. 'Hello. Monica? Yes, it's me. Everything all right?' Her drone reaches me in the dark and when the phone clamps down, it's my cue. I head for the kitchen door. Inside, tired tea towels hang over the chairs and a fine layer of condensation mists up the window above the sink. I watch the Parmesan bubble to a crisp.

'The princesses gone riding in the woods tonight?' I enquire.

'Sleepover at Carla's. Birthday party. They'll be back in the morning.'

I keep mum as I shall probably miss them for I am crossing the water back to the mainland on the first ferry.

'Overnight parties at three?'

'Four, Darling. Joelle's four, remember. Keep an eye on that gratin, Susie girl. Just going to change. Won't be a sec.'

Rosemary from the oven pervades her cavernous kitchen. I roll over my announcement with slow motion lips as she disappears upstairs. I flit between cleaning bitter green leaves for the spinach soup and grating strands of citrus zest for her Lemon Mousse Surprise. I decide to time my news carefully, with the champagne toast for the twins.

After Victor's last feed and Hubert's tucking-up duty, we settle around her pine oval table. The soup revives me, almost sates me. A wet spot where the milk seeps through the thin cotton blouse stains her aureole violet in the candlelight. The silver ring from Belinda shines like a good luck charm on my stubby finger. I twist it nervously under my napkin. I want to postpone the declaration and inevitable shock that will greet it. Only with the gratin steaming on the Portuguese tile I gave her do I know my time is near. I'll merely graze at the gratin so I can save a space for a smidgen of mousse. I never was a pudding person, more a dessert wine woman, but tonight I don't want to seem rude or put a foot wrong.

Hubert slowly removes the blue tinted glasses I selected for their wedding present, from the mahogany armoire, and does the honours with the champagne.

'To the twins!'

'To their future!'

'Their safe arrival.'

Emily glows in the yellow twilight, sitting radiant and blooming across the table from me. I feel sick to my stomach: the ease and comfort of Emily's idyll, wise cautious Hubert to protect her, a healthy brood. Pangs sweep over me for I know this will be our last supper for a long time. The fuchsia paper napkins set off her rose cheeks. It is that luscious pink, the colour of my Belinda's lipstick, that gives me courage to stand up and look her in the eye.

'By the way, it's all set. The date is fixed for the day after tomorrow. I'm off.'

She bolts upright, spills the champagne over her top and splutters.

'Off, darling! Where to? More filming in exotic locations?'

'Belinda. Back in Melbourne. She's asked me to join her.'

Her eyebrows draw a charcoal arc across her forehead. Reaching for her glass, she misses and with a slight knock, it splinters over the cork flooring. Her arms flop, limp at the elbows and her chest caves in. Only then can I divine the grapefruit mound where her leggings envelop her hips. Her mouth falls open, gaping. I gulp and twist my tongue searching out my words. Eyes fixed on his glass; Hubert downs the champagne without a murmur. Bemused, with a knowing smile on his lips, he looks up at me and winks. From his twinkling eyes and fluttering eyelashes I gauge his approval.

'Susie! Why, how could you?' Emily cries out.

I stare at her blankly.

'It can't be, Susie, really! You can't be serious. How can you go to Australia now, with the twins on their way?'

Lips pursed, I look down into my dessert bowl: yellow air bubbles beckon in the untouched mousse. I want them to swallow me up and drown out her voice. I sit down and light up a last cigarette, glance up at her and take a long slow drag.

'Afraid so, Emily. It's decided. I'm emigrating.'

'But you've hardly been together that long, have you? Aren't you rushing into it?'

'Five years, you know. Longer than it seems…'

'Not as long as us.'

'Well…'

'So, when did you…'

'…decide to go?'

'Yes.'

'Been thinking about it for a while.'

'You kept that very quiet. Didn't she?'

'That's why I came, to tell you *en famille*. I thought the girls would be here.'

Emily fidgets across the table.

'You'll have to come visit, all of you.'

Hubert's fingers twirl at his moustache and hide his mouth but his wait-and-see expression tells me what I have already guessed. As

Emily hovers to gather invisible slithers of glass, his arm stretches out to squeeze hers.

'I'll do it, Em,' he purrs.

She looks straight through me, flushed and drained at the same time. I sit tight and exhale. In a few months, when the twins emerge, I'll be down-under, living in Emily's hometown. A glassy sea lies between us, cold underneath yet warm around the edges.

Charlie

Jenny Sullivan

I suppose we weren't very nice kids, compared to some, but we weren't all that bad, honest. OK, admitted, we used to tease the life out of the daft kid up the road, and we weren't particularly nice to cats and dogs dumb enough to cross our path, but her, Mrs Pugh, we never even looked at her sideways. She looked like a witch, that's why. Bent almost double, her stick stabbing the pavement at each step, she watched us with sharp black eyes, her face a wrinkled, malevolent walnut, her nose hooked down, her chin bent up. She even had a hairy wart, honest to God, and Sy and me, we always walked past her hedge quick-like.

Not Charlie. Charlie always had to push it, didn't he? Charlie was the one that almost drowned swinging across the river on a half-rotten rope; Charlie who bust his leg falling off the roof of the girls' school; Charlie who got his ear clipped by Mr Patel for nicking Mars bars. I mean, old Patel's back wasn't even turned, asking for it Charlie was.

So, naturally it was Charlie who thought of the dare about Mrs Pugh's cottage. She was out, we knew that, we'd watched her shuffle-stab down the road to the shops, but Sy and me weren't what you might call enthusiastic.

'What if she comes back?' Sy asked doubtfully.

'She won't. She'll be gone f'rages. Come on, Mart, you chicken?'

I was, but. 'Nah!' I said.

'You are. Go on, I dare you. We could open the back window easy.'

'You wanna do it, Charlie, you do it.' Sy was nobody's fool.

Charlie curled his lip. 'Chicken,' he repeated, flapping his arms and clucking, and then he was through the garden gate and round the back of the cottage like a rat up a drainpipe.

I don't know if we'd've followed him or not, 'cause then Sy said, 'Oh, bugger!'

I followed his eyes. Mrs Pugh was coming up the road.

'She can't have got to the shops and back!' Sy groaned, 'not that fast.'

Sy and me remembered urgent business elsewhere and legged it. Wasn't anything we could do to warn Charlie: he was going to get caught.

We took turns to poke our noses round the corner, but it was five minutes, easy, before Charlie came through the gate again.

'What did she say, Charlie?' I asked. 'Did she belt you one?'

Charlie shook his head.

'She gonna tell your Mam?' This from Sy, who was mortally afraid of his, and with good reason.

Charlie shrugged.

'Didn't she do nothing?' Sy sounded almost disappointed.

'She give me something.' Charlie looked at us, a weird expression on his face.

'What?'

Charlie opened his hand. Across his grimy palm lay a small, grey-barred blue feather. We inspected it.

'What's that?' I knew it was a stupid question, the minute I said it.

'Du-uh,' Sy said, rolling his eyes. 'It's a feather, lamebrain. What's it look like?' He loved to score off me, 'cause my Mam talked posh, and his didn't.

'Yeah. But why'd she give it to him?'

'I asked her that,' Charlie's voice was creaky. 'She said "bird" and "you'll find out". I'm scared, Martyn.'

Charlie, scared? He was our main man. Charlie wasn't scared of anything. 'Chuck it, Charlie,' I said. 'Get rid of it quick.'

Charlie shook the feather off his palm, wiping his hand on his jeans as it spiralled slowly down. Then he ran.

I don't know what made me pick it up and stick it in my pocket, but I did. I made sure neither Charlie nor Sy saw me do it, though. I put it on the shelf in my room, weighted down with the jam-jar with the stick insect in, before I put my jeans out for the wash, and forgot about it. Mrs Pugh didn't tell on Charlie, after, so it looked like he'd got home free.

It was a couple of days later I noticed Charlie was different. Sort of quieter, you know? Sy and me, we'd be chopsin' away and I'd realise Charlie wasn't there. He just sort of stood, his eyes half-shut, kind of looking inside himself. Like he had a bellyache and was wondering what to do about it.

We were in the pictures one night: Sy'd paid and gone down the gents' to open the window for us to climb in, as usual. We sneaked in and sat halfway up the middle aisle so Flashlight Aggie wouldn't spot us.

Then Charlie started to squirm. He wriggled and twitched and fidgeted and grunted. He was driving me nuts, let alone the old bloke in the row behind. 'Cut it out, Charlie!' I hissed. Any trouble and Aggie would have us outside faster than the speed of light.

'I got an itch,' he muttered. 'I can't reach it.'

So I slid my hand round his back and scraped my nails up and down until he sighed with satisfaction. Every so often, though, during the film, he'd start to squirm again, and I'd have to give him another bit of a scratch.

'You picked up a flea in the pi'chers, I reckon,' Sy said as we can-kicked home.

Then Charlie and me went swimming, Sy having been hooked off by his Mam to buy new school trousers. We weren't supposed to swim in the river. My Mam said it was dangerous, but so long as we didn't go in the middle – and she didn't find out – we were safe enough. I stripped down to my underpants, but when Charlie took his T-shirt off, he had another one underneath. He inched into the water, hissing at the cold, then held his nose and ducked under. I could see him sitting on the bottom, his hair floating weirdly round his head, his eyes open and stary. His breath came up bit by bit in bubbles, and he was under f'rages, until I started to get scared. Me, I don't do stuff like that. I don't like the feel of water in my ears: I panic and that's it, then. But Charlie just sat on the river bed. He hadn't let any bubbles go for a long time, and he was starting to waver a bit, like he was losing his balance in the pull of the current. I lost my cool and grabbed his T-shirt, hauling him up in a flurry of water. He staggered, turning so that his back, bare where the T-shirt had pulled up, was towards me. His skinny shoulder blades stuck out like dinner plates and his back was covered in raw, red scratches. Before I could stop myself, I put out my hand and touched it, and Charlie shot round, yanking the T-shirt down, his face purple with cold, his teeth chattering.

'What's the matter with your back, Charlie?' I asked.

'Nothing. I been itching, that's all. I gotta rash. I'm getting out. I'm cold.'

We climbed up the muddy bank and shivered in a patch of sunlight until we were dry enough to dress. We didn't speak, and when we parted company at the bottom of my road, we still hadn't spoken.

I didn't see Charlie for a couple of days, but I thought about him. Then he phoned me one night. I was in the middle of my homework, and Mum wasn't best pleased. I hardly recognised his voice.

'Come round our house, Mart?' he pleaded. 'I gotta see you. I'm desp'rate, mate.'

Dread dogging me, I walked round the corner. His Mam let me in. 'He's in his room,' she said. 'I don't know what's the matter with him, lately.'

I scratched at his door and went in. He sat on his bed, knees drawn up to his chin, his face chalky. 'What's up, Charlie?'

He looked at me steadily. 'If I show you something, you gotta be honest, right? You're my mate, Martyn. You gotta tell me what you can see.'

I promised. Charlie got off the bed, turned his back and took off his T-shirt. His voice was muffled. 'What's on my back, Mart?'

Apart from the red scratches, which had multiplied, and some were bleeding, his back looked perfectly normal. I went close, and examined the knobbly round bones of his spine. 'You got a bit of a rash, Charlie. That's all. An' you scratched it, so it's bled.'

When he turned round, his face was anguished. 'I thought I could trust you, Mart! It's not a rash. It's feathers. I'm turning into a bloody bird, I am! It's that old woman. She's witched me, Mart! You gotta help me.'

He was nuts. 'Honest, Charlie. There's no feathers! It's just a bit tore up where you been scratching, that's all.'

'It's feathers, Mart. Feathers. Help me, Martyn, please?'

I backed away. 'I can't do anything, Charlie. There's nothing there, honest. Look, sorry Charlie. I gotta go.'

His Mam was waiting at the foot of the stairs. 'He's not himself, lately,' she muttered, tapping ash into an umbrella stand. 'He's off his food. Says he don't feel well.'

'I'm going now,' I said, shuffling past, my hand already turning the door-knob, 'I told my mother I wouldn't be long.'

I didn't sleep a wink that night. I know I didn't. I sat bolt upright, watching the moonshadows creep round my room. Maybe Charlie was going nuts. But then there was the feather…

Next day I got Sy over by the bikesheds. We had our backs to the playground so no one could see our fag. 'Charlie thinks he's turning into a bird, Sy,' I said, not looking at him.

He choked on smoke and passed the cigarette over. 'What you on about, Mart?'

'Honest, Sy,' I said. 'He's going batty. He thinks he's turning into a bird. We gotta do something.'

'Aw, pull the other one. What we gonna do, buy him some birdseed?'

'Sy, stop it. Listen, I mean it. I swear to God, he thinks he's got feathers growing up his back. We got to go back and see her, before he goes completely round the twist.'

Sy backed away. 'Who?'

'You know who. Mrs Pugh. It's obvious, isn't it? She's done something. With that feather. Remember the feather, Sy?'

He did, I know he did, but he shook his head. 'You're nuts, you. How could she do anything? She's only an old woman. You're as nuts as he is.'

I took a last drag on the dog-end and tossed it into a puddle. Down to me, then.

It took all the guts I had to knock on Mrs Pugh's door and wait while the stab, drag, shuffle got louder and closer. The door opened and the bright black eyes fixed me. I wanted to turn, run, forget Charlie and his problems, but my feet wouldn't work.

'Well?' she said, softly. She was smiling. 'What d'you want?'

My mouth opened and shut, but the words wouldn't come.

'I can't hear you,' she said, still smiling her terrible smile.

'Charlie,' I got out, at last. 'Charlie thinks he's turning into a bird.'

She nodded. 'Yes, he would. There was something about his face that just said "bird". Now you – Martyn Thomas, isn't it? You're more of a rat, Martyn. Yes. Definitely a rat. Wait here, my boy. I've got something for you.'

I found my feet. Honest, I reckon I bust the three minute mile getting away. I spent a week, after, feeling my bum, thinking I was growing a tail, before I calmed down. Then I went round to Charlie's. He was still in his bedroom, only this time he was sitting hunched on the head-board of his bed, his bare toes curled round the carved ivy leaves. His nose seemed sharper, longer, and his shoulder blades stood out like, like – wings. I blinked, and he looked like Charlie again.

'I asked her, Charlie,' I said, 'honest I did. I begged her to help you, but she told me I looked like a rat.'

He understood. His shoulders drooped. 'S'all right, butt.' He looked like a bony vulture, perched on the bed-head. 'That's it, then. I'm gonna be a bird. That's it.'

'Why don't you just go and apologise, Charlie?' I said, desperately. 'Maybe if you say you're sorry, maybe she'll stop it.'

He thought about it, then shrugged. 'Got nothing to lose, have I? Unless she turns me into a hen, so I start laying bloody eggs, right?' He cocked his head and looked up at me, almost crowing with hysterical laughter. Then, suddenly, he sobered. 'Come with me, Mart?'

Going to see Mrs Pugh wasn't the bravest thing I ever did, after all. Going to see her the second time was. We stood on her doormat, side by side, Charlie with his behind stuck out and his head poked forward, waiting while she stab-scraped to the door. When she opened it, Charlie didn't say a word for a bit, then, hoarse as a rook, he stumbled out his apology.

Me, I made sure I got behind him when she opened the door, just in case she slipped a rat-tail into my pocket or something. She stared at him for a long time, then looked at me.

'It's up to you, Martyn Thomas,' she said, 'you know how.'

'I bloody don't,' I said desperately.

'Language,' she said, automatically, as adults will. 'Yes, you do,' she said. She closed the door in our faces.

I stared helplessly at Charlie. 'I don't know what she's on about, honest I don't. I wish I did, Charlie.'

'That's it, then,' Charlie said. 'I'm a bird.'

Disconsolately, we walked back home. His feet, I noticed, were beginning to turn inward, like a pigeon's.

I didn't sleep much. I was thinking what the old lady had said. 'Up to you, Martyn,' she'd said. I tossed and heaved and bashed my head on the pillow with frustration. It had to be all in his head, right?

Then, suddenly, I remembered the feather. I got out of bed. It was still on the shelf (Mam had given up dusting my room ages ago) where I'd left it, although the stick insect had long since dropped off its twig. I turned the feather over in my hand and watched the light glint off the sheeny blue.

Next morning, early, I went round his house. He was perched on the bed-post, his eyes half-shut. He looked sick to me.

'You look terrible,' I said.

'I feel terrible. The itch is back. Give us a scratch, Mart.'

That was what I'd been waiting for. I lifted his pyjama top and slid my hand up. I was holding the blue feather, concealed in my palm so he didn't see it. I scratched, hard, then withdrew my hand.

Slowly I opened it under Charlie's nose. 'Look, Charlie!' I whispered. 'She must've forgiven you! She must've! Look! You're moulting!'

Tossed

Lesley Coburn

'Let's toss for it, winner decides.'

They were gambling on their next move. She wished for it, felt both bribed and expanded by leaving it to chance, cajoled even. But they were running out of time. What would Ben choose if he won? What would she choose? She waited, practising acquiescence. He took out a silver-coloured coin, a distant-land coin that he said he dreamed on. He spun it into the sorry air.

'Call, Sam,' he commanded.

'Heads.' She felt shaky now.

She gazed through desperate eyes, watched the disc flip, spin, soft – land on the polished table, top-laid with a square of felted cloth. For seconds, she couldn't see how her future lay. A moment of acid anticipation transformed to an instant of clarity – tails! Ends – ends and means – ways – he had won. Sam shrugged, life gives, takes.

Ben was irked by the turn of the coin, the responsibility. He never wanted to make this kind of decision – thought out, planned. He liked movement to keep up the momentum of his otherwise feeble interest in life. That's why he'd suggested the coin-flip – trying to escape the run-around of their ragged talk. Talk, talk, talk. His mind inchoate, he feigned attention. What would they do? When? How? He could be turning a corner, a page. Go left – right? Every day he had to choose. It wearied him. He had come to think of her as the leader, even when he staged his machismo moves. From their shared beginning, he'd given himself up. She settled him, eased the mishmash in his head.

He told his mother, months back, 'She's good for me, Mam, she's strong. She keeps me calm, on a clean road.' He made Sam feel like Mother Theresa, and she didn't like it. She was pissed off with the way he glorified her. She was beginning to realise that he was as see-through as her Christmas knickers. Fucking hell. They were facing changes that he'd rather avoid. Yeah, he's visible all the way through, she thought. He's afraid we're both losing control.

'You'd better come up with a good idea. We got to leave. Get on a road. What the fuck would Kerouac do?' She still had some style.

'Who? What? Fuck him, whoever. The coast, for fuck's sake. Let's leave this bloody place and head for the sea. Just walk, girl, walk away from this valley's shit.'

Ben and Sam raised their bodies and bags and paced out of the hotel lounge into the scary day. It had been her idea to hide there. No one would think to search for them away from the sad valley's low-life. They walked. And walked. Travelled south with loaded heads. She knew they were in heavy trouble. It tasted of dry metal in her mouth.

'Nothing's gone right since we got together,' Sam moaned. 'I bloody told you we shouldn't do it. We can't go back. The first time I listen to you and look at us. I'll never go back again. Never.'

She shuddered and the memories trapped her. She saw it all again, felt it all again. Like an old film on replay, she was soaked in every movement, colour, smell.

He knew how to get through a window. Chisel to the corner, sharp tap, it took out the whole pane, hardly broke it up. Handle the window right open, crawl in, almost silent. He knew what to do, no problem. It was so easy. The back door opened to where she stood shivering in fear and unaccountable excitement. He propped each door open to create a ready escape route. He'd known about all that. A scattered search of downstairs rooms. No money. No fucking money. There must be money. He got frantic, pulled the place apart. A few notes, tens, nothing. He pointed up, mouthing encouragement. Fuck no, not upstairs, she'd stalled. Yeah, yeah, it must be up there. No, no, no. She was filled with awareness and energy. There was a real person in the house. Upstairs. Didn't that mean something?

'Move it.' He was quickly mad, mad with her.

The stairs. Each step up, each silent step thudded instant remorse into her brain. No, no, no. Still she climbed. He was ahead. How could they do this? At last, a stop, a landing, feeling around her. The layout same as his Mam's. God, he was at home there. How? How could he? The old man's face as they entered his bedroom, his place of rest, his sanctuary.

The old man's face, scowling through the moon's gloom.

His crazy yells. He shook, pulled himself upright, arms flailing, helpless, enraged and helpless.

'Bloody kids, bloody fucking kids. Think you're so fucking clever, think you can do anything. I fought a fucking war for you lot, useless fucking lot.'

She was statue-still, facing him.

'I know you. I know who you are, you, you fucking bastards.' Their victim slumped. 'Take it, take it all. What do I care?'

He fell back, looked lifeless. And grey. Grey face into grey sheets. He closed his eyes in grim dismissal. Ben hadn't slowed a second; furious rummaging, while she was holding on to every particle of it, fixing it.

It fixed her. She couldn't move. The old man. She was defeated.

She wanted to stay.

Comfort him, reassure him.

Put it all back.

Tidy the place for him.

Make him a cup of tea. She wanted to stay.

He dragged her out.

Downstairs.

Run. Run. Run.

But they walked. She didn't want to forget it all, and couldn't anyway. As they walked she asked Ben, over and over, 'What do you think happened to him after? Do you think he's all right now? Do you think he got someone over to help him?'

At last, a bus stop, take a bus to the city. Big Cardiff city. He talked about football. She was silenced. They checked buses to the coast.

'Cardiff, I fucking hate Cardiff,' Ben managed. 'Only good thing about it is the team, yeah, the City. Hey, got a bit of time before the bus.'

She is thinking, thinking. She remembers again, slips on it.

'That poor old man –'

'Let's find some food, I'm starving –'

'I feel so bad about him, listen, please listen –'

'He'll be all right, I told you. Mam will sort him out, look after him, I tell you. For fuck's sake shut up about him. What do you want to eat?'

He was as harmless as drizzle, and just as pointless. No guile, no guilt, no promise. Sudden passion surged through her, strong as a thunderstorm. Anger and fear collided with sharp boredom. Sam pushed Ben aside and ran through the Cardiff people, on and on. Steady now. She was frantic to tell someone, share it. There was no one. She ran. On and on. Ran back to herself. Unable to speak it, she sat on a bench and felt almost better. There were people passing close by her, all around her. She began to feel safe. She liked the bench. She fitted it. She sat and tossed around plans, things to do, ways to go. Find someone to tell, someone to go on with, someone who'll listen to me now.

A young guy came over, eyed her, sat down. He looked easy, unencumbered. He looked right. She began it. 'You just hanging out then?'

They dribbled chat at one another. He showed a sliver of initiative. 'You seem okay, you do. What you doing later?'

Impulsive now, shaking, 'I'm not doing anything, but I know how to break into a house. I know exactly what to do.'

The Accident

Imogen Rhia Herrad

It all started so harmlessly. She'd been at work, bored, and started to surf the Web. Somebody had told her about webcams, and she fancied a look out into the world, somebody else's world. Her world wasn't bad, not really, but just every now and again she got to the point where, for the time being, she'd had just about enough of it, thank you very much. So she accessed a search engine and typed in 'webcam'. The number of hits that came back surprised her, even though quite a few turned out to be porn sites. But still, she had never imagined that there were so many of the things about.

From that day on, whenever the greyness of the office – grey filing cabinets, grey suits, grey computers, printers, desktops – threatened to drown her, Clara went on the web and typed in the magic word. She looked through webcams in Québec and Shanghai, in the Antarctic and in Shiraz. A woman in Shropshire had placed a digital camera in her garden so that the whole world could see her roses grow. A boy in Russia had put one on the roof outside his room that he only activated at night, because the lights of the factory complex across the road glowed so beautifully in the dark. She became a connoisseur of webcams all over the world, striding across the planet in seven-league boots, Samarkand today, Nairobi tomorrow, never the same place twice.

Then one day, she found herself transfixed by the image of a street corner somewhere in a Latin country. It wasn't a special street corner. There weren't any buildings of artistic or architectural merit there, no spectacular flowerbeds on the traffic island in the middle of the road. It was a perfectly ordinary street corner: a junction of two roads, zebra crossings, a bus stop, street signs. Buildings with shops on the ground floor and flats above, awnings, venetian blinds, flower boxes outside the windows, a café, pedestrians. There was a woman walking a dog, an old man with a stick, traffic she could see but not hear. She looked at the scene for a while, then her phone rang. When the call finished, she went on with her work, reluctantly returning to the here and now.

But the next day, instead of typing 'webcam' into a search engine and seeing where it would take her, she followed her footprints of the day before, searching for the same street corner. She couldn't even remember in which country the corner was to be found, let alone what city, but finally, there it was again: Rosario, Argentina – the junction, the zebra crossings, the shops, the awnings. There was the old man with the stick, walking along the pavement. When the image updated itself a minute later, he had arrived at the cafe and was sitting at one of its tables. With each reloading, the pattern of figures changed. A woman with a silly woolly dog was walking past. A bus arrived in one image and was gone in the next, having taken the knot of people waiting at the bus stop with it. During the siesta hour the flow of traffic thinned, and in some images the streets were completely empty. The shadows of trees and buildings wandered from left to right, morning to evening.

This other world enchanted her. It wasn't as exciting as some of the places she had looked at, it was smaller, more ordinary. Yet at the same time, it was exotic, foreign. It was somewhere else. She needed somewhere else. She'd worked in the same office for almost twenty years now; a rarity these days, people told her. A job for life was something to value, even to treasure. But Clara was getting fed up. She'd thought that life for a legal secretary would never really be dull. She imagined new cases constantly coming in, giving her glimpses into other people's lives, as exciting as the stories in the papers every morning, but somehow better, more real. She had always expected to see the world one day, but somehow time passed and it still hadn't happened. She had to make the most of this miraculous window she'd found in cyberspace, this window on another world, a real world. Her new world.

Clara's colleagues complained about her standoffishness. She used to be part of the office, they told her, a nice person, and now they didn't know what had got into her. Clara sighed. She was bored with their faces, their voices, the jokes that endlessly circulated round the office, never changing. She said that she suddenly had more work to do, what with the new guidelines and that big court case coming up next month, you know how it is. This was also a good excuse to give her husband. 'I'm afraid I'm going to have to work late again tonight. That big court case...' Her husband, a teacher who often worked long hours himself, gave her a commiserating smile over the breakfast table. Clara wished, perversely, that he would try to stop her, maybe do something unexpected.

Sometimes she worked late just to watch the sun set on her street corner, see the lights coming on in the flats and the café. She knew all the people by now. She had given them names. The old man with the stick was Héctor. The smart black woman in high heels who caught the eight-twenty bus every weekday morning was Celestina, the couple with the three kids were Gloria and Roberto. The woman who always walked the silly woolly dog and who was not much younger than herself was María. Clara had decided that she probably worked as a translator or writer, because she sometimes showed up at the café with a sheaf of papers and sat at one of the tables outdoors, chewing her pen and writing. Once, the camera captured the moment when a gust of wind picked up the papers and scattered them all over the pavement and the road. Clara pictured María and the café owner jumping up and running after them, rounding them up and collecting them before the next wave of traffic arrived. But she never saw them doing this, because by the time the image reloaded, the street and the outside tables of the café were empty. María must have collected her work and decided that it was safer to continue at home, or maybe she had moved to one of the tables indoors, and was now chatting to the café proprietor.

Clara felt left out, and for a moment wished she could join them, walk into the picture on her screen and into that other world. She realised that she thought of her people in the images as if they were characters in a soap opera. It was a shock to think that they were real, as genuine as herself, inhabiting the same world. The woman she called María might have just lost a day's work to a gust of wind, seconds ago, while Clara was looking on. This very minute, she might be climbing flights of stairs up to her flat, crying with fury, or else feeling triumphant because she'd managed to snatch a piece of paper from the jaws of an oncoming lorry. It had all just happened, it was real, it wasn't the Saturday repeat of Thursday's episode. Clara found it hard to get her head around that. She somehow thought of them as living in cyberspace, not in real time.

She went onto an online database of international information and, for the first time, looked up Argentina and the city of Rosario. She read about the country's history – from Spanish colony to dictatorship to republic to emerging market economy. She looked at a map of Rosario and saw where her street corner was situated relative to the rest of the place. Now she knew what the neighbourhood was called, she could find out more about that too. She started to visit other websites and learned more about her city, her neighbourhood.

Her husband finally did complain about the hours they made her work in the office, and for a while she tried to cut down, so they could spend more time together. One evening she realised that while she was with him, she carried on a conversation in her head with Gloria, exchanging confidences and complaining about their men. She was ticked off at work for spending too much time on the Internet. 'I was doing research,' she said haughtily, then fell silent as they showed her a printout of her exact movements online for the past four weeks. Clara promised to mend her ways. She looked over her boss's shoulder, memorised his password, and began using that to access the street corner.

Without telling anybody, she booked a Spanish class two evenings a week. She could have done it officially through work, but this was for herself alone and nobody's business. When she went away for a shopping weekend with a friend, she stole into a large record shop and bought a tango CD and another one of Argentinian folk music. She purchased a personal stereo, brought it in to work, and listened surreptitiously to her music.

The secrecy of it all gave her a kick. She felt as though she had taken a lover, perhaps a Latin toyboy. She felt like Zorro or Catwoman; she was leading a double life, one boring and known to all the world, the other brimful with excitement, known only to herself.

One day, there was a 'For Rent' sign on one of the flats in the house above the cafe. Clara pictured herself getting off a bus, walking past the café, pushing open the door with the determined shove she'd seen other people use as they went in, climbing the stairs, knocking on doors, talking to Héctor, to María, Celestina, to Gloria and Roberto. Saying, I'm the new tenant on the second floor. My name is Clara. I hope we'll be friends.

She checked out a website with cheap international flights. Then, with shaking fingers, she typed in places of departure and arrival, and entered a date four weeks in the future. This was all becoming entirely too real. She jumped when somebody came into the room to ask her if she fancied a bite to eat from the sandwich place round the corner, and surprised them by saying that she thought she'd come too, if they didn't mind.

It had been months since she'd done that.

And then it happened. She looked at her computer during her lunch hour, watched María run across the road, and saw a huge great lorry barrelling down upon her at a terrible speed. Clara watched, forgot to breathe, watched, watched, waiting with terrible desperation for the image to renew itself, so she would know what had happened – so that she could see María safely on the other side of the street, or see her having run back to the kerb, she didn't care which, but safe, oh please, let María be safe.

The next image showed the lorry, swerving, halfway across the street, María on the ground. Clara nearly rang 999. But she couldn't stop watching. In a series of snapshots, she saw other people arrive on the scene, several with mobile phones to their ears. She felt terribly bereaved. She was so far removed that she couldn't even hear the roar of the traffic, the screeching of tyres, the screaming of the ambulance. She watched, far away and helpless, as they picked up María and laid her in the ambulance. It all seemed to take hours, but the time print on the webcam pictures told her that less than twenty minutes had passed. She saw one of the ambulance men pick up the woolly dog, which had escaped unharmed, and carry it into the back of the ambulance to be with María. Clara liked this human touch, sympathy overriding the fear of germs. Her brain subconsciously registered the name of the hospital painted on the side of the ambulance.

All day, she wondered how María was. She worried. She would have given anything to be able to ring up Héctor, Celestina, Gloria, to be able to ask them how María was doing. But she was so far away. They had no idea she even existed. She had no idea what their real names were;

she didn't even have a phone number. Not even a phone number, she thought, and before she realised what she was doing, her fingers tapped out the address of an international telephone directory. She clicked on Argentina, then Rosario, typed in the name of the hospital, was rewarded with a switchboard number. She picked up the phone and dialled.

'*Buenos días*,' she said to the voice at the other end, moving easily into the Spanish phrases that she had secretly been studying every Tuesday and Thursday night for almost a year. 'There's been a terrible accident. My sister-in-law...' The lie slipped out before she'd had a chance to think it up. It seemed the most natural thing in the world. She stuttered, her tongue stumbled over words in her confusion while her clever brain cooked up lie after credible lie. She was put through the A&E department. She gave the address of the street corner where the accident had happened. 'And I'm so worried...'

'Well,' said the nurse, 'I can't really disturb Señora Arguedas now, not until I've spoken to the doctor.'

A name! She pounced on it. 'I haven't even introduced myself,' she said apologetically, her heart thumping like stampeding cattle. 'I'm married to Hernan Arguedas, her brother. We live abroad, and of course we're so worried. The neighbours just told me what had happened, and Hernan isn't even here, he's on a business trip...'

'That would explain it,' said the nurse, thawing. 'She said she didn't have any family.'

'Not in Argentina,' said Clara. She didn't even so much as make up her mind, she found it had already made up itself. While she was still speaking into the telephone, her fingers were telling the computer to go back to the cheap flights website. 'Can you tell me how she is?'

'She's not very well,' said the nurse, and Clara held her breath. 'She's got concussion, a broken leg, a couple of broken ribs and a lot of bruises; she'll take a while to heal. But she'll live.'

'Tell her,' said Clara, her fingers busy tapping out places of departure and arrival and tomorrow's date. She hit Enter, and a screen came up confirming her booking. 'Tell her I'm coming to see her. Tell her Clara's on her way.'

Across the Downs

Carolyn Lewis

The first time I met Molly was in the last week of May. I'm positive about that because the day I met her was my birthday, 28th May. I was 50 years old. The kids were planning a surprise party and they wanted me out of the house. The only thing I was surprised about was the fact that they thought anyone would want to come. I've hardly been good company since – well, not for a long time.

I told the three of them, Lizzie, Fiona and Andrew, that I'd be out for a couple of hours. 'I'll go for a long walk over the Downs. Then I'll drink two enormous mugs of cappuccino. Will that give you enough time?'

Andrew glanced at his sisters. 'That's fine, Mum. Enjoy yourself.'

I love the liberated feeling that comes from striding over the flat areas, smiling at people as they walk past. I suppose that's part of it too; we barely touch others' lives whilst we walk – we nod or smile but there's no impact. I don't make any connection with others and they have none with me. I like that, that freewheeling sense I get when I'm up there. The wind that tugs at my jacket, my hair, loosens me up somehow. I always start my walk hesitantly, feeling that people are watching, commenting on me, but then I feel that wind nudging, freeing me of those thoughts. I can stride out and, if I'm watched or judged, I don't care.

I'd got halfway around the Downs on that day, my birthday, enjoying the sight of a dog-training session. A row of wet-eyed dogs sat expectantly in an almost straight line, their gaze fixed upon the trainer. I was grinning at the sight of one dog; the frenzied wagging of its tail reminded me of the metronome that my over-enthusiastic music teacher placed on her piano. 'Keep to the beat,' she'd constantly demand. I felt sure that the longhaired dog with the energetic tail must have known her too.

'Bet you wish you had a dog.'

I hadn't seen who'd spoken, the voice came from one of the wooden benches set round the Downs. Some of these benches have got small metal plaques fixed to the wooden slats. I knew this particular one well.

I'd walked past it many times and I knew the wording on the bronze plaque. *In Loving Memory of Iris Walters 1919-2004*. I slowed down to watch the dogs and had almost stopped when I reached the bench. I turned at the sound of the voice. It was a woman's voice.

'Yes, you're right. They look so docile, so friendly.'

I smiled before turning away. I meant to continue my walk but the woman had left the bench in one fluid movement and stood next to me.

'Always had dogs, I did. House was full of them. Big ones, though, don't like the small ones, yap, yap, yap, can't be doing with all that yapping.' Her voice was light and sounded young but I'd guessed her to be in her mid-70s. She wore a raspberry red skirt and a dark grey cardigan. The buttons on the cardigan didn't look right and, after a couple of seconds, I realised why. It was a man's cardigan. She wore it tugged low over her hips and she'd pushed the sleeves up exposing freckled arms. Fine threads of grey wool had escaped from the buttonholes and they gently fanned out as she stood next to me.

Without understanding why, I took a step back. I wanted to get on with my walk but I found it difficult to pick up my pace again whilst the woman stood with her feet planted squarely on the path. I was at least a foot taller than she was and, as I glanced down, I saw that she was wearing gold shoes; they had a curved heel and sparkled in the sunshine. Her legs were slender, the ankles fine-boned and there was a faint sheen of gold glittering from her tights.

'I've seen you up here before,' she told me suddenly, holding out her hand. 'I'm Molly.'

My reaction was automatic; placing my hand in hers I felt the surprising strength of her handshake.

'Hello, I'm Valerie,' I told her.

'Pleased to meet you, why don't you join me here on the bench?'

I didn't want to do that, that's not why I go to the Downs. It was the one thing I wanted to avoid, contact with other people. Molly had her head on one side, as if she knew what I was thinking, waiting for me to make up my mind. She and I were still holding hands and I tugged mine away.

'Come on, just for a few minutes. I won't bite.'

She gave me a smile, her mouth was wide and the effect of the smile transformed her. I'd thought she was in her 70s, but the lines that criss-crossed her face, deep furrows from her nose to her chin, made me realise she was a lot older. I suddenly remembered my daughter, Fiona, telling me how we could all tell we were older and our skin had lost its elasticity by pinching the skin on the backs of our hands. If the skin fell back instantly, we were young, but if it took a few seconds to fall back into place, we were older. Molly's face took a few seconds to become smooth again.

She was an old lady, what harm could it do? I relented, smiling at her. 'Well, all right, just for a minute. I'm expected home soon.'

We sat on the bench, Molly's legs swinging slightly and, from where we sat, we could see the whole expanse of the Downs. It was a lovely day, wispy clouds threaded their way across the sky. There was no substance to them, the sun shone out.

'Lovely up here,' Molly said, and I murmured something in agreement.

'Where do you live then?' she asked. We'd been facing the Downs and I sensed her body shifting so now she faced me. I could feel her eyes on me; quick, penetrating glances over my faded tracksuit and loose jacket.

'Not far.' I waved my arm in front of the bench. 'Just down those roads, within walking distance.'

'Thought so, you're up here a lot, aren't you? Now, let me guess which road it is, the one you live in. Would it be St. Julian's or Church Road? No, I know, I've got it ! The Avenue. I'm right, aren't I?'

I glanced at her. I could feel her elbow touching mine. 'Church Road,' I said. I didn't live in that tree-lined road, but one leading off it. I knew that it wouldn't do me any good telling Molly where I lived.

'Like my shoes?' she asked suddenly, sticking her legs straight out like a child. In silence we both looked at her small feet in their golden shoes. I took Molly's silence to indicate her delight in the shoes. I was silent because those elegant shoes, with their fine leather T-bar extending up to her ankles, reminded me of the shoes my mother wore when she went dancing. She always said the same thing, 'I'm dancing to the music of Victor Sylvester,' before turning to wave at me, rustling in her best silk dress, as she went through the front door.

'Yes, I do, they're very pretty.'

Molly rotated her ankles, her head on one side as she enjoyed the effect. I tucked my feet under the bench. My trainers were an old comfortable pair I'd had for years. The laces were grey and fraying.

Molly placed her hand on my arm. 'I think it's very important to wear nice things. What I always say is why have them if you're not going to wear them and enjoy them?'

'Yes, you're right.' I shifted. I wanted to move on, away from Molly, resume my walking. Her hand exerted a slight pressure on my arm.

'I've seen you up here before, you know.'

'Yes, you said.' I stood up, dislodging her arm as I did so. 'Nice meeting you, Molly. I must go, must make a move.'

She stood up and I noticed again how short she was, she barely reached my shoulder.

'Will you be here tomorrow?' She wore large hoop earrings, they were so big they rested on her shoulders. The sun shone directly on her face and I could see blue eye-shadow she'd daubed on her paper-thin eyelids. Pink lipstick had been slashed across her mouth, blurring the edges of her thin lips. A greasy film of colour seeped into the tracery of lines around her mouth. I looked away.

'No, I don't think that I can. Look, I really must go.' I walked away quickly and didn't look back. No wave goodbye, nothing. I left her there.

To walk the whole path across the Downs normally takes me just under an hour. I pounded the path that day, my arms swinging, my legs marching to a definite rhythm. It took me 45 minutes. I decided against having any coffee and headed for home.

When I walked up the path to my front door, red balloons were jiggling around the branches of the silver birch in the front garden. A cluster of white balloons had been tied to the porch and through the front windows I could see a huge banner: HAPPY BIRTHDAY! FIFTY YEARS OLD TODAY!

Once I opened the front door, I could see that the kids had filled the house with balloons. So many balloons, they were hanging from prints on the wall, from light fittings, they cascaded down the wrought iron banisters. It looked wonderful. The kids had tried so hard to fill the house, and not just with balloons. The three of them had managed to work out a system whereby at least one of them would be at home with me each weekend. Fiona worked in Birmingham and Lizzie and Andrew were at Stirling and Warwick universities. God knows what kind of conversation they must have had about me. I can only guess at the pressure put on Andrew by his two sisters. You must take your turn. Or words to that effect.

When Simon walked out I didn't know what to do. It had been a long marriage – 26 years. It was a life, a habit, I thought it would go on forever. At first, I vacillated about everything: sell the house, stay, leave the city, find a new career, a new husband. I thought briefly about killing myself. A large glass of whisky, only I don't like the taste, perhaps wine would be better; a decent Chardonnay, nicely chilled, a massive quantity of tablets. Sad really, the only tablets I could find were in an unopened pot of multi-vitamins and Day Nurse capsules with a best-before date of 1997.

All three kids had been wonderful, telling me that it hadn't been my fault and they swore they wouldn't have anything to do with their Dad. That wouldn't have been right and I told them so, but I suspect they wouldn't have told me if they had seen him. I find it difficult to imagine anything hurting as much as those first months of being on my own.

My 50th birthday party was a surprise. The kids had contacted everyone, they must have gone right through my address book. Friends from university, the newspapers and magazines I'd worked on, even my first boss, Graham Robinson, turned up. I hadn't seen him in almost 30 years. He was very frail, but full of humour and memories. The house was packed with people. I'll always remember the sound of corks and balloons popping.

I didn't go up to the Downs again for over a week. I had a few lunches with old friends, then I sorted the kids out for their various journeys and really I revelled in the warmth that came from that party. I began to feel so much better about how I was coping on my own and so encouraged by the friendly faces that spent my birthday with me.

'What have you got to worry about?' Graham asked me. 'You're 50 years old, that's all. You've got no mortgage, the kids are off your hands. You're on your own. You're actually remarkably fortunate.'

Seems an odd way of looking at life, but when I thought about it, he did have a point. OK, so I'm a divorced mother of three, working from home as an educational consultant, no real money worries and not really on my own. I had an entire bank of friends to draw from, people who wanted to be with me and I with them.

My tracksuit looked worse than ever. I'd thrown it to the bottom of my wardrobe on the day of my birthday. I sniffed at it, thought I'd wash it on the weekend, but my socks were clean, and I began to walk towards the Downs. It was a Wednesday, a warm, sunny day and, as usual on a Wednesday, local schools and colleges were showing off their football skills. A mishmash of colours as lads shoved and shouted, running over the bright green turf. I felt a deep sigh of pleasure as I began my walk. It felt so good to be up there, walking across the Downs.

It was only when I reached the Iris Walters bench that I remembered Molly. She wasn't sitting there, there was no sign of her. I felt stupidly guilty. I was relieved that she wasn't waiting for me. I didn't slow down, just kept up a steady walking pace and enjoyed the colours and the sensation of being on my own up there.

On a narrow section of the path, I paused to allow a young mother with a pushchair to get past me. Then, as if from nowhere, there was Molly. She was smiling broadly at me, hands on her hips. She wore a white *broderie anglaise* blouse, the elasticised sleeves pushed slightly off her shoulders. The skin on her neck was exposed, stringy lines criss-crossing their way upwards, like railway tracks leading to a junction. A wide, gold belt was cinched in tightly at her waist and a full, gathered skirt in emerald green flounced out to her knees. She wore the same gold shoes and the enormous hoop earrings rested on the freckled skin of her shoulders.

'Aha, thought I'd see you today.' She grabbed my arm and began to tug, pulling me off the path. 'I've saved us a seat.' She gestured towards a rickety bench.

'No! No.' My voice was high and loud, the young Mum looked back towards me. I felt ridiculous, what was happening here? I wasn't being kidnapped. I took a deep breath and put my hand over Molly's. She was holding on to my sleeve. Her hands were freckled with rust-coloured liver spots. I could see shadow, a deep, green colour, like a bruise, on the inside of her wrist where her copper bangle had rubbed on her skin.

'Molly, it's nice to see you again, but I can't stop, I'm afraid. I only came out for some fresh air. I've got a lot of work waiting at home for me.'

Her eyes suddenly locked on to mine, the slight pressure of her hand deepened. I could feel her bony fingers squeezing my skin. 'One minute, that's all. Come and sit down, enjoy the view with me.'

I was angry with myself. Why couldn't I handle this? I didn't want to sit down, so why didn't I say so?

'No, really, I can't. Just a walk today, that's all I've got time for.' We'd been doing some sort of shuffle there on the path, Molly pulling, edging me closer towards the bench. It was an old one, vandals had attacked it, only two strips of wood to sit on and the ground underneath was littered with empty cans and used condoms. A pair of black tights fluttered like a sad banner from the wrought iron frame. A thermos flask was wedged on the seat – Molly's flask.

Oh, for God's sake. My shoulders slumped. We spoke at the same time. 'Please?' from Molly and 'OK' from me. I prised Molly's fingers off my arm and smiled at her. Her make-up was as garish as the day I'd first met her. Two daubs of blusher perched high on her cheekbones, her face looked like an artist's palette. I walked with her towards the bench. On the right hand side of the bench, almost hidden by an overgrown bush, Molly had folded her grey cardigan, the same one she'd been wearing the first day. She placed the neatly folded cardigan on her lap and pushed her hands into its folds. In silence she brought out two china mugs, one red, one blue. She held out the red one and I took it without speaking. She balanced the blue one between her knees. Still without speaking, she poured tea from the flask into my mug and we watched silently as the tea bubbled out. Molly smiled graciously as I thanked her.

'Would you like a biscuit with your tea?' As she spoke her hand darted into the folds of the cardigan again, this time she brought out a packet of digestive biscuits. Again I thanked her and we sat for a few minutes gazing at the expanse of the Downs.

Suddenly she shifted, half-turning towards me. 'Why haven't you been up before? Looked for you every day. Been ill? Is that what the problem was?'

I glanced quickly at her, her head was on one side. 'No, I've not been ill, I've been busy. My children have been staying with me and I work from home. I've just been very busy.'

I smiled at her and then turned back to look at the Downs. I took a gulp of tea. It was hot, I could feel it burning my throat.

'So what do you do then? This working from home, what's your job?'

The bench was really uncomfortable, we both perched on the edge of the seat and I edged myself forward. 'I advise the people who publish children's books on what children can learn from reading them – what suits each age group, numbers, how to spell words. How all those things will work for kids, that sort of thing.' I drained my mug of tea and placed it on the ground, close to Molly's gold shoes.

'Sounds a good job to me. 'Spect you need a lot of qualifications for that.'

'A few.' I levered myself up. 'I must be going, got a lot of work waiting for me. Thank you so much for the tea. It was very kind of you to go to all that trouble. Maybe I'll see you up here again.'

Molly scrabbled around in the sleeves of her cardigan. 'Have another biscuit. More tea?'

I shook my head. 'No thank you, I must go.'

She got off the bench much faster than I had done; her cardigan fell from her lap and dropped to the mud.

'When will you be up here again? Tomorrow? I'll make some cake. What sort do you like?' Again, there was that bird-like movement, her head on one side as she stared up at me.

'Please don't go to any trouble. I don't know when I'll make it up here again. I can't commit myself to any particular day. I just have to see what my work allows. Sorry.'

And I left her there holding her mug of tea and the grey cardigan lying among the empty beer cans and crisp packets. I didn't look back, I just kept walking, my head fixed, my eyes staring straight ahead of me.

I didn't go up to the Downs for a long time. There was a lot of work for me to finish. Couriers came almost daily holding large, brown envelopes addressed to me. I phoned friends, went out for supper a few times.

Graham came one Saturday evening and we chatted about old times. I talked to the kids about plans for the summer holidays.

Lizzie broke the news. 'It's Dad. He wants us to spend part of the summer in Italy. He's hired a villa near Pisa and, well, he wants us to fly over. He said something about wanting to talk to us. He sounded so upset, Mum. We've sided with you because we all hate what he did, walking out like that. But he's on his own, you've got us. Dad's got no one.'

Serves him bloody right.

Italy. We'd all gone to see the leaning tower of Pisa when the kids were small. Total and complete waste of time and money. Might as well have been in Blackpool. I wanted to shout, to plead, Lizzie, come with me, let me be the one to share it with you now.

My voice sounded calm. 'When? When are you going?'

I could hear relief easing its way into Lizzie's voice. She chatted away, telling me about their plans. She would be the first to spend time with Simon; then Fiona would fly out, then Andrew.

'So you won't be entirely on your own, Mum.'

'Don't worry about me, I'll be fine. Got masses of work to do. I'm way behind and the garden needs sorting out. It's not as if I'm never going to see you again.' I used these phrases like ballast for us both.

When we said our goodbyes, we replaced the phones at the same time. I remembered the games Simon and I played when we first met. 'You first, no you, no you...' Neither of us wanting to be the first to break the connection.

I wandered through the house, a glass of wine in my hand, staring out into the street as lights were switched on. I heard the sound of cars moving past, a horn announcing an arrival. I stepped back suddenly; someone was walking by. I must look such a sad figure gazing out into the twilight, holding a glass of wine. I moved back into the lounge and turned on the TV; then turned it off again almost immediately. I flicked through my collection of CDs, but settled for a book instead. I refilled my glass.

In bed that night I propped myself up on all four pillows; books and manuscripts I'd been working on were scattered over the duvet. I tidied the bed each morning, leaving the clutter of books like a crust on top.

My dressing table was opposite the bed. It had once belonged to Simon's mother. I'd never liked it – an elaborate fussy piece of furniture. Now I stared balefully into its triple mirrors. Simon had been standing by the dressing table when he told me he was leaving. He said I didn't need him, didn't need anyone. He kept saying that phrase again and again – 'you don't need anyone'. I'd watched him as he repeated 'need', his mouth stretching wide, a parody of a smile. I could see him in all the mirrors on the dressing table.

We'd only just returned from taking Andrew to Warwick University. Simon had barely spoken on the way back. A couple of grunts about petrol, a trip to the toilets at the motorway services, that was it. It was dark when we got home, the headlights of Simon's car flashed over the house. I remembered thinking that we should have left a light on, the house was so dark. I'd gone upstairs to change before starting supper. He followed me.

'Fancy cottage pie?' Hardly a meal for a dying marriage, but that's what I asked him.

'No, not for me. I won't be eating here tonight. I'm leaving.' He picked up my pot of night cream and opened the top.

I pulled the jumper over my head. I thought I hadn't heard him properly. 'What? Leaving? What are you talking about?'

He sniffed at the cream. 'I'm leaving you, this house, this marriage.'

He replaced the night cream and ambled over to his wardrobe. A suitcase was on the bottom, the big one we always took on holiday. He picked it up and it must have been heavy, because he grunted. I laughed. I remember doing that. I thought he was joking, some sort of moody, stupid joke.

'What on earth are you doing?'

He didn't turn, just lugged the suitcase across the bedroom. 'I've told you. I'm leaving, now.'

'Simon, stop. What are you saying, what do you mean?'

He came back to the dressing table and that's when he said it.

'You don't need me, you don't need anyone.'

I sat on the edge of our bed with a tumble of clothes around me and watched Simon's face as he listed my faults, everything he hated about me. All those words, all that anger. I couldn't speak, my mouth opened and closed, but nothing came out. Simon's words were hard. *Cold, mean, callous, frigid, sterile.* He used them like bullets, lining them up and firing them at me. They tore through any blanket of complacency I might have had about the solidity of our marriage. I can remember feeling how hard it was to keep breathing. It felt as if I'd forgotten the naturalness of taking a new breath.

Then he left.

A year ago. I'd had letters almost immediately from his solicitor; then it was over, our marriage dissolved. Divorced.

Everything hurt at the beginning; my head, my pride and I felt lost. But eventually the house settled around me. It seemed to sigh, shifting somehow, making up the space where Simon used to be. I took up all the room in our bed. I filled the wardrobes in an orgy of new clothes and I rearranged the bathroom shelves.

I found myself making excuses for not going up to the Downs. I'd had a lot of work to finish: the deadline for a book I was working on was suddenly brought forward, Fiona had boyfriend troubles and came to stay. The thought of bumping into that woman, Molly, bothered me too. I enjoyed the freedom I found on the Downs, not afternoon tea with an elderly, lonely woman. Instead I took to walking around the roads close to my home, looking at gardens and peeping into windows; it wasn't the same. I missed the space up on the Downs.

It was almost September when I went up there again. I'd bought new trainers, shockingly white, my tracksuit was clean and it was another bright, sunny day. Children were holding on to kite strings: lime green, tomato red and vivid purple kites flapped and soared in the wind. No sign of Molly. My arms began to swing, my legs found their rhythm as I started my walk. A nod, a quick smile to those I passed. Exactly as I liked it.

I had just about reached the end of my walk when I saw Molly on an open-topped bus. This city has many attractions and, on sunny days, one of these buses carries tourists on a pilgrimage round the harbour, along the sweeping Georgian avenues and then up here, across the Downs.

'Yoo-hoo!' There she was.

She was sitting next to a middle-aged couple on the long back seat of the bus. I could see the sun glinting on her over-sized hoop earrings. The man and woman who sat on either side of Molly gazed at me with little interest. I waved, but Molly had turned away. I could see her head tilted to one side as the bus passed me. I finished my walk. I might as well go home.

The children had gathered up their kites and, as I passed the bench, the Iris Walters bench where Molly had sat, a family opened up a picnic basket. No one looked up as I walked by.

Rash

Janet Thomas

Karen was one of the first to get a sun-lounger and she lay by the pool in jeans, a long-sleeved white shirt, wide straw hat, trainers and sunglasses. Every so often, she moved the blue umbrella so her hands and ankles were in shadow. Around the kidney-shaped pool, at least 50 other people, also tourists, almost all also British, lay around her, in swimsuits and bikinis. The Greek sun softened the tarmac on the road. People whispered, stared openly, nudged each other, but not as much as they had yesterday. Karen lifted her book and pretended nobody was looking at her. For all they knew she always sunbathed fully dressed. I don't care, she told herself, this is my holiday, my one holiday, and I'm not sitting in that little room any longer. Her skin, under her jeans, shirt and trainers, itched and raged.

The rep had said it was a photosensitive rash. 'We see them quite a lot, especially on British skins. An allergy to the sun, basically.'

'But I've sunbathed all my life.' Karen turned so the rep could see it was all over her back as well as her arms, legs and chest. Her skin was like pink sandpaper. 'I put on tons of cream.'

'Just keep covered,' the rep suggested. 'It'll go.'

Jim came walking up the beach with the group from Newport he'd palled up with while she'd been hiding in their room taking cold baths. She watched him from behind her sunglasses, as he chatted to the two girls, both wearing strappy tops and tiny shorts, their exposed skins honey and caramel. Her stomach clenched so hard she dropped her book. He'll sleep with one of them, if he hasn't already, a voice in her head whispered, sounding like her mother, as she struggled to find her page and look relaxed. You look repellent, he thinks you're infectious and you wince when he touches you, so what do you expect? He's on holiday. And how can you be allergic to the sun? It's like being allergic to life.

She smiled as he came closer. He was going pink along his freckly cheekbones. 'You might burn a little, love.'

He waved his hand, dismissing this. What idiots can't handle the sun? The Newport lot looked at her, the freak, one tilting her head to get a better look. Karen pulled her sleeves over her hands. The movement stung. 'I was thinking of going shopping in Corfu Town. I'm fed up of wearing these, thought I'd treat myself.'

Jim pointed to the others. 'We're going paragliding. We've booked.'

'That's fine, love.' Karen smiled brightly. 'There's a bus trip. I'll get that.'

'Oh,' one of the girls said, 'that's going in a minute.'

Karen hugged her bag. She didn't want to leave him with them, didn't want to walk away alone. But what was the option? Stay in her room in the bath? Watch them paraglide, dressed, scratching? She had four days and eight hours of this holiday left. 'Right. Well, I'd better move then.'

She stood and Jim leaned an inch away from her. She hurried off, holding her hat, smiling away as if a bus trip alone in the heat was the only reason she'd come to the island.

The stuffy coach swung back and forth along the twisting roads. The hill dropped down at the side, small stones skittering into nothing as they passed. Six boys from Birmingham drank beer in the back seats and sang obscene songs, mostly insulting Greek men's balls. Karen picked at her nail varnish and wondered what everyone at home was doing, how work was managing without her. She imagined facing them all, with no Jim, no tan, and felt sick. She closed her eyes, blaming the swaying bus. She itched.

About half an hour later the bus stopped, and she looked around for Corfu Town, but it was just scrubby hillside. The Greek bus driver stomped to the back and shouted at the boys from Birmingham in Greek. Karen sank down in her seat. The bus started again and so did the singing. Everyone else pretended to be deaf. Another ten minutes and the bus shuddered to a halt. The bus driver shouted, got off the bus and walked down the road. The boys cheered.

Karen was sweating, sticking to her seat, itching and itching. The boys kept singing. Soon they started to sound bored, looking for the driver, egging each other on for Round Two. Ten minutes. Fifteen minutes. OK, he'd made his point now.

All the British tourists sat in the bus for half an hour. The singing had finally mumbled into silence. Karen knew she'd scream if she had to sit there itching against the plastic seat any longer, so she got up and everyone looked at her. Desperate to move, she climbed off the bus down on to the dust road. The olive trees twisted their branches around themselves in grey-green rows. The sun stared down at her, burning her centre parting. There was no sign of the bus driver, or anyone else, or any houses. Her phone played *I predict a riot* when she turned it on, making her homesick. No signal. What the hell did she do now? Her skin seethed, nagging her on. She was wearing her trainers, so, unfolding her sunhat, she started to walk. There would have to be a village with a phone eventually. Behind her, she was aware of people spilling off the bus.

'Hey, you gonna walk all the way?' A Birmingham accent. Noisy scuffing footsteps followed her down the hill.

'On your own, darling?'

'I saw your man with those Welsh girls, didn't I? That why he's not with you?'

'Aw, I'll keep you company.' Sniggering.

She carried on walking, eyes ahead, as if nobody was saying anything.

'Hey, don't be unfriendly.'

'Why'd you come, if you just want to be so fucking miserable?'

They caught up with her, moved around her, their shirts off, showing their soft flesh. They had bottles in their hands, their eyes covered by big ugly sunglasses, like flies' eyes. The lager smelt like sweat. Why didn't the sun turn their skins pink and spiteful? Her body remembered a party when she'd suddenly been circled by gatecrashers, when she'd had to be rescued, and trembled. She stared desperately at the horizon, trying to show nothing on her face at all.

'Bitch.' One grabbed her left arm. They all stopped. She realised they had walked out of sight of the bus. Why had she thought they were boys? Her tongue was too big in her throat. 'That's more like it,' he sneered, pushing her back against the wall of his friends. 'I've seen you, stuck up, avoiding everyone, thinking you're so fucking great.' His grip bit into her rash, stinging. The rash that was why Jim wasn't here.

'Careful,' she said, her voice shaking. She pulled back her sleeve and the spots glowed in the sun. 'It's catching.'

He let her arm go. She pulled back her collar, showing her shoulder round. They all stepped back, one scuffling on the edge.

'That's why my boyfriend couldn't come. Nothing yesterday. Today he's covered. *Everywhere*. And he'll be scarred.' The thought of Jim burning added bite to her voice.

'Fuck.' The man wiped his hand on his shorts.

She took a tiny step up the hill and they backed off. She wanted to laugh. Move, her brain screamed, and she slipped through them and ran for the top, her breath rough. Her legs were so tense it was hard not to trip over herself, waiting for a hand on her shoulder, in her hair. The bus was at the top – and the bus driver, beckoning her. She grabbed the bar and swung herself on after him. He was talking away in Greek. 'Those men,' she panted.

He waved dismissively and drove off, his smile stretching his moustache wide. None of the others said anything about the group left behind. She sat on the seat behind the driver, clinging to the rail. I'm all right, she told herself, shaking.

After the hotel complex full of British people, Corfu Town felt Greek. She bought a glass of white wine in the first bar she saw and a pudding she couldn't pronounce, all layers of pastry and nuts and honey, sweet enough to make her fillings ache and yet dry on her tongue. It was the first thing she had eaten on this holiday that she couldn't eat at home and she felt a little heartache of joy, as if it was a mini adventure just eating it, but it didn't still the shakes. She drank her wine and licked honey from her fingers, and all she could think of was the way she'd stared at the horizon as if nothing was happening. Why do that? That was always how she handled the bullies at school, that was how she'd handled those men at that party, before she'd been rescued. Pretend it isn't happening – why was that her defence mechanism? When had that ever worked?

But I did something this time, she thought. I'm here. She stretched out her hand and smiled at her raw angry skin.

And she thought of Jim – pretend everything is fine. Pretend you aren't bothered. Ignore it and it isn't happening. Why did she do that? When had it ever worked?

The waiter offered her another glass, smiling, and she felt an urge to flash her rash at him, just to see the start in his eyes. Surprised at herself she almost giggled. She nodded to the wine, and pointed at random to something on the menu. It came back deep-fried with tentacles. She laughed openly then. Was she really going to eat that? She looked around for someone to notice that she was about to eat tentacles, but everyone else was caught up in their own business. She stared. What did these people do on holiday, away from the beach, seemingly sexless and so dressed? She bit into her seafood, which was crunchy and chewy and didn't particularly taste of anything, and waited to feel sick. She thought, I am alone, foreign, repulsively pink and crusted, and waited to feel afraid.

And instead, like a loosening, she had this sense of Corfu Town spreading out around her, and beyond that other towns, other countries, on and on, like a map unfolding. It was a weird feeling and she didn't know quite what to do with it. But she knew what she wouldn't do.

She sat in the bar, swaying in her chair, eating tentacles, until she knew the bus would have gone. She rang Jim, left a message at reception for him as he was out. She rang her mother at home, shouting to her over the music. And as she told her mother about her allergy, stretching out her arm, she realised she wasn't itching any more. As she listened to her mother panic, the phone clamped between her cheek and her shoulder, she scratched her arm and waited to feel the pain. She picked at her spots, dug her nails in, attacked them. She wasn't ready yet to lose her rash.

Flora

Sarah Todd Taylor

Roses yielded the best. Their long necks snapped or sliced off, he could crush them softly between sheets of vellum, silk petals folding into one another as entwined limbs. The seed pod would offer the natural resistance of the mother, but a careful press of the thumb would break its womb, crushing any hope of new life into the waiting page.

His books were his delight. He loved to leaf through their pages, admiring his past loves on their deathbeds. Lilies bending over to give frozen kisses to aquilegia, snowdrops curling round the margins, a riot of bluebells and harebells stolen from woodland to preserve for antiquity. The roses, though, were his darlings, and on them he lavished the most care, arranging them as Botticelli might have done his nymphs, letting them dance across the page for him, layering cotton leaved paper over them before condemning them to months of darkness, pressed under his most precious volumes till they were completely subdued and their youth was captured forever.

She watched him, seated in his chair in the morning sun, hat tilted to shade his fading eyes. He was watching for the yellow rose to open, and she poured herself a lemonade, knowing that he would not thank her for disturbing him. He would sit like this for hours, waiting, while the bees hummed around his feet and the sprinkler wept mechanically across the lawn. Only when his chosen bloom was at its moment of perfection would he leap forward, knife quivering with anticipation. Buds fully open, petals splayed as he cupped its soft beauty, the rose would plead silently for its life, not understanding that it was destined for immortality.

She would not disturb him. He believed, as he had often told her, that a moment's hesitation would ruin his beloved, and she had no wish to anger him. Instead, she went to her work in the living room.

Others had often commented that there were no flowers in the house. 'The garden is such a *blaze*,' her mother had said on her first visit, 'we really *must* bring some into the lounge.' The younger woman had begged her not to, but on returning from a trip to town one morning, they had found a cut glass vase filled with his choicest blooms, dusting the air with their scented pollen. He had retired to his study with a face of thunder, and when she had passed by with coffee an hour later, she had heard the steady crack of turning pages as he sought solace in his books. Her mother had left, accepting the flowers, with bemusement, as a gift, and she had seen to it that the vase was quickly disposed of.

They did not understand, she reasoned. They did not know him as she did. He hated to see decay. His flowers did not stand in vases, wilting, making a decoration of their death throes. The moment of perfection was what captivated him. The point between growth and death. That precious time where the flower was fully alive, at its most beautiful. If he could capture that before the bloom began to fade, he could render them immortal, eternally perfect.

She heard his footsteps on the stair, and knew that he was heading for his study with a fresh specimen. The little yellow rose of which she had grown so fond. Today she would become a goddess. She strained her ears, and heard the opening chords of *O mio babbino caro*. It was the music he always played for his most beautiful subjects. The common flowers were treated to jazz, or light operetta. Only the roses were serenaded with the light soprano voice which she now knew almost as well as she did her own.

She knew what he would be doing. He had mentioned it at breakfast. 'I'm going to draw her,' he had said. 'The leaf shapes should be good, and I already have a pressed yellow. The magazines might take a few new drawings, you never know.'

She had nodded, encouragingly. It was good to think that he was taking an interest in work again. He had been quite a successful artist, before the accident. Before the night that had taken their daughter and their hopes away in a mess of spinning wheels and shattered glass. She could not recall whether, before that, he had been so interested in capturing what he now called 'the moment of absolute life'. They had just been flowers to him then, plants to strip apart and record in minute detail. He had built a comfortable life for her with the income to be had from botanical magazines, and his work had graced the covers of several bestsellers and popular *flora*.

He had used pen and ink in those days, but now he worked only with charcoal, sketching quickly to draw the vitality of his subject into the page. He refused to consider paint or pastel and even chalk, with its chemical hues, was tasteless to him. 'Nothing false,' he had insisted one Christmas when she had offered to buy him more materials. 'Only nature can appreciate her own value.' His drawings were death redeemed into life. The dead crushed wood fused by his expert hand with the dead pulp paper to create a perfect image of the living. Once finished, the model would be cast into the fire to be consumed in an instant. He would not suffer decay. This was how it should be, he reasoned. Beauty should exist for beauty's sake. He sought to protect his loves from time, from death.

It pained her that he had never chosen to draw her. In the early days she had arranged herself in the garden, amongst those flowers that she knew he loved best, inviting him to take out his sketch book. She had cherished the thought that she could hang the piece in their front room, reminding herself in later years of how she herself had looked in her prime. He had ignored her suggestions, and she had taken, of late, to haunting the sycamore trees at the end of the garden. Their thick trunks were not to his taste and she felt safe with them. There was no danger of harsh comparisons being drawn with the more delicate blooms nearer the house. She was aware that her own beauty was fading.

'You should get them fixed,' her sister said one afternoon. They were enjoying a rare afternoon out and she had insisted on going to her favourite teashop – a faux Victorian affair with *ranunculus* and *alastromeria* gathered in ornate vases, impossibly fashioned nymphs draping themselves round the handles. She had chosen a table in the centre of the room and was enjoying the sensation of being surrounded with flowers. She gazed at the centrepiece placed between their teacups, tracing the line of the paper-thin petals, admiring the curve of the *ranunculus* head, the variety of blooms, noting without pain the curling edge of one leaf, which had passed its perfect moment and would soon begin to shrink from this world.

'Seriously, June, you'll hardly notice it. I go every few months and it's done wonders, look.'

She peered at the soft, plumped skin where the crease of her sister's eye had once settled. She had become far more aware of late of the lines around her own eyes. She no longer recognised the texture of her brow, and where her cheeks had once easily betrayed her blushes, there was now a translucency under the rouge that she had taken to using. It would only be a matter of time, she thought, before he noticed as well. She had not, until now, considered such drastic action.

'Was it expensive?' she asked.

She was booked in for the next Friday. A simple procedure. She did not expect to be away long. She had told him she had a lunch date in town. He was waiting for a carnation to open and would not miss her. She had left him, newly sharpened blade in hand, circling the flower stem impatiently.

She lingered in town to allow the swelling to go down. On the way home she bought a large bunch of sweet peas, drawn by their frivolity, and breathed in their scent until, drawing near to home, she forced herself to abandon them on top of a wall. She checked herself in a hand mirror, marvelling at the smoothness of the skin around her eye sockets. It was not so hard after all, she thought, to preserve that moment of beauty.

She could hear Puccini playing as she walked through the gate: '*…mi piace è bello bello…*' She knew he must be preparing for a favourite bloom. One of the roses must have matured unexpectedly.

As she passed the carnation, she noted that it was in flower, but untouched.

Inside the house, the aria swelled. He was busy in the study and would not wish to be disturbed. Tired, she made her way to their room and lay on the bed, smiling to herself, listening to him in the next room.

He found her there an hour later. He watched her for a while, noting the fine leaf-veins on her cheek, seeing how her skin had become paper-like, as if inviting his craft. He had not noticed, before, that her bloom was failing.

The eyes were plumper than they had been that morning. He knew why. He had seen the card as it fell from her bag onto the path. It pained him that she had gone to another man. This was his specialism, his art. What had this man done to his love? He peered closer, anxious not to wake her. The clumsy attempt at artistry was repellent. There was no honesty here, no true framing of nature in her prime, only an ugly world seeking to lie about its own fragility. He would have done better for her. Why had she not waited for him?

He reached for the pillow.

The carnation had opened later in the day than he had thought. She lay now, crimson petals nestling into the cream parchment he had selected for her. He would arrange her later.

Now, he was busy with his first love.

He had broken her arm in the struggle. It hung limply, torn nails snagging the Persian rug she had bought him for their crystal anniversary. He winced and turned from the sight of it. She, of all of them, should have remained perfect. He turned her face towards the window so that she could look into the setting sun, and smiled at the glow that settled across her cheek. Already, the bloom was returning, her skin brightening as the last rays reflected their life in her staring eyes.

He carefully re-arranged her hair, combing each lock, placing them precisely to frame her face like a halo. She was so beautiful. He was glad that he had been given this chance. He would make amends and would turn her into an angel. Not since last summer, when an orchid had flowered unexpectedly, had he taken so long with one of his loves. He remembered how she had been angry with him for locking himself away for hours, working into the night to capture the orchid's matt beauty, painstakingly recreating the droop of her head, the fading shades of each curved petal. They had gone into town later, for dinner. An apology that he felt was expected, but that only underlined for him how little she still understood.

He cradled her feet in his hands briefly as he put them in place, toes pointed downwards to the foot of the bed, knees bent as though running through the air. An attitude of flight, he thought. He was sad that she was wearing brown. She had a white summer dress that would more befit a divine being. He wondered if he could draw her in white, against a background of sky, a Jacob's ladder showering light onto her warm, dark head. He looked across at the broken limb and frowned. He would have to lie anyway – in his pictures she would be whole.

He curled her good arm across her chest and lifted her locket into the palm, marvelling, as his fingers intertwined once more with hers, at the softness of her still warm flesh. He stroked her fingers, humming lightly in time with the soprano serenade from the next room, where the crimson carnation waited patiently for him.

'*Babbo, pietâ, pietâ.*'

The aria was drawing to an end. He did not wish to draw her tonight. He only wished to admire her. He lay down beside his love, careful not to disturb his creation. She would hover between life and death forever, his angel. She would never age, never decay. He would hang her in the front room. He thought she would like that. He wished he could join her.

He had never loved her more.

Unwrapped

Lara Clough

Within seconds Cara's feet and flip-flops are soaked. Rain is running down her legs and bouncing high off the pavement in big messy drops. Car headlights pick out the choppy new torrents pouring into the drains. Good, she thinks mournfully, as she turns into the high street. At least one part of her is clean. She hasn't had a shower for days. David is knee-deep in plumbing, obsessively talking to himself and ringing up about immersion heaters. The pile of copper piping grows between them, as do the silences. He won't tell her how it's going unless she tells him what she has sold in her gift shop and she can't bear to. Now at least in the rain she is getting clean, Welsh water clean, soaking, Atlantic, chapel-thundering clean.

'Shit.' She stumbles over a loose paving stone. How she hates this mid-Wales town. Hates smiling in her shop over one modest purchase all afternoon. She hated smiling in the café at lunchtime, when it felt like people were whispering about her. It rained then too. She lit a damp cigarette, ordered another coffee and smiled grimly at the woman serving.

Now she hugs the cagoule tighter around herself. It is her son's and inadequate. Why is the chip shop stuck at the end of the high street when it's doing far better than hers ever will? Her shop will go, an eighteen month wonder, incomers here for a try out. She knows she has to face up to that.

She glances across at two men pausing briefly by the pub. She thinks one might be Wynn. Why does she care? He is nothing to do with her, absolutely nothing. Except that he keeps coming in with his little girl, Rhiannon, who has blond hair, melting brown eyes and such clean, clean clothes. He does a slow, tinkering tour of her handmade cards (too expensive), handmade felt bags (too small), local paintings (not really good enough) and then only spends a pound on a tiny item like a pen with a fluffy top.

'Bit expensive for us all this,' he commented, grinning, that first time. 'You wouldn't do some cheaper jewellery? Or some of those transfer tattoos? For the kids?'

She folded over his smart paper bag and gave it to him with the change. 'That's not quite our thing,' she said from behind her counter.

Now she winces – such ignorant, misplaced smugness. They were going to sell real crafts, beautiful toys and gifts for real prices. To whom exactly they hadn't quite thought. They would be discovered, sought out by people spending over fifty pounds. But now she knows it's only one or two: there's the prosperous lady with the dog kennels and the numerous relatives, the doctor's wife who buys two items in the course of an hour's anguished chat over her very lonely state.

Wynn is someone. He knows everyone, is always chatting in that hour long Saturday talking spree down the high street. He always comes in. He has a new jacket, more money than them, and inquiring blue eyes. His brown fingers handle her things, those things that are spending far too long in her shop, abandoned, mutely accusing her. Why doesn't he buy something? Why does he come in if her things are not to his taste?

David says he wants to talk, a serious talk with accounts books open. His picture framing business has taken off while her takings are abysmal. In black and white on paper there is no breathy enthusiasm to hide behind. And she knows her Christmas stock, ordered naively, won't sell.

She turns into the chip shop, the door closed against the driving rain, and she shakes off her cagoule. All week she's been dreading it and now it's come, the serious talk, and on a Friday night, worst luck. It will be nothing like those slightly drunken Fridays of laughter on the sofa, long out-of-time kisses and a trail up to bed. They seem an age away and she misses them. She misses the old David that went with them. The smell of vinegar and frying food hits her forcibly. Dai's pungent vinegar is a joke in the town. Water has somehow made its way into her bra and she blows down her collar, trying to get more comfortable. A button is missing on her blouse, there's a stain of ketchup showing. She remembers scrubbing at her blouse haphazardly at tea time, angry with David.

'Cara, it's so stupid. You're not facing reality. Take those back.' He gestured to the highly decorated pink package he found in their bedroom.

'But –'

'But what? That'll buy us a new radiator for Con's room. Surely you can see?' He stared at her, accusatory and slightly shocked. David, her co-dreamer and supporter in their venture into Wales, has turned into a down-to-earth business man with no imagination. So the lacy camisole and French knickers must go back.

'I see.' She was clearing the table. 'It's fantasies about central heating all the way, welding, gravity feeding, whatever. Very sexy, completely erotic.'

David looked past her, overtaken by his new obsession. 'Maybe I could connect – what did you say?'

Cara stared at him, stupefied and very tired.

She had bought the lingerie because of Wynn. She had been waylaid in Llandrindod, drawn against her will to look at underwear in the shop round the corner because she didn't want Wynn to spot her in the main street. The camisole lured her, draped awkwardly on the old fashioned dummy with the vile grey-green wig. Long thin straps and a lacy appliqué style of green leaves all around the neckline. The rest was made of the lightest sheer white fabric with two simple darts on each side. The matching knickers mirrored the same design. They looked simple and elegant and gorgeous. They spoke of a woman with time for a lovely long bath, time to arrange herself on the bedclothes to advantage. She came closer, looking for the price tag, and jumped.

Wynn was there, right beside her, hands in his pockets, grinning. 'Lucky man, Dave.' He slipped her a glance. 'Bit of a goddess in that.' Her mouth dropped and he winked. Winked at her and laughed and backed away. 'Bye Cara.' And because he kept watching her, she stalked into the shop and got out her card.

At least he isn't in the chip shop. She casts a glance around. She's late tonight, some are from the pub.

She tried the camisole and knickers on in their half-decorated bathroom. Her skin gleamed very pale in the dim light. She looked thinner, her dark hair lank by the sides of her face. She was an underwater nymph, in a swirling, confusing autumn tide. I won't survive in the real world, she thought. Not in this grim, you must sell cheap tat or die world. Barabrith and Welsh cakes and drunken farmers driving very slowly down the middle of the road world. Oh God, she must get a grip. But what can she sell in the shop? Won't she compromise herself, selling items from Lord knows where, probably made with child labour abroad? She wants the shop to have beautiful things in it, items which will seduce people into her world – but what is the point if nobody buys them?

There are bottles of chemical pop on a shelf high above the dripping white tiles. One is electric blue – she stares at it. Maybe it will help her brain cells congregate and then she'll survive here, because she wants to, really. Because nowhere is as lush as the green park by the river after the rain, nothing is as voluptuous as the clouds, driving back with her son Con from swimming.

Idly she watches Dai's boy wrap the chips. He must be new because he hasn't the knack, that twist round and flip after each wrap so that that they don't fall open. Dai chides him gently in Welsh as his parcels spring open again. It is so touching somehow, the chips that won't be wrapped and Dai's quiet intervention. She realizes the lad must be slow and looks up into his face and then down at the chips again.

They nestle there, exposing themselves, their long brown succulent fingers of potato awash with vinegar and salt. Dai is generous. They are so ready and she experiences an immense and rather painful need for sex, for reassurance, for that feeling of hope and comfort afterwards. She glances up and sees someone at the door. It could be Wynn, but the jacket is different. She turns back to the chips, and through to another world. She's behind her shop counter, selling herself in a hazy sort of seduction. Someone comes up behind her and very gently parts her white jacket and top. They come apart like silk, in shivering layers, and underneath is the leafy camisole, but now it's the most incredible, ornate top made up of beautiful designs, a dragon at her shoulder, a butterfly, stars, Celtic swirls. A little girl comes in the shop and whoever is behind Cara, talking in Welsh, peels the dragon delicately away from her skin. It floats across the counter and onto the girl's arm, iridescent and sparkling. The girl hands over four pounds. Two lads come in and off come the Celtic designs. They are black and red, intricate and curving. Then three more girls. The till is looking better. They don't seem to see her becoming naked, just stare with delight at their temporary tattoos and tell their friends. From behind her, the fingers reach over and she realises they're Wynn's. And still people keep coming and the tattoos float over...

'Five pounds seventy five, Mrs Phillips.'

'What?'

There's a snigger and she peers round, startled. Wynn is there but he's not looking happy, and his jacket doesn't fit. She spills her change onto the counter and scoops up her parcel. Breathless, she pushes past Wynn out of the shop and pulls up her hood. It's still raining.

'Hey!' Someone has her arm. It's Wynn. He pulls her along to where an alley heads off from the High Street.

'Wynn, you'll lose your place, go back.'

'He doesn't mean any harm, he's just trying. You've got to give him a chance.'

'Who?' Cara is lost.

'Oh my God,' says Wynn, 'make a joke do you, all inbreeding and that sort of shit? He's my cousin, Aled, in the shop, the one you were staring at. He's a bit slow, that's all, not an ounce of harm.'

'Oh, no, I didn't mean to…honestly, I was thinking about something else. He was great, he'll get better.'

Wynn stares at her in silence and then releases a slow wry smile. 'You look shattered. Better get home with those.'

'Yes. Well, if you call it a home, no hot water, plumbing in pieces, David *is* trying and the shop… Well, you know, we won't be here long.' She shifts her feet, she is really so very tired.

'Cara, listen, I'll get Jack to call in, first thing tomorrow, he'll see you right. And my sister, she's packing up her shop in Llandod, want to see her stock? I've helped her a bit, you should have a look, it's a real variety, honest. She's got some great transfer tattoos.'

'Oh, has she?' she manages to say in a high voice and can't meet his eyes.

'Not your style, hey?' His face is settling into disappointment.

'No, you're wrong, it's just I – I don't know what my style is, just now.'

'Wednesday then, I'll take you. No point opening, is there? Wednesday's a dead loss, market at Machynlleth, you know that. Don't you?'

She sniffs. He is so patronising, but he reaches out and lays a hand on her arm. 'Oh Cara,' he says and she notices he is tired too. 'Rhiannon's sick of your shop but I can't pass it, I have to bribe her to go in.'

'You're a terrible Dad.'

'Yeah, but let me help you. Please?' And he leans over and kisses her cheek, his breath very warm on her ear, brown fingers on her arm.

She settles back onto the pavement and gives him a small smile. 'Maybe,' she says slowly and then she turns into the swirling autumn rain and is gone.

Swimming

Sarah Jackman

'Ready?' Lisa asked.

'Yes,' Mattie said slowly, but she didn't move. She was thinking that even though Lisa was dressed in a brand new tracksuit and was carrying a brand new sports bag, she didn't look like she was about to go swimming.

In fact, if Mattie had opened the door and found Lisa's disembodied head bobbing in the air in front of her, it wouldn't have been at all surprising to hear it start grumbling about how, once again, Mattie had misunderstood the arrangements and impatiently telling her to go and get changed for the disco.

Lisa's hair was secured in place at the back with a clasp and held neatly off each side of her face with heart-shaped diamanté clips so that Mattie had an unimpeded view of Lisa's blue eyes nestled in thick mascara.

'Have you got your cossie on underneath?' Lisa's tongue flicked across her bottom lip, then the top, making the lip-gloss gleam.

'No.'

Lisa frowned. 'It saves time when we get there.'

Mattie seriously doubted this was true, but she recognized the casual certainty of Lisa's declaration and knew it would be best to keep quiet. It had been the same yesterday when Lisa sprung the idea of swimming on her as they were walking home from school.

Lisa had said, 'We need to get fit.' She'd said, 'Swimming's good exercise and there's nothing else to do on Wednesday evenings anyway.'

Mattie fished her costume out of her bag and shut herself in the downstairs loo. She sat on the toilet seat to remove her trainers. Outside Lisa had started singing and Mattie knew that she'd be practising the dance that went with the song; Lisa only needed to see the video once to be able to copy the moves. Mattie struggled to pull her sweatshirt over her head. She tugged it to and fro but it was stuck on her scrunchie, and the more she tried, the worse it seemed to get. She was panting with the effort, her arms felt weak held above her head, her ears hot from friction.

Outside Lisa stopped singing. Mattie froze.

'Matt? Have you died in there or what?'

Mattie's muffled laughter filled her top with warm, minty air. She pictured it frosting the inside like a coating of icing sugar. She yanked herself free and stood up giddily to take off her tracksuit bottoms and knickers.

Mattie eyed the photo on the wall in front of her, picked herself out in the middle row without intention or hesitation. For the millionth time, the desire accidentally to knock the photo to the floor swelled inside her, but she knew it was futile; it would only be promptly replaced by one of those plastered all over the living room. She noticed the costume that she was wearing back then was the same one she was now about to step into; she seriously doubted it was going to fit.

Swimming had taken up too much time.

There had been practice at least four times a week and then competitions most Saturdays, which meant that she could never go shopping in town with Lisa and the others. It meant going to school on Monday and having to ask Lisa to fill her in on what everyone was talking about until Lisa started snapping at her and saying, 'You had to be there, Matt.'

She glared at Tony's face on the photograph, her face reddening with the thought that she had once nearly fancied him and at the memory of that evening when he'd turned up at the house.

She'd heard the doorbell and people talking hush-hush in the hall, so when her mum had called her downstairs with a strange urgency in her voice, Mattie had burst into the living room full of anticipation and excitement. Three serious faces had turned towards her and stared, until her dad said, 'Where are your manners? Say hello to Mr Mills, Mathilda.'

It had taken a moment to register that he meant Tony.

The moment she sat down Mum started throwing accusations and questions at her: *She'd lied to them. Where had she been going on Saturdays all this time? What had she been doing? Who was she with?*

Then Tony had his go, telling her that she'd need to be dedicated and how there were plenty of others to take her place if she wasn't. Perhaps not as good, he'd added, but reliable members of the team. As he spoke he kept looking at Dad, who had jumped in as soon as Tony had finished speaking. 'What do you have to say for yourself, young lady?'

When Mattie said that she didn't want to swim anymore, she was sick of it, she hated it, Dad leapt up.

'You're an idiot for wasting a gift,' he shouted, grabbing one of her cups off the shelf and holding it aloft as if he'd just won a race himself. 'Look at what you're giving up, look at what you're giving up,' he kept repeating. When Mum started crying, Mattie had closed her eyes. Anyone would have thought she'd been doing something terrible instead of just shopping and hanging out. She couldn't understand how swimming had ever got that important.

With a final wriggle, the costume was on. It was way too small and cut across her cheeks so that they bulged out like the lumps of raw dough they'd made pizza bases with at school. Mattie tilted backwards, which loosened the material on her bum but tautened it across her stomach and tits which, with nowhere else to go, started to ooze into her armpits. Mattie squished them back in as best she could.

Outside Lisa was singing, 'Why are we waiting?'

On closer inspection, Mattie saw with alarm that sprigs of pubic hair were also escaping down below. She poked those back in too.

'What *are* you doing in there Matt?' Lisa rapped crossly on the door.

Mattie went straight to locker number 193 without thinking and the same queasy feeling came over her as it had in the ticket queue when she inhaled the familiar smell of rubber and sweat and cleaning fluid. Her heart was beating fast, like it used to before a race. She stuffed her belongings inside and stood for a moment trying to breathe deeply, but her lungs felt like soggy sponges soaking up the warm, damp air.

She wrapped her towel around her; tying it at her waist; she stared at the bump her stomach made which seemed to be growing bigger every second. She clenched her muscles and sucked it in when Lisa emerged from the cubicle.

'Do I look OK?' Lisa turned this way and that in front of the full-length mirror.

Slice Mattie in half and there would still be more of her than Lisa. She reminded Mattie of one of those brittle shavings Dad planed from hunks of wood in his workshop and which Mattie liked to pick up off the floor just to feel their fragility.

'You look great.' She tweaked the elastic that had cut grooves into the top of her thighs and rubbed at the red marks. 'Mine's too small.'

Lisa made Mattie undo her towel. Under her scrutiny, Mattie clenched and sucked so hard her muscles trembled and her jaw began to ache from holding her breath.

'It's not too bad,' Lisa announced after a long pause.

The air was bitter with chlorine and tainted sea-green, so that Mattie felt as if her eyes were open under water. Ahead, Lisa handed her ticket to the lifeguard attendant. He peered at Mattie as she approached. 'Haven't seen you for a long time.'

Mattie felt caught. 'I've been busy,' she finally said, hanging her head.

She walked past the baby pool filled with tiny children splashing along in their armbands like wind-up toys let loose; past the cordoned-off inky-blue diving pool where she'd always imagined if you dove down like an arrow, you could break through into a magical world. When she came to the main pool she was shocked by how busy it was; there was barely a centimetre which didn't contain a body part; the water was so thrashed up that the black lines on the bottom looked as if they'd been painted by someone who couldn't keep their hand steady. Everyone was shouting and somewhere a child was crying, jagged shrieks which reverberated around the hall.

Mattie had always tried to be the first to arrive for training. She liked nothing better than treading through the echoing quiet early in the morning to stand at the deep end and look across the motionless blue of the pool. She would dive into the exact middle and once she'd reached the other end, look back at the perfect 'v' trail she'd created unfurling across the water until it bumped into nothingness at the sides and stillness was restored.

'Come on, Matt,' Lisa shouted. She was sitting on the edge with her legs dangling in the water and her arms hugged around her.

Mattie threw down her towel and angled her body sideways down the steps so that neither her bum nor her stomach faced the pool. She plunged into the water and spotting Lisa's feet, came up with her mouth gaping, pretending to chomp at her toes. Lisa squealed and Mattie splashed her – only once, but it was a big mistake. Lisa hissed a single word, '*Don't*,' before retreating to a bench at the side of the pool where she sat shivering until Mattie promised not to do it again.

'Are you really wearing those?' Lisa asked, looking down at Mattie as she adjusted the goggles to sit tightly over her eyes.

'How else will I see under water?'

'Why do you need to?' Before Mattie had a chance to reply, Lisa spoke again. 'You go away,' she instructed, 'until I'm in.'

Mattie held her nose as she sank down, feeling the water close over her head. She began a slow glide along the bottom, her tummy grazing the floor. She swam through a forest of pasty legs to the other side and then back again before surfacing.

Lisa was a couple of metres away swimming with jerky strokes, her neck stiffly arched, her chin pushed forward, her nose held high. In the swimming club they'd called the people who refused to get their heads wet 'snouts'.

Mattie dove down and surfaced just behind Lisa, touching her leg to let her know she was there. Lisa yelped, began flailing around, gulping for air and kicking out plumes of spray as she headed into the side.

'If I'd known you were going to muck around so much, I wouldn't have asked you to come.' Lisa's face was screwed up and pink with anger. 'I could have drowned,' she said, clutching the rail of the steps, her voice shrill and her eyes wide.

'Sorry,' Mattie said. 'I was only…'

'Has my mascara run?' Lisa cut in. 'It had better not have.'

Lisa's hairline at the back of her neck was damp and Mattie watched as a single drop of water slid slowly down her forehead; but the mascara and lip-gloss were untouched.

'No, it's fine.'

Mattie turned back to face the pool. Without thinking, she pushed off and began to swim, keeping alert to the gaps between people. Her body stretched and curved as she dipped and rose. Then she altered her stroke and began to cut through the pool, narrow and fast. She'd forgotten how strong her body was, how her skin felt coated in silk as it slipped easily through the water. People cleared a pathway for her as she tumble-turned and began another length.

Mattie counted twenty more before easing to a gentle halt in the shallow end. She looked around for Lisa, felt a bump of guilt when she saw Lisa hadn't moved but as Mattie started towards her, she noticed Lisa wasn't alone. She was talking to Robin and Sammy from their school.

Mattie quickly submerged herself but as soon as she came up for air, Lisa started waving to her. She swam reluctantly forward.

'Robin and Sammy come swimming every Wednesday,' Lisa told Mattie and giggled. Mattie remembered Lisa fancied Robin. 'Mattie used to be in the swimming team. But I'm useless, half a length and I'm exhausted.'

'You need to build up some muscles,' Robin told her and Mattie watched him gently squeeze one of her thin arms; they both laughed as if it was the funniest thing in the world.

Mattie quickly lowered her arms out of sight. She had bigger muscles than either of the boys and now that she was stationary her whole body seemed to be expanding; her tummy was ballooning, the fat on her thighs was rippling with the flow of the water. She sank deeper and half-listened to the others chat.

Mattie didn't know what to say to boys anymore. In the swimming club it had been easy, she just talked to them about techniques and times and normal things too, like what they'd watched on television the night before. There wasn't a big deal made about girls and boys like there was at school where you weren't supposed to forget about it for a single moment.

Whenever a group got together, Mattie felt sick with nerves, much worse than she ever felt before competing. At least then she'd known what the rules were and that her team was always there cheering her on, calling out her name, wanting her to do well. Now, Mattie was constantly confused and was always in danger of getting it wrong. Girls who were friends one minute were no longer talking to her and Lisa the next; and one time Mattie had made the big mistake of just chatting with a boy only to have Lisa drag her away, whispering how she was causing loads of trouble because he was 'somebody else's'.

It was safer, Mattie had decided, to look stupid and stay silent.

Lisa giggled again and suddenly Mattie saw how it was.

She left the side without saying a word. She would not, she promised herself, stop swimming until Lisa had stopped talking to the boys.

At each turn when Mattie checked whether they were still in the same spot, the words 'she knew, she knew' bubbled through her. She had to force herself to forget, to concentrate on placing her body within the water, getting the stroke exactly right. She was too out of practice to achieve this all the time, but whenever she did, it felt good and purposeful.

She stopped to catch her breath and couldn't resist glancing over. When she saw them huddled together, the words swept through her: 'She knew they'd be here.'

She swam over.

'I'm getting out now,' she told Lisa.

'Me too. See you later, you guys.'

Mattie was up and out in a flash. She retrieved her towel from the bench and set off for the changing rooms. The lifeguard called out to her as she passed, 'You've not lost the knack, I see.'

She slowed her pace, smiled over her shoulder. 'Thanks.'

'Don't leave it so long next time,' he said and winked.

In the shower, Mattie closed her eyes as the water cascaded onto her head, over her face and shoulders. She could stay like this for hours.

'Was that lifeguard chatting you up?' Lisa stood shivering at the entrance to the shower room, her towel wrapped tightly around her shoulders.

'No.'

'What did he say then?'

'Nothing. He remembered me from before that's all.'

'I think he fancies you.'

'He was just being friendly.'

'He's old anyhow,' Lisa said. 'He'd be a perv.'

'Aren't you having a shower?'

'I haven't got any stuff with me.'

'You can borrow mine.'

'It's OK. I don't want to get my hair wet.'

Mattie began shampooing her hair.

'I told them we'd meet up after, in the café,' Lisa said.

Mattie said nothing.

'Sammy says you're a great swimmer. I think he likes you. Do you like him?'

Mattie began rinsing her hair. She couldn't think there was anything to like about Sammy. He was shorter and skinnier than her, and spotty. He told jokes that weren't funny. She peered through the streaming water at Lisa. 'You knew they'd be here.'

'I thought they might, but I didn't know for definite.'

'I think it's out of order, that's all. Not telling me.'

'Don't get stressed Matt, OK. You wouldn't have come if I'd said.'

'I might.' Mattie paused. 'It's out of order, that's all,' she repeated but less firmly. Lisa's attention was drifting; she was looking towards the changing cubicles.

'Sammy's a wet,' Mattie said, turning the shower off. 'But Robin's all right. He fancies you.'

Lisa waited for her. 'He doesn't.'

'He's mad about you. It's obvious.'

Lisa touched Mattie's hand and they stopped, centimetres apart; face to face. 'Do you think so, Matt, really?'

Mattie hesitated but only for a second; it was her chance to make Lisa smile. 'Yeah, I really, really do.'

In the cubicle, Mattie peeled her costume from her body, kicked it off her feet onto the floor.

'I do feel,' Lisa shouted over a long hiss of aerosol spraying, 'kind of good, you know, having made the effort. Do you know what I mean? We'd only have been stuck indoors otherwise, watching television or something.'

Mattie felt suddenly tired; her stomach growled. 'I'm hungry.'

'You can get something upstairs in the café.'

'I fancy a tomato. A lovely, red, juicy, fresh tomato.'

Lisa laughed. 'You're mad, Matt.'

Mattie imagined the tomato, perfectly round, with a perfect green flower stalk on top. She pictured biting into it, the juice and pips squirting onto her tongue, the sweet, meaty flavour.

'They might sell spicy tomato flavour crisps in the café,' Lisa called out.

Lisa had changed into jeans and her best black top. Mattie had on the tracksuit that she came in. 'OK, ready?' Lisa asked.

'I've got to dry my hair a bit. You go ahead.'

'I'll wait for you.'

'Don't bother,' Mattie told her. 'I won't be long.'

'OK.' Lisa paused by the door. 'I'll get you a coke, and some chilli crisps or something.'

'Great,' Mattie said. 'Thanks.'

She inserted twenty pence in the slot for the hair dryer which roared into life, then settled into a low drone. She aimed the lukewarm air at the top of her head. She wished she'd asked Lisa to wait after all. She saw she'd been mistaken to think that it was better to go up alone than to stand side by side with Lisa. Now she'd have to break into their group, interrupt their laughter, their chat. They'd all three turn and look at her and there would be no one to hide behind.

'You are a great swimmer,' she said out loud. 'You are a better swimmer than all of them, put together.'

The dryer came to an abrupt halt.

What worth did swimming have, anyway? It would be more useful to be good at practically anything else. She looked in the mirror. Her hair was frizzy and the goggles had left a red impression round her eyes. She placed the tip of her index finger on the glass, traced the outline of her face, then along the bridge of her nose. Or – best of all – why couldn't she be pretty?

She returned to the cubicle and looked at her swimming costume which was still lying on the floor. Water had seeped out and formed a puddle around it like a shadow. Mattie pushed the toe of her trainer into the costume and watched it squirm before walking away.

Son and Lover

Lesley Phillips

On the kitchen wall I've got one of those twee blackboards that's meant for writing messages, menus and appointments. If I lived in an elegant uptown loft conversion, it would read 'Collect wine, buy flowers, baked halibut, Eurostar 4.30 Friday'. But I don't and it doesn't. In my case, now that my son Gareth has left the nest and moved in with the lovely Zoe, it reads, 'Don't forget the bin, pay milkman', and (in case anyone is interested in my whereabouts) 'up the garden'.

However, this little blackboard and a packet of multi-coloured chalks recently became the object on which I would vent my anger, shout my joy, spill my beans, express my doubts and rue my actions. It all began with the fish, of course. Doesn't it always?

Gareth and the lovely Zoe arrived one Saturday morning with a hexagonal aquarium, complete with filters, pump, lid and lights, and a background picture of underwater rocks and ferns that was equal in tweeness to the blackboard in the kitchen. To complete this encapsulated underwater wonderland, there were two goldfish, only one was small and black and the other was twice the size, very pale with orange patches. Both had lots of long floaty fins, like wedding veils.

It was a lovely gift, kindly meant, but after an hour of moving the furniture to accommodate this tank, filling it with water and fish, and turning on the lights and the bubbles, Gareth and Zoe departed for lunch in the pub and I was left feeling as though I'd just been paid off: 'Thanks, Mum, for the last twenty-odd years – here's a few fish.' Churlish of me or not?

'So what are you going to call them?' asked Zoe the following day, tapping on the tank with talon-like fingernails.

'Oh, I hadn't thought.'

Well, I should have, apparently, and there followed what seemed like hours of suggestions.

Ant and Dec

Posh and Becks
Morecambe and Wise
Noddy and Big Ears

It went on and on, and I have to say – unkind, I know – at the time I just wasn't interested.

Chas and Dave
Jack and Vera
Bill and Ben.
and, Heaven help me
Charles and Camilla

The fact that the poor damn fish may not even be a pair had obviously not occurred to either of them. After they'd left I noticed that on the blackboard Gareth had written:

Tom and Jerry
Homer and Marge

Zoe had just signed her name and drawn a little smiling face underneath.

Having fed and watered them and having been left, again, with the washing up, in a wave of defiance, I put down the dirty dishes I was carrying, picked up the chalk and wrote:

Cheese and Pickle
Postage and Packing
Dustpan and Brush
Spark and Plug

And so it began, this fish naming game. It became quite competitive and obsessive with the three of us. I would come home gleefully clutching a list of names I'd thought of during the day:

Cup and Saucer
Odds and Ends
Thick and Thin
Rough and Smooth

only to find that Gareth had called in earlier and already added:

Bangers and Mash
Fish and Chips
Socks and Shoes

The message on the answering machine was not, as it seemed, a message in code from the KGB, but Zoe's contribution to the game:

Pick and Choose
Stop and Start
Nip and Tuck
Wet and Windy

It was all getting out of hand and it was to get a lot worse.

It was the week of my nearly-sixty birthday.

Time and Tide
Lift and Separate

Gareth and Zoe arrived looking sheepish and silly and very pleased with themselves and announced that I was to be a grandmother.

Thunder and Lightning
Hugs and Kisses
Tears and Laughter

We spent the afternoon wetting the baby's head. Well, Gareth and I did, Zoe had tea, and, to be fair, Gareth only had one because he had the car. But I made up for their abstinence.

Gin and Tonic
Ice and Lemon
Brahms and Liszt

Late that same week, while I was still getting used to the idea of grandmotherhood, I wiped the blackboard clear of stupid fish names and wrote the date of Zoe's first scan and the predicted date of the baby's birth. Nice idea this blackboard. It was this same week that I – me, nearly sixty, nearly a grandmother – fell in love.

I was standing looking in at the butcher's window, half-heartedly trying to decide between lamb chops and some fish, but the day was too spring-like and the queue too long. I decided to go home and take pot luck.

Scrimp and Save
Make-do and Mend

I turned and there he was. As gorgeous as I'd remembered him. An old flame who, if I was to be honest, had been smoldering away in my heart for years. All he said was, 'Hello, I thought it was you.' My pulse leapt, my face blushed and my tongue refused to put two coherent words together, and I'd fallen in love, like a silly sixteen-year-old, right there in the street, in front of the butcher's.

Hot and Cold
Hard and Fast
Open and Shut

We went for coffee and talked and talked the morning away. My brain registered what he was saying but my heart, diverted by eyes which were bluer than I remembered them, had its own agenda.

High and Low
Bits and Pieces
Sweetness and Light

As we got up to leave, Himself touched my cheek with the back of his hand and said, 'You know the little picnic place up behind the old mill? Shall I meet you there tomorrow after work?' I nodded, and all the next day I kept drifting off into daydreams of blue eyes and smiles, of lips and bare skin. And when I arrived at the car park his car was already there. I hurried down the path and, as he saw me, he opened his arms and I walked straight in. I breathed him in and I knew I'd come home.

Safe and Sound
Home and Dry

I lay in bed that night grinning into the darkness. I could hardly believe what was happening to me. What had I done to deserve all this happiness? Gareth and the lovely Zoe were together at last, and obviously so happy and settled, the baby was on its way – and love, love at sixty? I was, as the song says, bewitched, bewildered, but not the least bothered. I had been on my own a long time and, until now, I hadn't realized just how lonely and unfulfilled I'd become.

Suddenly, wonderfully, here he was, in my heart and my life with his blue eyes and that amazing smile. Someone who cared just for me. Someone to take my side. There were letters, poems, late-night phone calls and plans. I was, I realized with an ear-to-ear grin, embarking on a full-blown affair. Grandma was in love.

Bill and Coo
Fun and Games
King and Queen

We became lovers. Maybe it was our age, but we so enjoyed the lying in each other's arms afterwards. There was a gentle reassurance in the afterglow. The drifting, the dreaming and the planning.

Willing and Able
Hearts and Flowers
Slap and Tickle
Bed and Breakfast

But nothing is ever that easy or straightforward. Himself had a family. Our meetings, our lovemaking, were always in secret. Our times together were stolen and never long enough. We would manage to meet 'by accident' at a car park, a station, a supermarket, at a car boot sale.

Cloak and Dagger
Secret and Lies
Kiss and Tell

We managed, though, with a lot of laughing and talking, mainly down the phone, and our letters got longer and longer.

Rough and Smooth
Me and You
Thick and Thin

One stolen Sunday afternoon, we were naked and abandoned in that glorious afterglow, when Himself rolled over and whispered the bubble-bursting words of all clandestine lovers, 'I've got to go.' We'd dressed and were downstairs kissing goodbye as if he was off to war, or at least the moon, when the backdoor opened. 'Yoo-hoo, Mum, it's only us.'

I went hot, I went cold, my heart stopped, my heart raced and my palms sweltered. Ignoring my panic and the pale face of Himself, I called, 'In here, love.'

I met them in the kitchen, giving Himself time to tuck in his shirt. 'This is a nice surprise.' I made hurried, vague introductions, 'An old friend from away.' I threw together a pot of tea, while Himself said to my son and the girl who was carrying his baby, my grandchild, 'I hear congratulations are in order.'

Zoe sat and assumed the position and attitude of imminent birth, while Gareth chatted happily about scans, natural childbirth and breast feeding. I couldn't, as I handed out mugs of tea, look Himself in the eye. I didn't know if I should laugh or cry.

Bow and Arrow
Blood and Guts

Cock and Bull

The compulsory tea finished, Himself said his goodbyes to the expectant couple and, at the front door, with a quick peck on the cheek and a look that I couldn't quite read, he was gone.

Tea and Sympathy
Touch and Go
Hit and Miss

We'd got away with it, or so I thought – hoped – prayed.

I had decided to re-decorate Gareth's old bedroom, turn it into a spare room-cum-sewing room. After all my grandchild would need somewhere to sleep when she came to stay. So later that week, Gareth, at a loose end, came to give me a hand with the painting while Zoe was with her Mum. We'd been working away for a while and I went downstairs to make a pot of tea. I can, even now, only hope it was his DIY frame of mind that had inspired him to write on the blackboard:

Fast and Furious
Tongue and Groove
Hammer and Tongs

It seems funny now, but I just panicked, terrified I'd been found out. My God, what did he think of me, the grandmother to his precious 'bump', getting her leg over? His own mother for heaven's sake! My embarrassment was overwhelming. I grabbed the tea towel and rubbed off the accusing chalk and, in an attempt to appear calm and innocent, I wrote:

Chalk and Cheese
Hat and Coat
Bucket and Spade

In a vain attempt at morality I added:

Right and Wrong

The incident upset me. I drank several glasses of red wine before drifting into an inebriated sleep, when the phone rang. Himself. I wept. I told him everything and then came the blow of blows. He too had been rumbled. We had been spotted at the car boot sale the weekend before. Whether it was the fact that we were the only ones at the secondhand book stall and weren't looking at books, or whether someone spotted the pinched bum, the stolen kiss or the touching of hands at the hot-dog van didn't matter. Nothing mattered any more, nothing would matter ever again.

We had one last tearful secret meeting. During the following dark and empty days and weeks, I wept, I didn't eat, I drank too much, I couldn't concentrate. I listened on purpose to love songs on the radio and they made me cry all over again. I was too bereft to write on the blackboard.

Shit and Fan
Hell and High Water
Bitter and Twisted

and on one particularly bad night:

Wither and Die

I've regained some of my self-control – only just, and only in public. And a car boot sale, a secondhand book, smiling blue eyes or a butcher's window will have me weeping big hot tears whether I'm in public or not. I try to tell myself it's better to have loved and lost but it doesn't work. It isn't true. I still love him. He never was mine 'to have and to hold', but it's a hard lesson to learn.

Battered and Bruised
Cheap and Nasty
Tired and Emotional
Grin and Bear It

The blackboard in the kitchen has a new list of names now, because, according to the latest scan, 'the bump' is a girl bump. I hope they call her Isabelle. The lovely Zoe is blooming and Gareth is flourishing on fatherhood. Himself, well, he's gone back to smoldering in my heart. Alone at night in the wee small hours when sleep won't come, I take him out and dream and cry about what might have been, but I always put him back, safely, where he belongs, where he's mine. And I know Gareth and Zoe will never understand, and I'm certainly not going to explain, but I've finally named the fish.

Almost and Nearly

How to Murder your Mother

Patricia Duncker

Nobody takes any notice of white-haired women in their mid sixties, especially if they are wearing flat shoes and carrying unfashionable handbags. But these two are desperate lovers, hiding out in a chic, slick café, on the watch for Maman, who might, at any moment, come rampaging down the boulevards, dark glasses lowered, the prize bull at the corrida, entering the ring, late in the afternoon. One of the women crouches near the window on the first floor level of the café, keeping her glass of unsweetened tea close to her face for protection.

'You must involve the clinic now, *ma chère*,' she hissed. 'If she does commit suicide it will all fall on you.'

Maman had thrown a dramatic fit that morning at breakfast, armed with a large bottle of whisky and sixty paracetamol, spread out on the tablecloth in symmetrical rows. She had even yelled, 'When I'm dead, you'll be sorry!' The elderly lovers remained divided.

'She'd sick the lot up. She can't bear whisky. It's all theatre.'

'Don't be so sure. She's working up to something. I know it.'

The lovers lived two houses and one cul-de-sac away from each other. At first, when Maman still possessed most of her marbles, this had been extremely convenient. What could be more natural than close neighbours becoming closer friends? In and out of each other's houses, watering plants and feeding cats, putting out dustbins and sharing builders, even perusing the January Sales, first through the catalogues then ransacking the shops. But now the problem was Maman. The old lady, eighty-four, sporting a cluster of white hairs on her jutting chin, looked small, thin and frail. Poor dear, sighed the district nurse, not long for this world. But Maman's duplicitous physique disguised a lithe and wiry energy; she simmered with bottled-up aggression. The early stages of Alzheimer's glittered in her milky eyes. Her mother and her mother's mother had both been carried off by the disease, at first forgetting to eat and to wash, and eventually forgetting how to breathe. But both these women had first passed through a lengthy stage of murderous venom, when their native selfishness, egotism and savagery knew no limits. At last, the end of respectability and good manners. I can do what I like, say what I like, mangle everything within reach. For who shall fathom the depths of a woman's anger? Who will contain her ingenuity? For every calm old biddy rocking her ancient wisdom to her wizened chest, there are ten, no, dozens of frustrated, ageing witches, who glimpse their diminishing territory and fading powers, and who decide to explode, one last time, in a Catherine wheel of malice and hatred, conducted with volcanic intensity. My daughter is my victim, mine to denigrate and criticise, mine to persecute and destroy. Before I dwindle into darkness I will wreck your life too, and if I can I shall take you with me.

The doctor who suggested that Maman should eat more fruit and vegetables and drink two litres of water every day, decided that the old girl was not yet mad enough to be sectioned. He rationalised the situation. The daughter could hold on for a few more years. The old lady was still in good health and nippy on her pins. She might make it to ninety before being banged up in one of the locked wards. But this cruel diagnosis took no account of that successful hell on earth that two women, living in domestic proximity, can create for one another, especially when their family history is one of silent animosity and undercover guerrilla tactics.

The descent presented itself as a gradual, uneven degeneration into muddle and gloom. Maman sometimes sat nodding peacefully at the television games shows or crouched over her table concocting crossword puzzles, which never quite worked. She even dabbled in a little embroidery. There were days when the old woman watched her daughter and the beloved neighbour leaving the house armed with shopping bags and umbrellas without uttering a murmur; no snap interdictions or threats, no emotional declarations of menace or blackmail. But as the weather improved Maman's internal engines began to ratchet up the scale, increasing from a low growl to a gigantic roar. The beloved neighbour served as the main target.

'Get that woman out of my sight,' she shrieked at her daughter. 'She wants you to enchant you away from me. She's trying to persuade you to put me in a home and lock me up.'

This was true.

'Do you think she really cares about you? She hasn't got a car and she can't drive. Why do you think she circles round you like a buzzard? She only wants someone to drive her around and take her out shopping.'

Most of this was true too.

'She hopes I'll die. And that you'll get the house. Then you'll both be cosy and rich with all my money. And you can dig a swimming pool in my vegetable patch.'

This idea had indeed been mooted as an eventual possibility. Maman had abandoned her vegetables years ago and the browned grass waving in the patch, unsightly and abandoned, figured in vague future plans hatched by the daughter and her beloved neighbour. Maman's cunning seemed to respect no earthly boundaries. She overheard secrets even when she was not present; she divined their thoughts like the shrivelled sibyl at Delphi. She lurked behind doorways in kitchens, thwarting their careful arrangements. She went on hunger strike until the holiday bookings for five meagre days in Spain were cancelled. She rang up her grandchildren and wept down the phone, then sat, tranquil and malicious, while her daughter fielded their legitimate anxieties.

Maman no longer allowed her only child to leave the house alone. She settled like a black widow spider on the back seat of the car and complained about the heat, the air conditioning, the journey, the shops, the obligation to walk ten yards to the chiropodist. Her paranoid accusations blossomed into colourful fantasies of conspiracies and plots, hatched by her daughter and the beloved neighbour, to whisk her into the clinic and abandon her there or to eliminate her altogether in a carefully devised accident. Her behaviour became so atrocious that at last they left her screaming on the doorstep and drove off at speed to take tea in town.

They crept home at five only to be confronted by the fire brigade, two police cars and the SAMU parked before Maman's door, with all the neighbours gathered in the street, whispering.

'*Mon Dieu*,' breathed the daughter. 'She's done it. She's killed herself.'

Their horror and relief bloomed before them, like an emergency air bag. A neighbour rattled the car window.

'It was me,' confessed the excited *voisine*. 'I saw the smoke and called the fire brigade.'

And lo, there was Maman, bristling with courage, wrapped in a blanket, supported by two handsome men in uniform, applauded for her daring enterprise and startling strength. Stranded on the terrace stood the daughter's favourite armchair, still smouldering gently, the springs charred and hot.

'She must have fallen asleep with her cigarette still alight,' explained the *capitaine*. 'We found the whole place full of black smoke. It's a wonder that she wasn't asphyxiated. She had the presence of mind to cover her face with a damp towel and pushed the thing out onto the back terrace. The neighbours saw the smoke and called us at once.' He lowered his voice. '*Excusez-moi*, *Madame*, but I don't think that you should leave a fragile old lady of eighty-five completely alone all afternoon.'

'She's eighty-four,' snapped the beloved neighbour, 'and she doesn't smoke.'

But the daughter stood, white-faced, confronting her mother, who took a few faltering steps, tottered unsteadily, then gasped, '*Ma fille, ma fille*! Thank God! My daughter has come back to me.'

The smoke damage was so bad that the entire household, Maman, her daughter, two cats and one poodle were all forced to move into the beloved neighbour's house while the painters set to work. Maman had the whole thing redecorated in vile greens and pinks; she oversaw the improvements with sinister zeal. The grandchildren dove past on their way to the rented beach villa and made a fuss of her. The old lady basked in their attentive warmth; she had forgotten all their names.

Maman took a taxi to the Inner Peace Emporium and returned armed with josticks and incense, which she lit in every room of the beloved neighbour's house, claiming that it stank. Yet she settled in, grim and intent, despite her discomfort in the slandered slum, and consented to be waited upon from dawn to dusk. She had her own property re-valued.

'Lovely place,' declared the *notaire*'s agent, looking at the new tiling and polished wooden stairs, all paid for through a lavish insurance claim. 'There's enough space in that vegetable patch for a swimming pool.'

Maman hired a gardener to clear the rampant weeds. Was she enjoying a late burst of rational behaviour? Alas, when the gardener arrived bearing strimmers, forks and shears, she accused him of intending to bury her in the wasted patch. Everybody heard her screaming from the terrace steps. 'It's the fire,' they agreed, 'it's affected her brain. Poor thing. She's still in shock.'

Maman commandeered the beloved neighbour's television set to follow her game shows and soap operas. She reorganised the kitchen and the furniture. She threw out all the potted plants. The daughter found her beloved friend sitting cross-legged on the bedroom floor, staring at a Tarot pack.

'What are you doing?'

'Working out how to murder your mother.'

The date set for their removal back into the redecorated house was September 1st. Maman refused to purchase any furniture and the plush, fresh rooms stood empty, reeking of paint. Instead she took to walking the streets of their *quartier* with her arms and legs wrapped in bandages, a hat pulled low over her dark glasses.

'Are you going out disguised? You look like the Invisible Man.' Her daughter refused to let the old lady wander the streets alone and traipsed along just behind her, carrying handbags and parasols.

'It's the radiation,' growled Maman. 'The radiation levels have risen to a dreadful height, well beyond the permitted maximum. I must protect my skin.'

These Chernobyl fantasies persisted for weeks despite the heat. Maman even appeared in the Post Office with her face swathed in white cloths. Shoppers stared. A crowd of Arab children ran after her, begging a peak beneath the mask. The beloved neighbour seethed within her corset of self-control as the chorus of well-aimed casual insults, delivered daily by Maman, began to rise towards an evil climax.

The showdown came during the August fiesta. The streets were filled with drunken revellers dancing on the boulevards, brass bands, rock bands, a symphony of accordion players and a twirling gaggle of flamenco gypsies. Juicy smoke rose from a thousand open-air grills and the cicadas roared amidst the magic paper lanterns strung between the trees. Come on, get drunk, enjoy yourselves.

Maman forbade her daughter to go out. She turned on the neighbour.

'Why don't you go by yourself for once?' she snapped at her daughter's elderly lover. 'Then we can have a pleasant evening without you.'

There was a dreadful pause. And then, for the first and only time, the beloved neighbour answered back.

'This is my house. And you are a guest in my house.' The woman's voice gurgled forth in a ghastly whisper. Maman glared at her adversary, egging her on.

'It's not a house. It's a tip. It's full of rubbish and it stinks.'

She began chanting abuse, each barbed slur more vicious than the last, and rose up from her post at the table, pointing at the other woman's chest. Everyone began screaming. The neighbour's hand closed over the kitchen knife.

Nobody knows what happened in the kitchen, but hundreds of people saw an elderly lady, swathed in bandages, apparently leaking blood from every crevice, yet surprisingly agile and dynamic, tearing through the fiesta crowds and actually dancing before the Polynesian musicians to the tune of 'Everybody loves Mambo!'. The old lady's body could not be found. Her house had been sold weeks before, her accounts drained, her savings spirited away, her passport vanished. The plot was utterly clear. The daughter and her malevolent companion had cashed in and hidden all the old woman's assets, then planned to bump her off. Both protested their innocence, but they would, wouldn't they? Maman's signature was there on the *Compromis de Vente*. You forced her, didn't you, argued the Inspector. Maman herself, covered in bandages, had removed all her savings. But she had given an appalling hint to the now tearful cashier that the bandages masked dreadful incriminating bruises, meted out at home when she had refused to eat up her lettuce. She seemed so vulnerable, pathetic, wailed the cashier, I blame myself. I didn't report those two monsters.

No blood was ever found at home. Not even on the kitchen knife, despite all the latest forensic techniques. The daughter and her companion were remanded in custody as the circumstantial evidence against them mounted beyond reasonable doubt.

But where had they hidden the body?

Every centimetre of the neighbour's flagstone patio and rose garden was ploughed up in the great search for final proof. The abandoned vegetable patch behind the old house became a crevasse beneath the digger's jaws. Nothing, of course, was ever found. But the new owner was delighted and instantly created the blue tiled swimming pool of his dreams.

Where, oh where is Maman?

The clinic overlooks the sea and the old French lady, perched on her sunlit balcony, surrounded by palm trees, can no longer remember her own name. She likes the island's traditional music and whenever the nurse comes to check her blood pressure or to help her eat, she turns up the volume and sings along with her favourite band. 'Maman loves Mambo!'

The Red Dress

Brenda Curtis

The young man could not get the red dress out of his mind. Every evening, going home on the bus, he made for the upper deck, hoping for a seat on the nearside. If there wasn't one free, he waited for somebody to get up and dived for the empty place. There it was, in the shop window, glowing under brilliant spotlights. Several times he jumped off the bus early, just to stand and gaze through the shop window. Tonight, he was determined he would go inside the store. His stomach churned with excitement and sweat pricked his armpits. A fine drizzle floated down through the light from the street lamps, giving the road and pavements a black sheen. The bus accelerated away and, jostled by crowds, he hesitated at the entrance before marching forward through the invisible barrier of warm air.

On the first floor of Cowley's Bazaar, Gwyneth, a young assistant, leaned on her counter, raising first one foot, then the other. Her size six shoes felt like size fours, her legs ached and she was hot. There were few customers about, it was February, tail end of the sales and near closing time. She rubbed her dry eyes and wandered over to the window to watch the crowds below scurrying like silverfish in the rain. She was bored at Cowley's and longed, as every day, for something in her life to change. She bent forward to get a better look at the street below.

There he was again, gazing into the window, always near closing time. What was he looking at, so intently, every night? Leaning even further over, she realised that he was coming inside. That was different, wasn't it? Her concentration was interrupted by the piercing bark of her supervisor, reprimanding her for leaving her post. She turned and, with folded arms, dawdled back to her till.

Inside the store, he was surrounded by curved glass counters stacked high with jars and bottles in glossy wrappings, rows of bullet-shaped lipsticks and little pots of nail varnish, a dazzling blur of white and gold and a million shades of red. Female assistants in white coats with alabaster faces, black-fringed eyes, perfectly arched brows and sharply drawn scarlet mouths stared at him as he hurried towards the shop directory. It took him a few seconds to focus as he struggled to control his panic. With relief, he saw that Ladies Fashions were on the first floor and he stepped onto the escalator. At least, he thought, he had broken the daily routine of paper pushing in Leggatt's Office Supplies. He had escaped.

Too soon, the escalator arrived at the first floor and he had to step off. He squeezed along the narrow aisles that ran between closely packed rails of coats and dresses and was glad there were so few customers about. Background music hummed, and, breathing in the warm, clothy smells, he began to feel calmer. In the distance he spotted a sign that said 'Pay Here'. Behind the till he could see a solitary assistant. She was young, about his own age, seventeen or eighteen maybe. Her pale face was bare of make-up and framed by curtains of straight dark hair. She looked like he often felt, tired and bored. Just then, she glanced up at him. His heart jumped and he veered away, pretending to browse, but the rack ended abruptly and he emerged at the cash desk. The assistant was looking directly at him, smiling. There was no escape now. He had difficulty breathing.

'Can I help you?'

He gripped the edge of the counter to stop his fingers trembling. 'Yes.' His tongue seemed to have swollen to twice its usual size. 'Yes, please. The red dress, the red dress in the window.'

'Yes, sir. It's the last one. What size did you want?'

Fireworks exploded behind his eyes. He couldn't remember.

'The one in the window looks about right.' He dug his hands into his pockets.

'I'll have to go and fetch it. Please wait. I'll be as quick as I can.' She disappeared.

The staircase was her nearest exit and her mind raced as she ran downstairs. So, he had come into the shop at last. Was the dress for his girlfriend? Men rarely had any idea of women's dress sizes. He reminded her of a greyhound ready to bolt out of its trap, but men were often unnerved by the overwhelmingly feminine atmosphere of the store. She reached the window, eased off her loafers, slid back the partition and stepped into the glass space. It was like going on stage, the spotlights deepening the darkness outside. She loosened the pins that secured the fabric, working quickly and carefully, then gathered up the dress and backed out.

Left alone, marooned in a sea of fabric, hot under fluorescent lights that winked and flickered, the boy wiped a hand across his upper lip. Should he just go, make a quick exit while the assistant was absent? He retraced his steps and realised there wasn't a down escalator in sight. Could he jump on the one going up and take refuge in soft furnishings and beds? He felt a sudden urge to pee and was about to run, when the girl reappeared through swing doors with the dress, a cascade of scarlet satin draped over one arm.

'Is it for your girlfriend?' she asked, suspending the dress from its hanger for his inspection. His brain seemed to have turned to jelly and he could not speak.

'Perhaps she's about my size?' She held it up against her own body. Instead of answering, he put out his hand and slowly stroked the slippery fabric, until raising his gaze, he saw that she was watching him. He felt his face suffuse with a deep blush and withdrew his hand. He saw her draw away, shock clear on her face. She knew. He would have to leave, run, now. He had a horror she might start shouting at him or screaming. And then her expression changed.

As he watched, she went to a cubicle, drew back the curtain, hung the dress on a hook inside and beckoned to him to walk in. His legs propelled him into the tiny, warm, scented space and he saw himself framed in a full length mirror. A soft draught ruffled the back of his hair as the curtain closed behind him. She had understood; had realised what he wanted and wasn't going to call the manager and have him thrown out or arrested. She had helped him. He hadn't felt this mixture of terror and joy since the first time he'd penetrated the forbidden territory of his mother's wardrobe. He swiftly removed his jacket and, without undoing the laces, slipped out of his shoes and trousers. He clawed at the knot of his tie and tore at his shirt – a button pinged off. His hands seemed to have turned into clumsy paws and blood pounded in his ears. Standing in his briefs, he took the dress off its hanger, stepped into it and pulled up the silky swathes of fabric. He looped his arms through the shoulder straps and held the dress against his body. The back zip was open. Sweat trickled down his breast bone. He felt both hot and cold and goose-pimples peaked amongst the black hairs on his arms. How did girls manage back zips? In the mirror he saw the curtain move and the girl's face appeared behind his shoulder. He heard a 'zizz' and felt the cold of metal as she ran the zip up his spine. She settled the folds across the top of his arms and her touch was cool and feathery on his burning skin. Then she was gone. He was inside the red dress. He glided his hands over the heavy, slippery fabric that hugged his body and spread his fingers out into the flowing stuff as it flared down round his legs. The curtain drew aside and he shut his eyes, but opened them again when he felt something cold and heavy placed around his throat. The girl's hands slid back to reveal a crescent of glittering diamante that hung in the hollow of his neck. In the mirror he saw her smile of satisfaction and she withdrew, leaving him alone again. He felt transformed. His everyday self fell away like a discarded chrysalis and he smiled triumphantly at his glowing reflection.

Gwyneth returned to her cash desk, trembling, her heart thumping and banging in her chest. She needed to sit down, but felt compelled to look out for customers or, worse, her supervisor.

Oh my God, she thought, this can't be happening. Not to me, not late on a wet, February Friday night. She'd begun to feel uneasy when he'd started to stroke the falling folds of the skirt, but when she'd seen his expression, a vivid mixture of fright and desire, somehow it had moved her. She'd thought, If I let this lunatic try the dress on, I'll lose my job for sure, but her curiosity had been aroused and seized by a sudden impulse to rebellion, she'd thought, What the hell! This was the most interesting thing to happen to her for months – if ever. Something of the boy's passion had communicated itself to her and, after a moment of indecision, she'd scanned the shop floor and, breathing a fervent, 'Please God, keep the supervisor busy elsewhere,' she'd turned towards the nearest cubicle and beckoned him to follow.

Curtain rings rattled and he emerged carrying the dress. He avoided her eyes. 'Yes, I'll take it.'

Glad to have something to do, her hands flew in and out and over the red satin, folding and smoothing, tucking soft rustling tissue paper between its layers as he reached into his back pocket for his wallet. Fumbling, he dropped it, and she ran round the counter to pick it up. As she scooped up the cards, she caught sight of an address.

'Sorry,' he stammered and ran his fingers through his hair, finally meeting her gaze. She found herself mirroring his gesture and drew a tress of hair away from her face.

'I get like that when I'm tired,' she said with a smile as she gave him his change.

He drew breath as if to say something but, changing his mind, picked up his purchase and walked away. She felt a pang of regret. Was that all? Having glimpsed the scenery of another world, could she let it go so easily?

He was the last customer to leave the shop. The china dolls had disappeared and a burly uniformed security guard stood rattling keys. The drizzle had turned into a downpour, and, hugging his purchase close to his body, the boy turned up his collar and escaped into the street. Shoulders hunched, he ran towards the bus stop, peering down the road for sight of a bus. Cars sped past, splashing through puddles, tyres hissing on wet tarmac and minutes went by. No bus. He shifted from foot to foot. Rain trickled cold down the back of his neck.

'Hello.'

It was the girl who had served him. She was wearing a shiny black mac and held up a large umbrella. He looked down the road. Still no bus.

'Hi.' He took a deep breath. 'Thanks for your help.'

'That's OK. I hope you enjoy the dress.' She moved closer and held the umbrella over both of them. He scanned her expression. Was she laughing at him? 'I like dressing up too. On my Saturdays off I go to the flea markets to hunt down antique clothes. I love old-fashioned ball gowns and the old fur coats – there are hundreds of them in second-hand shops.'

'Yes.' He felt animated, remembering his mother's furs, the feel of the slippery, cool, satin linings on his skin, the lingering smell of his mother's perfume as he buried his nose into their soft warmth. 'Yes.' He stole a glance at her face but her expression of friendly interest didn't falter. The rain beat a steady thrum on the canopy of the umbrella.

'My name's Gwyneth, by the way.'

A bus pulled up, its doors opening with a clunk. 'This is my bus. Goodbye.' He leapt onto the platform.

'And mine.' She jumped on after him. The top deck was empty. He made a beeline for the front seat and settled his parcel firmly on his lap. He stared at it. He'd bought the dress. He was certain he would remember this day for the rest of his life.

Gwyneth sat next to him. He wondered if she would talk more about clothes. He looked down at the shop window as the bus pulled away and wondered what he would look out for tomorrow.

One Little Room

Sue Morgan

Julie woke to find it was summer. A blue unblemished sky was calling out to her to come and bathe in early morning sunshine and dew. She knew dandelion flowers would be crowding the grass verges on the way to school, as if summoned there to watch a royal procession: hers. She loved the way they held out their bright yellow heads like silly bath caps and the back-to-front fishhook look of their leaves, even the bitter white sap that oozed from broken stems to make you wet the bed. Old wives tale she knew, but it was good all the same, the thought of letting go. And all the dandelion clocks, just like the fluffy white heads of old men, there to be picked up and blown away to smithereens.

There was no telling what lay in store for her as she walked to school with her bare legs and her school bag bouncing at her side, full of the day's books. Even Mr Roberts, who tried to pull greasy strands of hair over his bald patch, even he couldn't spoil a day like this. If she kept her eyes averted as he dictated his old History notes, surely she could pretend to be somewhere else? Limbs spread-eagled, body browning nicely on bone-white seaside rocks in the sun.

In English they were doing John Donne. Poor thin hunched-up Miss Davies would try her best to inspire the class with all her powers of suggestion, but it was a hopeless struggle. Julie might like to think about metaphysical questions herself, but she would never talk about such things in public, for fear of being hounded out of town. Forced to adopt the same blank stare as the others, the only safe way to discuss such matters was to write about them in essays. Miss Davies and she communicated through the written word, sharing their shameful minority interest in secret.

No, it was only Dr Francis, Geography, who was brave enough to make something happen, something extraordinary enough to satisfy even a young girl's wildest imaginings. Only last week he'd told the class about a play on the radio they should try and catch. Taking herself early to bed, Julie stretched out her legs and closed her eyes with a wonderful sense of anticipation. As she listened there grew inside her head a scene in midsummer: a man lying back in a small boat, in the flickering light under a weeping willow on a lazy brown river. Water birds croaked, insects buzzed and things were made to sound so hot and sleepy that she felt drowsy herself and let her limbs fall aside in an awful indolence.

He was looking back, the man, at a terrible mistake he had made in that exact same spot, in his long lost youth. It was all to do with a girl he should have kissed. Like saying no to the offer of wild strawberries picked straight from the hedge, warmed by the sun and eaten unwashed, he had failed to act on his truest impulses when he had the chance, which was why he was destined to live for evermore in sad dreams and futile regrets.

This particular gem of a day, Dr Francis went out of his way to surpass all Julie's expectations. Their double lesson fell before lunch and with half the class away on a French trip and others taking part in a sports event, he hatched up a plan which he called 'The Great Escape'. The peerless blue of the sky suggested boundless possibilities as they shouldered their school bags, and with rolled-up maps tucked under their arms, followed their teacher out to the staff car park. Passing unchallenged beneath the Headmaster's sentry box, slipping effortlessly through coils of barbed wire, they walked towards the school minibus in an untidy snaking line. As she climbed up into the front seat Julie was sure she heard the clink of a bottle when Dr Francis plonked a shopping bag on the floor by her feet. Martin Rowlands, more than a head taller than the rest of them, folded himself onto the seat next to her, while the others squashed in as best they could on hard wooden benches in the back.

Dr Francis gave a whoop of delight when they got through the gates without being machine-gunned and joined the flow of traffic heading for the coast. He pointed out a fine example of ribbon development: a straggling line of bungalows, which petered out when they reached the common where farmers let rough-looking sheep and ponies roam free. Looking at the moving scene through the wide windscreen, Julie felt something snap inside her, as if she was being let off a leash. She could smell the sea before seeing it, as they turned a sharp corner to go down a steep hill. A warm wind came in at the open window and lifted her hair from her face. There it was: a deep greeny-blue flecked with glinting white, stretching up to the finest black line of a horizon, and an oyster-white sky tinged with yellow from the chemical works out east. The bay was one great curving grin of sand, hemmed in by tree-topped slopes that ended in seaweed-darkened rocks. A large hotel had bagged the best spot, well clear of the caravan park and there was a breakwater, a boat ramp and a row of peeling chalets that on weekends and summer holidays opened up their shutters to become beach shops.

Officially, the students had come to study Raised Sea Beds. Dr Francis knew they hadn't actually got round to doing landforms yet, but he thought this experience would give them a taste of the geomorphology to come.

'What I want you to think about,' he said, as they stood in an awkward semi-circle on the sandy beach, feeling conspicuous in their stiff school uniforms, 'is that what looks permanent and everlasting is actually in constant motion or flux. The hardest most static looking rocks and cliffs are never the same from one moment to the next. They're on the move, constantly changing.'

The children shrugged off their blazers and ties as if they couldn't care less. Julie had to suppress a sudden impulse to strip off and run down to the sea for a shockingly cold swim.

As the teacher walked his pupils round the base of the cliffs, looking for signs of weathering and evidence of changing sea levels, even the most reluctant children began to relax and enjoy themselves. Scrambling up the rocks, they found a footpath that trailed around the coast which they followed for several minutes, before sinking down gratefully on a soft green slope overlooking the sea, amongst that year's first growth of ferns and wild flowers. This, they learned, was the Raised Sea Bed. Carefree blue and yellow butterflies danced above their heads as if drunk. Out on the horizon heavily loaded cargo ships made slow progress to and from the docks, while closer to shore a tiny sailboat scudded about like a toy. Small brown waders dodged the waves at the water's edge and a black cormorant on a rock held out its wings as if being crucified. The vapour trail of a jet fanned out like a feather, and lying back to watch it evaporate, Julie felt dizzy with joy, just to be there, out of school.

Dr Francis pulled a bottle of red wine from his bag, along with a bunch of grapes, a packet of bread rolls and some strange-looking soft cheese. Most of the children mumbled they couldn't when he offered them 'a slug', preferring their bottles of 'pop'. Though at the time Julie was on a strict diet that forbade the eating of anything at midday, bar one apple and one small pot of fruit-flavoured yoghurt, she decided to try some wine and cheese, if only to look grown up. When Dr Francis finally lay back, folding his hands on his belly, he groaned and closed his eyes. It was Siesta Time.

In the midday sun, small birds piped from hiding places in the ferns and invisible grasshoppers scraped their wings like so many insistent machines. It was one of those rare moments when you know you are happy and Julie was just basking in this thought when Martin suddenly sprang to his feet, his gangly frame blotting out the sun as he swayed about in panic. 'Sir! It's a quarter to one and we're supposed to be in registration! In school, right now!'

'Oh hell's bells,' said Dr Francis drowsily. 'We'll have to get going then, I suppose.'

The children grabbed their bags, blazers and ties and started to hurry back the way they'd come, muttering about it not being fair if they got into trouble, it wasn't their fault and if they did, they knew who to blame, stupid waste of bloody time, call it a geography lesson? Julie stayed behind to help Dr Francis pack his shopping bag. 'I'm in for it,' he said. 'Go straight to jail. Do not pass go.'

'Do not collect two hundred,' the young girl said, bursting out laughing. She felt strange, as if her voice belonged to someone else, as if the wine and sun had turned her head and worked her tongue loose.

'When we get you back, young lady,' Dr Francis said, looking at her closely with what she considered to be a rather strange expression on his long, mournful face, 'you'll need a good strong cup of tea to sober you up. Can't have you turning up to your next class tipsy!'

Julie splashed her face with water from a rock pool when they got down on to the beach, giggling when she sent a shower of salt-water drops flying over Dr Francis. The others glared at them from the breakwater, where they stood brushing the last of the sand off their shoes.

One of the school governors phoned Julie's father that night, to tell him about Dr Francis being hauled before the Headmaster for taking the class out without permission on an unofficial school trip and getting them back late for afternoon registration. There was talk of alcohol being consumed, which was when Julie's name came up. The governor wanted her to come with her parents to the Headmaster's office first thing the following morning to make a statement. There was a strong chance the teacher might be suspended.

'See why I wanted you to take French?' her mother wailed. 'I've never been sure about Dr Francis. You hear things about him.'

'Stories,' Julie scoffed. Did she mean the one about his nervous breakdown, which was why he was teaching in a school even though he was a doctor of philosophy and used to teach at universities all round the world? Or the one about being shipwrecked in the Indian Ocean, where his daughter drowned, which was why he had the nervous breakdown? 'I thought you told me never to listen to gossip, just take people as they come,' she said.

'Don't talk to your mother like that! Sounds like you've caused more than enough trouble already,' said her father menacingly, before sending her to bed.

When they got back to school Dr Francis sat her down in his stock cupboard at the back of the geography room and made her a cup of tea. Julie was perfectly happy to perch on a stool, spin his globe, swing her legs and examine his rock collection, while he talked about a philosopher called David Hume. Hume, he said, thought that where we imagined the 'I' or 'self' to be, there is actually a series of fleeting impressions, sensations, fancies, pains and pleasures. Julie liked this idea; it explained things. Like rocks, she was in constant flux. Dr Francis said the trick was learning not to hold on too tight, or expecting anyone or anything to stay the same. Not to fight change. The most you could expect was to come together, however fleetingly, to share an experience. Describe and discuss.

Julie said David Hume reminded her of John Donne. Dr Francis also liked Donne, in fact he tracked down his copy of *Songs and Sonets* so he could read Julie his favourite lines: 'For love, all love of other sights controls, And makes one little room an everywhere.' Julie was startled to see tears making their way down his rough-looking cheeks. To her relief, he wiped them away, coughed and said she was lucky, the world being her oyster. Julie said she hadn't even tried oysters yet. Dr Francis said one day she should. Some people make you happy, just being themselves, she decided. What kept her awake that night, as her parents raised their voices in the room next to hers, was the thought of those who try to stop them, always thinking the worst.

Gasping

Jo Verity

Lizzie opened the front door and peered at me. 'Thank you, thank you, thank you.'

'For what?' I followed her into the kitchen.

'For not bringing any bloody flowers. It's so inappropriate. And unimaginative. White lilies, for God's sake. The study's full of them and the smell's turning my stomach. Are they fast rotters? Because they're going straight on the compost heap.' She was wearing grubby jeans and her old tie-dyed T-shirt. I knew she wouldn't be dressed in black but I was expecting her to look changed. Damaged. Distorted. Mutilated.

'Now, what I could really do with, if anyone asks, is food. Apple pies, casseroles, pasties, that sort of thing. Big bars of dark chocolate, of course. I don't want to have to think about what we're going to eat. Not that I've been doing much of that. Poor Phil's been living on takeaways for weeks. He's taken out a debenture at The Golden Lotus.' While she talked she fidgeted around the kitchen – folding a tea-towel, putting crockery back in the cupboard.

She meandered towards me, sandals slapping on the quarry tiles, and, as if her brakes had failed, ploughed into me. The collision turned into a hug and she sagged against me, succumbing to gravity and the other less specific forces that had been pounding her for months. 'Grace. Gracie. It's good to see you.'

'I was going to come yesterday but I thought you might not be feeling up to visitors.' I paused. How convenient and unconvincing that sounded. I held my hands up. 'Pants on fire. I chickened out.'

She clucked gently. 'I've got a soft spot for chickens.'

The house was still, as if it was holding its breath. 'Where's Phil?' I asked.

'Collecting Rachel from college. Then they'll pick Sam up, on the way back. They volunteered to come on the train, but I think Phil was desperate to escape. I don't blame him. I *did* think about going with him, but I could see that a jolly jaunt to Southampton wouldn't be quite the thing. Silly really because all I've done is sit around here, debating whether I should clean the lavatory.' She shook her head. 'Don't worry. I haven't.'

I produced the foil-wrapped fruit cake from my bag and put it on the work-top. 'It's sunk. Too much brandy, probably, but I think it's edible.'

'Just the job. Mmmm.' She closed her eyes and sniffed the cake, then cut two generous slices.

There was no need to tell her how sorry I was. She knew how much I'd liked and admired her father. He was a wonderful combination of wisdom, humour and open-mindedness. The children treated him as one of them and kids can always spot a phoney.

We drank black coffee, ate cake and indulged in our favourite game. 'OK. If you could be anywhere in the world now, where would it be?' she quizzed.

The only rule is, whatever the question, you have to answer straight away. 'I'd be crouched in a yurt … with Mongolian nomads … drinking yak milk.' I was pleased with my reply. 'You?'

'Somewhere warm. Not lying on a beach. Doing something useful. Maybe on a dig. Just outside a hill village in Tuscany. Lots of pasta and olives and red wine.'

'Dark-eyed lads? Tousled black curls?'

'You've got it.' She smiled but I could see she wasn't in Italy.

I waited whilst she dabbed at the willow-patterned plate, gathering the last few cake crumbs on her middle finger.

She took a deep breath. 'People say that this bit, between death and burial, is the worst part. But the whole thing is the worst part. Think about it. If you're ill, you get medication. If you're bankrupt, you get money from somewhere. If your husband screws his secretary, you throw him out. No matter how bad things are, there's always *something* you can do to make it better. But my father is dead and there is nothing at all I can do. Why does that come as such a shock?'

She wasn't expecting an answer.

'It's not as if I haven't been through it before. It's not that long since Mum died. I must have blocked the memory of it. Like the pain of childbirth.' She paused for a second. 'No. It's nothing at all like that.

Anyway, the circumstances were so different. At one o'clock she was eating lunch and by teatime she was dead. I'll never forget driving back from Accident and Emergency, in the rush hour, with her wedding ring in my purse and Dad, in the passenger seat, just staring straight ahead. "Great way to go but a terrible shock for those left behind." If I was told that once... This time I'm getting, "It's a blessing." I want to smack them in the mouth.' She banged her fist down on the table. 'And don't tell me that anger is a perfectly natural emotion.'

The kitchen was thick with the smell of coffee. A neat pile of ironed clothes sat on the chair; a card for a dental appointment was propped against the fruit bowl. We were sitting in the eye of the storm.

Lizzie reached across the table and patted my hand. 'Sorry. Sorry. I shouldn't take it out on you. I'm just a bit frazzled.'

'Don't be daft.'

She carried the dirty cups to the sink and had her back to me when she asked, 'What would you do, if someone you love begs you to help them?' She was standing with one hand on the tap and I knew she wouldn't move until I answered.

'What sort of help are we talking about?'

'Isn't it obvious?' She came back to the table, still carrying one of the cups.

'Perhaps it's not the right time to have this conversation, Lizzie. Why not wait until the funeral's over? Give yourself some breathing space.'

She dipped a spoon into the brown sugar, lifted and tilted it. We both watched the amber granules slither down, dropping onto the glistening mound in the bowl. The fridge hummed, the wall clock ticked, and I congratulated myself on catching the bombshell before it hit the ground.

But I hadn't caught anything because she continued. 'He never moaned or grumbled. But he did once say that life without Mum was a meaningless interlude. Then, when he became ill, I don't think he could find a good enough reason to keep going.' She paused. 'Let's have a drink.'

She filled two sherry glasses to the brim and I took a sip. The liquid burned my throat and numbed my tongue. She'd poured whisky, not sherry, so I knew things must be serious. 'I can't guarantee I'll remember a single word you've said after this.' I held up my glass.

She took a gulp, screwing up her face, like a child swallowing medicine. 'When he started to go downhill, as you can imagine, he demanded to know the truth. I can't explain, but from the moment the doctor told him that, at best, he had a few months, he seemed relieved; as if she was giving him permission to die; as if he didn't have to keep up the charade, put up with being messed about.' She picked up the bottle and raised her eyebrows, but I covered my glass with my hand.

'Dad never had much patience. Always wanted to get on with things. I suppose I realised he'd decided to give up when he agreed to come and stay with us. Then he started making lists, in one of those spiral-bound pads. People we had to notify. Hymns he hated. Where he'd hidden the key to the bureau. Who should get the really precious things, like his garden fork and the Christmas decorations. And he labelled up whole shoe-boxes full of photographs. *VE Day party. Auntie Nellie at Colwyn Bay. My first car.* Wrapping up a life. Signing out. And all the time we were reminiscing about Mum. That was good for both of us.'

I tried to say something, to give her a chance to pull back, but she held up her hand and stopped me.

'Then, last Wednesday (was it only three days ago?) he stopped making lists. He sent me to fetch his briefcase, from the bungalow. Remember that tatty old thing he used to use for school? It weighed a ton but he'd never let us buy him a new one. Said it was perfect for his sandwich box and apple. D'you know, Mum made him a packed lunch every day in term-time.' She lingered in a memory before going on. 'Guess what he'd been up to? He'd been stockpiling sleeping tablets, probably since he knew how ill he was. Stashing them in the briefcase, in one of those little black tubs that you get thirty-five millimetre films in.'

She stared at her hands, twisting her wedding ring, and described how she had crushed the tablets on a saucer, with the back of a teaspoon, then dissolved them in sweetened tea. How they'd sung bits from *Oklahoma* and *My Fair Lady*, while she'd held his hand, waiting until he drifted into sleep.

'Have you ever watched a dying goldfish? They lose their shine and swim round and round, sort of on their side, just below the surface. Gasping. It's horrible. Once they get to that stage, it's kinder to flush them down the loo. But you can't flush people down the lavatory, can you? I couldn't bear to think of him, gasping his life away.' She shut her eyes and ran her hands through her short hair. The glass in front of her was empty and her cheeks were flushed.

'D'you realise, it took me longer to make up my mind what colour to paint this kitchen than whether I should kill my father?'

'That's a bit melodramatic, Liz. Anyway, how can you kill someone who's dying?' I knew there were flaws in my reasoning, but I continued before she could spot them. 'And there *was* no reason for you to agonise about it. You only need a second to make a decision when there's obviously a right answer. There's probably a lesson to be learned there, if I were sober enough to work it out.' It came out like dialogue that someone else had written, although I meant every word of it. 'What does Philip think?'

'He doesn't know. I need him to be rock-solid for me and I can't take the risk that he'll –'

'Look, Phil knows, we *all* know, how much you adored your father.' It sounded woolly and weak. I took another tack. 'Besides, the doctor signed the death certificate, didn't she? There couldn't have been the slightest doubt in her mind that he was going to die, or she would have ordered an inquest. Wait until you're seeing things straighter,' *straighter* – is that a word?, 'then tell Phil what you've just told me. I think he'll love you all the more.'

She nodded and yawned.

'You're right, as usual. God, I'm so tired. "Sleep no more! Macbeth does murder sleep." I know how the man felt. Every time I shut my eyes, I've got all this stuff going round in my head. Whizzing around. Remember those candyfloss machines on the pier? How the man twirled the stick and gathered up the spun sugar? The inside of my head feels like that. Pink and fluffy and sticky. Have you been to the seaside recently? The stuff comes pre-packed in plastic bags these days. Not even on a stick. That's not candyfloss.' Lizzie folded her arms on the table and flopped her head onto them. The sun caught a cut-glass vase on the draining board, throwing a rainbow on the wall above the cooker. A few streets away, an ice cream van jangled 'We'll Keep a Welcome in the Hillside'.

Lizzie lifted her head and started laughing.

The Essence of Kasyapa

Alexandra North

Ranjid's voice stirred me from my thoughts. I heard Buddha number six and I smiled. Ten miles per Buddha. Dez thought I was smiling at him, so he moved his hand to rest it on my inner thigh, his little finger clumsily shifting back and forth just inside the opening of my shorts. It felt inappropriate and uncomfortable, but I remained still. I tried to recall times when I had enjoyed his touch, but it was too long ago. I looked out of my window and returned my attention to Ranjid's chant-like guide of Sri Lanka.

His was the only voice to be heard for the rest of the journey. The two other couples on this tour had been silent apart from the odd belch from one or a yawn from another. The seats were too close, the heat was suffocating and the smell of each other was oppressive, but still I felt isolated. There was nothing threatening about it. It was liberating.

We were on the main road north – the only road in fact – to Sigirya. The tourist guidebook had labelled it 'the palace in the sky'. The loose rocks made the ride uncomfortable at first, but after a while I felt a sense of reassurance. The jolts gave rhythm, regularity.

Another hour and six Buddhas later, we stopped. Ranjid turned round for the first time that morning. Until then I had only seen his ebony eyes in the rear-view mirror. A well-groomed moustache sat proudly on his upper lip and when he smiled he revealed a mouth overcrowded with teeth, trying to burst out. Though his complexion was healthy he looked tired. It couldn't have been the drive, he took this tour almost every day. Perhaps he had young children, or problems with his wife, or perhaps the war kept him from sleeping.

'Do not let anyone touch your hand or arm. Must keep them like this' – he crossed them – 'or like this' – he put his hands in his pockets – 'but only necessary until you get on first step. Then it doesn't matter who touch you. If someone touch you before first step, they become your guide, will want money at top. I have got you guide. Romesh. You pay him donation, yes? He take you to top of Sigirya. Eight hundred and one steps. Now, you go.' He opened the sliding door at the side and we piled out. I watched everyone enjoy a satisfying stretch.

'Remember your arms, no?' He laughed as we simultaneously folded our arms.

The path leading to Sigirya was almost a mile long. There were remnants of what used to be the Royal Water Gardens either side of this dusty airstrip. Romesh was excitable about these. But there were no flowers, no herbs, no colours, no water.

The Rock itself was impressive in size, 656 feet high apparently. And it could be dated back seven thousand years, Romesh told us. I heard the words *rock-shelter monastery, 3rd century BC, impregnable fortress, palace*, but I was more concerned with getting to the first step. I barely lifted my head for the mile for fear of making eye contact with another guide. I could hear them chanting 'Me take you me take you' and 'Me please me please'. Their feet trooped in front of me. There were Reebok trainers, beige sandals with ageing sports socks peeping through, Doc Martens, even a polished pair of brogues. Suddenly I felt the breath of one of the guides on the back of my neck and I shuddered. I looked to Dez, who walked with his head up, mainly to catch the sun, but with his hands firmly tucked into his armpits. I wanted to ask him to move closer to me, to protect me. But I didn't. Couldn't.

Now my head was up I noticed a large number of native women carrying children. The toddlers going in our direction were behaving intolerably – screaming, hitting. Their mothers ignored them. But the children returning were hushed and calm. I made eye contact with one. He was a child of about three being carried away from the Rock by his mother. He wore a blue and white striped T-shirt, black shorts and no shoes. He did not take his eyes off me as he twiddled a pendant around her neck. My pace slowed and as they got closer he placed his index finger vertically across his lips. Sh sh sh. After they passed he looked over his mother's shoulder and waved. As I raised my arm to wave back, Dez grabbed hold of me. I said I was sorry. When we rejoined the group I glanced back. The boy was gone.

I freed myself from Dez's grip and let my arms fall by my sides. We had reached the first step. I noticed how, even with my toes flush against the next stone, the back of my heel hung over the edge. I could feel myself slipping. 'Is it safe?' I asked Romesh. 'Has anyone fallen from the climb?'

'It is over a thousand years old,' he replied. 'It took seven years to build.'

But was it safe, I asked again.

'Many thousands died.'

'This King, what did he promise these people? He must have been some leader if they were prepared to give their lives just to build his palace.'

'Fortress!' Romesh snapped.

'Impregnable fortress!' I snapped back.

He smiled. 'There are two stories of Kasyapa. One is inscribed on stone slabs by monk called Ananda in fifteenth century. I tell you people's version. It is first story every child on island is told. Taken from Mahavamsa, the ancient historical record of Sri Lanka.' He continued his climb. I followed closely.

'His father was King Dhatusena. Kasyapa wanted very badly the throne. But he not rightful heir. Mogallana, his brother was heir. Kasyapa was what you call bastard child.'

'Who was his mother?'

'She was maid servant to Dhatusena. No one know which one. He liked them all.' When he smiled he showed a mouth like Ranjid's. Teeth everywhere. 'Legend tell us Kasyapa was bitter man. Alone. Afraid of truth. He wanted to be liked, like Mogallana. He saw no other way. He commit parricide.' He placed great emphasis on this word, pushing out the *p*, rolling out the *rr*s and spitting out the *d*. He nudged me, as if asking for praise.

'He killed his parents?' I played his game.

'Yes!' He clapped his hands together. 'Well, just his father. He murdered him alive. Walled up. Left to die. Yes?'

'Yes.'

'Then took throne. Mogallana heard news and was angry. Kasyapa knew he must flee. His brother was building great armies to kill him. So Kasyapa came to Sigirya to build retreat at top. Told people it was palace, but it was fortress. He promised people he would be good King, provide food and water and make lives better if they help him build. So, thousands came to help Kasyapa. Carrying these bricks, dangerous, yes? Transported on their back. Wearing no shoes. Even young children help him.' He stopped and turned to face outwards. We all stopped. The mountains in the distance seemed to reach up in praise of the gods, the jungle bowed its head in prayer and the gentle breeze carried hallelujahs across the sky. Romesh looked across the land as if it were the first time he had seen it. His whole bearing changed: head up, shoulders back, chest out. It was if the spirit of Kasyapa and his men had taken him. A different man stood before me. He wore that same proud look as Ranjid.

'Good so far, yes? It get better at top.' At regular intervals he would come to a stop so we could rest and drink. At first I thought he did this out of consideration, realising that Westerners struggled with the climate. But after a while I believed he was doing it to give us time – to think about Kasyapa, about the men that died.

'Did he have a Queen?'

'He was like his father. He like women. He have five hundred women, more, live here with him.'

'Surely that's just an exaggeration over the years?'

'No. He have every girl painted on walls. At one time, all women painted would have covered entire western face of Rock. Only twelve frescoes left. You will see. Come, come.' We climbed for twenty minutes until we reached a level platform leading into a cave.

'This is first pocket. You take picture, but no flashy flashy. Please meet Apsaras. The Heavenly Maidens. Also translate Cloud Damsels.' On the wall were paintings of three women, all offering one hand skyward. The other hand rested, curved with palm upwards, just beneath their slightly swollen bellies. Their breasts fully exposed. Each dark nipple was perfectly round and erect. The colours were as sharp as the day they had been painted. Golds, emeralds, sapphires and rubies all made, Romesh said, from honey, clay, termite mounds and rice flowers. And the smell – I could not put my finger on it, but I knew it.

Romesh pointed out the jewels entwined around these frescoes. All gifts from Kasyapa. Heavy bracelets encased their forearms, hooped earrings illuminated the gentle outline of their neck, pendants hung towards their bosoms and I realised that it was the towering headwear, filled with treasure, which forced their heads to bow. One of the women was carrying a basket of flowers. Her fingertips, beneath her belly, were almost touching the petals. There was such sadness in her face. She bore her fertility like a burden. Though these women sat side by side, they looked alone.

Then I remembered. That smell. Lilies. I looked around for where it could be coming from.

'Come, come. Nearly half way.'

Another twenty minutes and we reached the Plateau of Red Arsenic. There was a stall here, as promised, selling Cola, Fanta and bottled water, Western survival in an Eastern world. Dez bought a bottle of water and told me I could share it with him, if I wanted. I declined.

Though there was more of a breeze at this height, the heat was still blistering. As I smoothed my hair back from my face, I noticed how gritty my skin felt. The red dust was settling on its visitors, whispering its history in their ears. The others in the group were showing signs of agitation and discomfort, but, to me, this felt right. The locals were not complaining. I understood it was a privilege. Had Dez paid more attention to Romesh, he wouldn't be sitting on the edge of a rock, picking the dirt from his treads, a Lambert and Butler hanging from his mouth.

I turned away from him towards the mountains. I imagined Mogallana's armies trooping relentlessly towards Sigirya; the horizon ablaze with their armoured coats, the hammering of their marching feet, the forbidding war-cries bursting from their lungs. And I pictured Kasyapa, watching them, knowing deep down that this colossal retreat could only protect him for a while. His enemy would find him. Truth would find him.

There were small lakes, randomly scattered in the distance. 'Wells formed from tears of Cloud Damsels.' I felt breath again at the back of my neck. Romesh. 'Story tells us they knew Kasyapa's fate. And they wept, yes? Even Sri Lanka looks like teardrop. On map?' He leaned in close to me and whispered, 'Not even Lion save him.'

'Sorry?'

He swung me round. Right in front of me was the next four hundred steps. The King had built a great Lion, which had stood majestically against a granite cliff, facing North, to fend off the enemy. Its open mouth led to a once-covered staircase. All that remained now of the stone Lion were the enormous paws. They looked worn and scarred but Romesh assured me that they were once as bright as the blazing star itself. He stood me against one of the claws, which was bigger than any of us, and called for Dez to take a picture. I suddenly felt my insignificance. A click and a flash and I was back.

'Come, come. You finish rest, no? Next is Kat Bitha.'

This turned out to be a lime-plaster wall which enclosed the walkway. It was so highly polished you could see the reflections of the fresco paintings from the opposite side. When the sun caught it, this screen could be seen from miles away. Was this Kasyapa's way of showing his greatness or did he want to guide his brother's armies to him?

This mirrored wall had been veiled with graffiti. A script in ancient Sinhalese told the story of how the palace was built. But, Romesh told us, there was no one left to translate. The Rock was shrouded in secrets.

The air was getting thinner and I felt my breathing becoming short. I could not control it – it was controlling me. I looked around to see if anyone else was struggling. Dez had another fag hanging from his mouth, but it was not lit. His face seemed a little swollen and his forehead gleamed like Kat Bitha. This made me smile. I inhaled deeply through my nose. Romesh turned to me and told me not to fight it. 'Meditation good, yes?'

When I stopped thinking about my breathing it became much easier, and my other senses burst into life. I could smell salt in the air, taste it, feel the cooler air drying the grainy sweat from my hands. I could see for miles around, overwhelmed by the height we had already climbed. I was exhilarated. I felt alive.

Looking below I could see two great stones, both shaped like elephants, at the base of the Rock. Romesh said that these stones were natural, nothing had been added, merely emphasised. It was as if these elephants had been born to protect Kasyapa, that they knew of the palace's conception before its birth.

'Why elephants?'

He told me they were the symbol of strength and memory. The remarkable size of their ears showed they were widely knowledgeable – this played significant role in warfare, yes?

'Does he represent Ganesh?'

He laughed. 'Only if you are Hindu.'

I apologised. I hadn't meant to cause offence. I thought carefully before I asked another question. 'If you had to sum Buddhism up in one word, what would it be?'

He took my hand. His skin was hard, like parchment paper, and stained different shades of brown. His fingers were small and wrinkled, yet the creases in them were fresh and white.

'Truth. That is the one word. For if you can find it you will one day reach Nirvana. Follow the Four Noble Truths, yes?' He let my hand slip from his. As we continued to climb I raised my hand to my nose. I could smell bread. I could smell him.

The rest of the ascent was silent. We heard no more of Kasyapa. All we could hear were the rhythms of our sighings and wheezings. And finally, two hours after leaving the minibus, the island knelt before us.

It seemed to open something inside Dez. Just when I was trying to feel the emptiness, the solitude, he came up close behind me.

'I can feel it, you know... the resentment.'

I told him I didn't know what he was talking about.

He grabbed my arm. 'Look at me.' He pulled me round to face him and cupped my cheeks gently in his hands.

I looked through him.

'Please. Look at me.' He was calm. 'Even now, you can't help it – judging, criticising, tearing me to pieces with that look.' His voice was unthreatening. 'Two and a half years I've waited for that look to go away.'

I focused on the mountains, the sky.

'When it's not in your eyes, it's in your lips. When it's not in your lips it's in the palm of your hands, the base of your spine, the top of your thigh. You can't conceal it. But you could explain it.' He lowered his hands, took a step back.

I told him I couldn't explain. I had already tried. He never listened.

'No.' His voice was trembling slightly. 'You run. You always have.'

'You can't force me to...'

'I'm not the enemy.' His shoulders sank, his head bowed, and there was no towering headwear to weigh it down. 'I've never been the enemy.'

'This is ridiculous.' I tried talking through a smile, so that no one else could see our awkwardness.

'Ridiculous?' He raised his pitch, but not his volume. 'The way I smoke my cigarettes disgusts you. When I clean the crap off my shoes it makes you angry. I make your stomach turn when I touch you. When we do make love you look the other way.'

'You're exaggerating! I don't care about your cigarettes or your trainers or...'

'Me? You don't care about me?'

I walked away from him.

'There's nowhere to run to,' he shouted. He was right of course. But a few feet was as good as a hundred miles. I tried to lose myself in the landscape. The mountains looked like whales, diving through the ocean of sky, the curve of their backs never quite escaping the surface.

'Graceful, yes?' Romesh was stood behind my right shoulder.

I nodded. 'What happened in the end to Kasyapa?' I kept my gaze on the mountains.

'He kill himself ' There was no passion in his tone. He was simply matter-of-fact.

'What about his frescoes, his men, his brother?'

'Some live, some die. Mogallana become King.'

'And that's it? That's the legend of Kasyapa? You build him up like some kind of idol and then you tell me he commits suicide. And this is the first story every child is told? What can that possibly instill in them?' I felt betrayed.

'The pocket I take you to, what did you smell?'

'Lilies. But what has that –?'

'Me, I smell fresh bread. My grandfather was in England in 1920s. He come home and teach grandmother to bake bread. She die in 1974, but every time I come here, I smell same smell. Everybody smell something different.'

'That's a nice story, Romesh, but ...'

'You not listen. I come here every day, sometimes one, sometimes two. I enter pocket and I remember who I am, where I come from, what is important to me. What are lilies to you?' He rested his hand on my shoulder.

'I don't know. I just like them.'

'No. That not it.'

'What would you know?'

He turned me to face him. 'You must face truth. That is what Kasyapa tell us. We teach our children that he was remarkable man. We show them greatest monument to his memory, the palace in the sky. But he could have been greater man if he faced enemy. No running away. No time for falsehood. Then you move forward.'

I felt sick and faint. A stream of cold air entwined itself around my neck. I asked him if Kasyapa's spirit was in that first pocket, that first cave.

'No, no. It is in you.'

I looked across at Dez. He had lit the cigarette which had been clinging to his lips. As he exhaled the smoke spiraled in front of him, thinning into nothing. He looked across at me. I was still shaking. We met each other in the middle.

'You never cried for him.' I felt as though we were completely on our own.

'Not in front of you, no.'

'You never talk about him.'

'Not out loud.' He went to put his half-smoked cigarette out on the ground.

'You don't have to ... the cigarette ... I don't mind.' My voice was hushed. 'I lost my boy and you did nothing.'

'I lost him too and I did everything I could to make it easier for you.'

'I went through it alone.'

He replied that he was always by me. I just never saw him.

Romesh broke our silence and called us over to him. 'Give me camera. I take picture, yes? You must stand here.' He pointed to a large stone slab which lay alone. 'You have climbed eight hundred steps, no? This, eight hundred and one. Please, me take picture.'

Dez took the camera from round his neck and handed it across to Romesh. We looked at each other for a moment, unsure as to what to do next. I held my hand out to him and together we climbed the last step. He rubbed his little finger against the joint of my thumb. I did not mind.

'Big smile.'

We could see for miles around – the jungle, the main road, the narrow dusty airstrip at the start of our ascent. I looked at the people who stood with us at the top. A mother began to climb back down the Rock, a young child in her arms. He was about three years old, wearing a blue and white striped T-shirt, black shorts and no shoes. He looked over his mother's shoulder straight at me. I raised my finger and placed it vertically across my lips.

'Who are you looking at?' Dez asked.

I turned him in the right direction, but the boy and his mother had gone.

Romesh called our group together to begin our journey back down. As we descended the first steps, I asked Dez if he had smelt anything in the first pocket with the frescoes. He told me he could smell my perfume. I wasn't wearing any.

The Cat's Real Name

Cal Walters

Bix wandered to the edge of the field and turned his head towards the west, where he believed the sea to be, and thought of his wayward brindled cousin. Jubl lived his life at sea, lucky one, with all the adventure his wild heart could desire and all the fish he could eat.

Mum says that cats are usually given people's names, like Tom or Suzie, or are named for what colour they are because their owners have small imaginations and the cats put up with it gracefully. Or they're named after dayatees. I don't know what that is, she says it's a bit better; but no one knows the cat's real name, the name he calls himself. And then she said that I was really clever and could probably find out. She told me that Brambles already had that name when we got him and he didn't really mind us using it. Then she called him, and I could see that he did look at us as if he thought we were a bit stupid, but didn't mind.

'Animals have to put up with lots of silly human ways,' she said, 'but they're very patient and understanding.'

Some people are too, but not many.

Bix regarded the furry insect with an expression of hauteur.

Miss Williams told me to try to read other books instead of just animal books. I don't know why. Why would I want to read about what people do and think? That's boring. I know people, I know what's in their heads. Dad wants a new car and Kirsty wants to kiss that older boy in school. Why would I want to read about stuff like that when I can read about animal's adventures? Anything Bix does is much better than anything my stupid sister could ever do.

He follows me to school every morning and waits at Laylock Corner until I come back. I don't really think he stays there all day, but he's always there when school finishes. I cross the playing fields and Leigh Road and turn into our road and there he is by the old stone wall. Sometimes he's sitting on it so he can butt his head against my shoulder before jumping to the ground and walking home with me. Those parts of the walk to school and the walk home are the best, with Bix at my side. Bix doesn't need to go to school. He's clever enough. And when I cross Leigh Road I always look back at him as he sits watching me. I look for as long as I can, before I turn the corner and lose sight of him. I fix him in my mind to protect me when I enter that other place, the chaos of the classroom and the playground, with shouting and sneering and games I don't understand, far from my secret world at home in the gardens and fields with Bix. Some mornings, leaving Bix is so hard and so cruel, I go off into a corner of the playground and cry. But most of the time I get my strength from him; the way he watches as I walk on, as if he's saying don't worry, all of that isn't real, it's our world that matters. And I can't wait for school to end so I can run across the green and over the road to Laylock Corner to meet him.

Bix paused at the edge of the garden by the weeping willow, one paw raised, because he knew he was nearing the territory of Ohb.

I found a way to discover a cat's real name. I tried it with Bix first, of course. Dad had a strange pack of cards which had letters instead of numbers. I sat on the floor with Bix and turned one card over. It was a 'B'. I thought it might spell out 'Brambles', the dopey name he had when we got him. But then I turned over 'I', then 'X', and he butted my knee with his head. So that was it: 'Bix'.

I said 'Bix?' and watched his expression carefully. He smiled. Cats smile by blinking very slowly, as if happiness to them is partway to sleep.

I found the names for all the cats in our part of the village in the same way. I had to reuse the vowel cards so that the names would make sense in human language. The cat would give a sign when you had turned over enough cards: by looking at you suddenly and directly, or the more talkative ones would meow, or they gave you a sign just by walking away. I would say these names to myself when I left Bix and continued on my way to school alone: Bix, Lise, Teva, Aku, Jubl, Mazer, Ohb.

I don't think it would go so unremarked these days – a child spending so much time alone. Maybe nobody realised. When I wasn't at home I was at my grandmother's and there wasn't much communication between her and Dad, despite the fact that her house was only a couple of streets away. She gave up trying to help him when he started drinking. So neither of them knew what I got up to. Dad thought Nanna was looking after me and Nanna thought Dad was, and I didn't say anything to correct them. These days there would have been child psychologists and god knows what else making sure I was okay. Nanna had an endless stream of visitors and was happy to let me do my own thing. Most of the time I would just run in through the front door and straight out the back. Dad only seemed interested in whether or not I was eating.

'You eaten?' he would bark from the front room, and as long as I recounted my meals he left me to it. It never occurred to me to wonder if he was eating. Kirsty was eight years older than me and hardly ever at home. She had a boyfriend who lived in town and she was always staying with him. At the time I wondered briefly why Dad hadn't gone nuts about that and made her stay at home, but then he didn't seem too bothered about anything. It wasn't long before she'd left home completely.

Marianne showed me her teenage diaries the year before we married. They were sensible and grounded, with only the occasional teenage flight of fantasy about a teacher she idolised or her own future as a brilliant doctor. When she asked me if I had kept anything similar from my childhood I told the truth – that I had only written stories about my cat.

Marianne was secure in the centre of life, whereas I was haunting the edges. I knew that it didn't look like that to other people because I involved myself in everything, especially where the children were concerned. But that was just it – they were my way of clinging to childhood; they could have been anyone's children. I liked to look at them from their bedroom doorway, peering around the door to watch while they were absorbed in their own worlds: James so busy and practical like his mother, Katy so dreamy and distant, like me, I supposed. But I found it hard to think of them as mine. Of course they were my children, and I could see it in them, those flashes of personality or gesture, but, if they sometimes looked like me, they didn't feel like mine. I couldn't possess them. If they were anybody's, they belonged to Marianne. She wanted children, a boy and a girl, the boy first, which is what she got. I hadn't not wanted them. She got herself pregnant, really, by doing whatever she had needed to do – by taking something out or not putting something in. Of course, Marianne knew how I felt about the children, she wasn't stupid, but I'm not sure how seriously she took it because, as she often pointed out, we were happy. She told me I had hidden depths, and I thought she was taking the mick. She told me I was a good man and I believed that a bit more. I'm not aggressive and I'm a bit shy, which might translate into good. It didn't matter how close I was to the children, there would always be something more between them and Marianne. Something I couldn't ever share. I could be warmed from a distance and that was all I hoped for.

Marianne had always been comfortable in her flesh. I saw each of them ripped from that flesh, hardly able to tell where she ended and they began. It changed her, no matter how many preparations she had made for motherhood, being a mother somehow made her self – her soul – bigger. I felt smaller by comparison. I had wanted becoming a parent to change me for the better, but the most noticeable change I felt was a more pronounced sense of fear. I was afraid for the children, as new parents should be, I suppose, but I was also afraid of them, of their unabashed primal vitality and humanity, their unspoken but absolute claim to life. And their flesh was hers; mine remained insubstantial.

This was love, I told myself, as I watched the children playing. They were love. But I felt empty, emptied. I wanted to cry, but I didn't know where to start and feared I might never be able to stop.

In bed with Marianne I still yearned for the peace and security when I could feel the discreet weight of the cat on my bed, curled at my feet. If I ever had a bad dream I could reach down and dip my fingers in the warm, breathing fur. I almost couldn't bear to remember it now. Sometimes I would reach out in the night for Marianne, but it usually woke her up and she would say, 'Darling, you're lying on my hair again.'

I tell stories to the children, stories about a golden cat called Bix. Simple stories with titles like *Bix's Battle* or *Bix Dreams of Ships* (Katy's favourite) or *Bix Annoys a Bumblebee*. Marianne thinks I'm inventive for making them up, and a good father for telling the children stories every night.

But I need to tell these stories more than they need to hear them; I think James is already starting to believe that they're too childish for him. I wonder how I'll feel when they both want more than the adventures of a magical cat. Soon they'll be hooked on the more convincing magic of computer games and I'll be left to remember Bix on my own. Will I then slip back to that silent, introverted little character I was as a child? Or will I lose touch with childhood completely, their childhood, my childhood, and be stranded in the adult world? Without this haven, this blissful bedtime moment, the enchanted half hour when I can watch the barrier between reality and fantasy break down in the children's minds, as their eyelids flutter, as their eyes slowly close. There isn't a single night that I don't wonder how I got here, a father of two children, clinging to their childish minds as the only link back to my own. And I think of the strange, isolated child I was who could never have imagined the life he has now, who was frozen within that little world of paths and hedges and gardens, of that walk to school with a golden cat.

I've always been tracing and retracing that walk, in my mind's eye, in my dreams, in my stories. It's all starting to feel like something else, something separate from me, like a myth or a children's story and nothing more. Marianne thinks I should write them down and turn them into a book, but that would only drive my memories further away. Maybe by telling these stories to the children, in an attempt to hold on to my childhood, to Bix, I've actually lost it, turned a corner and lost sight of how it really was. When they get older, I doubt if I'll have much of a relationship with them. But they'll always be close to their mother, so they'll be alright.

Bix died when I was eleven. He was hit by a car on Leigh Road and I was convinced he must have been coming to find me, that he had finally decided to leave Laylock Corner and cross the threshold into the world I had to face every day. I never saw his body; a neighbour read his collar and told Nanna and she disposed of him. It was only then that I gave in to a vast and nameless darkness that had been waiting somewhere just out of my field of vision. I can't remember much about that time; it was probably only a matter of days that I stayed in my room, lost in grief. I remember the sense of relief from Dad, Nanna and the other grown-ups around.

'He's finally coming to terms with Sarah's death' they were saying. 'We knew it would come in time, the shock of losing his mother so young was too much for him. He'll be all right now he can grieve.'

But it doesn't feel like some kind of emotional progression, ordered like the passing of days. It's all jumbled up and grief, like a painter's wash, has tinted everything. I can say: my mother died, then my cat died, and I could grieve. I could grieve and I could remember her, whispering from her cracked lips, her drawn colourless face, 'Bix will look after you, yes, I know his name.' But it's the same as having to remind myself what day it is, or what season. All the summers melt into one, one summer chasing a golden cat through a field.

Biographical Notes

Patricia Ace was born in Cleethorpes in 1969 to a Welsh father and West Indian mother. Many of her family still live in Swansea. Patricia has had many poems and stories published in magazines all over the UK and has won prizes in several poetry competitions. In 2003 she published *Intensive Care*, a short collection of poems in pamphlet form. A second collection comes out from Happenstance Press in 2006. Patricia is a member of Lippy Bissoms who perform all over Scotland with their cabaret-style poetry show. Patricia is currently living in Crieff, Scotland, where she teaches yoga and creative writing and continues to write herself.

Linda Baxter used to live in London. In 1990 she gave up teaching Modern Languages in order to write, but suffered a subarachnoid haemorrhage which damaged the language centre of her brain. She began the slow and arduous process of re-learning her mother tongue. In 1996 she moved to west Wales and found the inspiration to write again. When her son Timo was murdered writing became a release valve for her grief, pain and anger, and her book *Losing Timo* was published by Honno in 2004. *A Journey to Berlin 1964* is her first published fiction.

Lara Clough started writing seriously after attending a course at Ty Newydd writing centre in North Wales. In 2004 she was awarded a writer's bursary from the Academi to complete her first novel, *Facing into the West Wind* (Honno 2006). Lara lives near Presteigne and is now studying for an MA in Creative and Media Writing at Swansea University, as well as running writing workshops in her area.

Sue Coffey was born in Aberdare but fetched up in Cyprus on a 'three year posting' that lasted twenty years. She caught the writing bug there and had several stories published in magazines. A writing week in Ty Newydd led to her joining the South and Mid Wales Association of Writers (sadly missed) and she won awards in 2004 and 2005. She's also had all of seventeen syllables published in *Mslexia*. She is now happily living in Cardiff and commuting to Swansea University for the MA in Creative Writing course. She is a member of Writers Bloc – an eclectic collective. This is the first of her stories to find a home in an anthology.

Lesley Coburn says, 'Over the years, my academic prose became more open, less objective. After the death of my father, Ron Berry, I was moved to write creatively. My obscure poetry and prose make me laugh, my realistic stories make me cry. I suppose it all comes down to a reflective attitude, watching myself play language games with myself. It matters.'

Brenda Curtis has lived in mid Wales since 1985. She originally trained as a nurse and midwife and has since worked in a variety of jobs. She had three children, gained an Open University degree in Social Science, and is still arguing with the same husband. Her chosen writing fields are poetry and short fiction.

Nicola Daly studied English and History at Wrexham and now lives in Chester. She has had several poems and short stories published in small press magazines, and a story in Honno's previous collection *Mirror Mirror*. In 2002 her science fiction novel *Thinking of England* was published by Pegasus.

Patricia Duncker has edited two other short fiction anthologies for Honno with Janet Thomas *The Woman who Loved Cucumbers* (2002) and *Mirror, Mirror* (2004). She has published four novels, *Hallucinating Foucault* (1996), *James Miranda Barry* (1999), *The Deadly Space Between* (2002), and *Miss Webster and Cherif* (Bloomsbury, 2006) as well as two collections of short fiction. She is now Professor of Modern Literature at the University of Manchester. She lives in Aberystwyth.

Vanessa Gebbie spent a large part of her childhood in Merthyr Tydfil, where both her parents were born. She went to boarding school in Dolgellau at 13, and can still sing hymns in Welsh. She now lives and works in Sussex. She is a journalist; her fiction has been widely published in print and on the web. Her competition successes include a First Prize awarded by Zadie Smith. Her work has been broadcast by the BBC. She teaches creative writing as therapy at a drugs rehab in Brighton, and leads a writing group for the homeless run by a community publisher. She is founder and editor of *Tom's Voice Magazine*, a specialist web based literary magazine for writing from people whose lives have been touched by the traumas of addiction. She is married with two sons. For further information: www.vanessagebbie.com or www.tomsvoicemagazine.com

Imogen Rhia Herrad is a freelance writer and journalist based in London and Berlin. Born in 1967 in Germany, she has also lived in Wales and Argentina. She writes about travel, social and cultural history and politics for German public radio in German; and fiction and non-fiction in English. Her work has been published in Germany, the UK and Canada. Imogen has written a book of short stories, *Lives of the Saints* (Seren, 2007), and a mystery novel set in London and Wales for which she is now seeking a publisher. She is currently working on a book about her Patagonian travels. Imogen's story 'The Accident' was shortlisted for a prize at the Quality Women's Fiction 10th Anniversary Competition in 2004, and the 2006 Raymond Carver Awards.

Sarah Jackman was born in Berlin and has lived variously in England, Germany and France. She moved to Wales in 2004 and to Swansea in 2005 where she intends to settle. Her first novel *Laughing as they Chased us* was published in 2005 by Simon & Schuster (Pocket Books); who will publish her second novel *The Other Lover* in January 2007. She is a recipient of a 2006-2007 Academi Writer's Bursary and is currently working on her third novel and a collection of short stories. Sarah also works part-time for the fine arts organisation, Swansea Print Workshop.

Ruth Joseph from Cardiff graduated with an M.Phil in Writing from Glamorgan University, and was approached by Accent Press to publish *Red Stilettos*, her collection of short stories. She is a Rhys Davies and Cadenza prize-winner, and won the Lichfield Short Story prize. She has had work published by Honno, Accent Press, *New Welsh Review*, *Loki*, and *Cambrensis*. Her memoir, *Remembering Judith*, chronicles her situation as child carer to an anorexic mother traumatised from the after-effects of the Holocaust. Her husband Mervyn, family and rescue

Labrador are a source of inspiration, and comfort.

Dahlian Kirby was born in a small industrial town in the North-east of England and moved to Cardiff in 1976 to attend the Royal Welsh College of Music and Drama. After several moves around Cardiff and to London, Sweden and Leeds, she now lives in Boverton in the Vale of Glamorgan with her husband, son and pets. She teaches part-time, writes part-time and occasionally gives a lecture in philosophy at Cardiff University. Dahlian enjoys sitting in her garden with a glass of wine talking to her hens.

Carolyn Lewis was born in Cardiff in 1947. Married twice with three daughters and six grandchildren, she now lives in Bristol. Writing since she was eight years old, her work has been published by Honno, Accent Press, Redcliffe Press, *Mslexia*, *QWF*, *Route* and *Libbon* magazine. Her stories have won a number of national and local competitions. Last year she came second in the Mathew Prichard Award and she was also shortlisted for the Asham Award. Currently working on a novel and a collection of short stories, Carolyn also teaches creative writing. In 2003 she graduated from the University of Glamorgan with an M.Phil in Writing.

Barbara MacGaughey was brought up and educated in Wales and spent the first few years of her career teaching English to the English in London and overseas. She returned to Wales in the late 1960s. Now retired, she lives in Swansea. She has a daughter, a son and three grandsons.

Melanie Mauthner is an Oxford graduate. She studied French and Spanish Literature and has worked as a television researcher and social science lecturer. In the 1990s she was involved in setting up and teaching Women's Studies at Swansea University. She spent many years talking to women about their sisters and then wrote *Sistering: Power and Change in Female Relationships* (Palgrave 2006). She started writing short fiction in 2002 and her first story, 'Prudence', appeared in *My Cheating Heart* (Honno 2005). A second story, 'The Runner', was published in *Parenthesis* a year later (Comma Press 2006). She lives in South London.

Sue Morgan grew up in various parts of the world including Swansea, studied English at Sussex University and trained to be a teacher in Brighton. She moved to Cardiff to raise a family in 1990 and now works part-time as a tutor in adult education. One of her classes takes place in the National Museum, where she also designed a writing trail inspired by objects on display in the archaeology department. She has written short film scripts and her stories have appeared in previous Honno anthologies and on Radio 4. She is writing a novel, with the help of a bursary from Academi.

Laura Morris, having completed an MA in Creative Writing, worked as a bookseller, fruit-picker and proof-reader. She is now an English teacher, living in Caerphilly and struggling to learn to drive.

Alexandra North teaches in Cyprus. She completed her M.Phil in Writing with the University of Glamorgan in 2006, having finished a collection of short stories and a novella entitled 'Running the Whiteboard', the latter based on her experiences as a Moneybroker in London. She has also published *Adagio* with Leaf Books (2006). She is now married and has a dog, a car and a garden.

Lesley Philips was brought up as part of a large family in the South Australian outback. By the time she returned to Wales with her family she had completed her primary education with the Australian School of the Air. She has now nestled contentedly and permanently into her beloved Pembrokeshire. Lesley has two grown-up sons and one granddaughter. She works for a local woollen mill in the workroom. Lesley went to her first creative writing class with a friend who persuaded her she would enjoy it and it would do her good. That was six years ago. This is the first story she has ever had published…so far. Lesley drives around in a beaten-up old Mazda called Gladys, and prefers red wine to white, tea rather than coffee. Loves log fires, bonfires and the beach in winter.

Angela Rigby was born in Kent and has lived in Wales for twenty-eight years. After obtaining a Diploma in Public and Social Administration at Oxford, she worked for a voluntary Children's Society and then for a local authority in an experimental project in residential child care. She now lives in Cardiff. Her work has been published in *Social Work Today, Cambrensis, New Welsh Review*, the *South Wales Golfer*, the *Collins Anthology of New Christian Verse* (1990), the *York Poetry Society Magazine*, and in Honno's short story anthology *The Woman Who Loved Cucumbers* (2002).

Penny Simpson began writing full-time as a journalist in Sussex. Gomer Press published *DOGdays,* her debut collection of short fiction, in 2003. She now lives in Cardiff and works for Welsh National Opera. She has just completed a new collection of short stories with the help of an Academi bursary – and her friends in Llanos de la Cruz, Andalucía.

Jenny Sullivan was born in Cardiff, the fourth daughter of six children. She left school at 15 without qualifications and at the age of 50 bit the bullet and did an MA at Cardiff University. She gained a PhD there in July 2002. She is a prolific children's author – her many published books include *Gwydion and the Flying Wand, The Magic Apostrophe* and *The Caterpillar That Couldn't* – and won the Tir na n-Og Award in 2006 for *Tirion's Secret Journal.* She has also had several short stories published and her work has featured in five previous Honno anthologies. Jenny has three grown-up daughters, one adorable grand-daughter, Daisy, and one lovely and long-suffering husband.

Sarah Todd Taylor moved from Yorkshire to Ceredigion at the age of eight. She graduated from the University of Wales, Aberystwyth in 1998 with a PhD in early modern ballad writing, which has yet to feed into her fiction writing. Her short stories have featured in two previous Honno anthologies and she has ambitions to finally finish a larger piece of work. She lives in Aberystwyth with a supportive husband and a succession of hamsters.

Janet Thomas is a freelance editor, living in Aberystwyth. She has edited previous short story anthologies including two with Patricia Duncker, *The Woman Who Loved Cucumbers* and *Mirror Mirror.* She has published short stories and her children's picture book *Can I Play?* (Egmont) won a *Practical Pre-School* gold award.

Stephanie Tillotson is a native of South Wales. After university Stephanie originally trained as an actor and spend some time specializing in the portrayal of mad queens, usually of the Greek variety. She worked for over a decade in theatre, radio and television – including a period in television production at the BBC – before co-founding WellMade Theatre, a classical company based in Cardiff. It was during this period that Stephanie experienced a road to Damascus moment whilst exploring *Macbeth* with a group of students at a school in Merthyr Tydfil. Since then she has worked almost exclusively with young people as an actor, writer, director and teacher. For the past three years, Stephanie has taught Acting at the Department of Theatre, Film and Television Studies, University of Wales, Aberystwyth. She is a performed and published playwright and poet. 'One for Rose Cottage' is her first short story to appear in print.

Jo Verity began writing in 1999 – mainly to see if she could. In 2003 she won the Richard & Judy Short Story Competition and in 2004, the *Western Mail* Short Story Competition. One of her stories was broadcast on Radio 4 and many have appeared in magazines and anthologies. Her first novel, *Everything in the Garden*, was published by Honno in 2005 and her second, *Bells*, will be published, also by Honno, in May 2007. Jo lives in Cardiff.

Cal Walters has lived in Aberystwyth for almost half her life, having originally studied at Aberystwyth University for a BA Hons and M.Phil in English Literature (on Virginia Woolf and Anais Nin). She has been running her own secondhand bookshop Aber Books & Collectables in Northgate Street, since starting it with her partner in April 2005, and is very happy that her life revolves around books. She writes short stories and poetry and is currently working on a novel.

Short story anthologies also from Honno

Mirror Mirror

Edited by Patricia Duncker and Janet Thomas

The wars between women – wife and mistress, first and second wife, moth and daughter, Welsh and English, the stay-at-home and the working moth – are fought out with fresh energy in this collection. Equally vivid is th longing – for lovers, fantasies, mothers, dreams, and for the other women w wish we were.

Includes stories from Patricia Duncker, Elin ap Hywel, Jo Mazelis, An Oosthuizen and Jenny Sullivan.

ISBN – 1870206576 EAN – 97818702065

My Cheating Heart

Edited by Kitty Sewell

There's nothing foreign to the human heart, but there's lots that's forbidden a plenty that's hidden...

This anthology, collected on the theme of infidelity, includes work by Jo Veri Jenny Sullivan, Ruth Joseph, and Melanie Mauthner, and each of the writ has fashioned a gem from the grit in the oyster of the human heart.

ISBN – 1870206738 EAN – 97818792967

First Fiction from Honno

·acing into the West Wind

.ara Clough

'ell is glad to be back at her family's summer house on Gower, after losing ·t another job. Here she can be safe. But this year, her brother has brought is friend Jason to stay. Jason has a gift – a face people confess to. Nell finds erself drawn to him, as do her brother and her mother. But is Jason strong 1ough to handle the confessions he's going to hear?

An evocative first novel about family, secrets and love.

ISBN – 1870206797 EAN – 97818070206792

.verything in the Garden

Verity

'Clear winner' Richard & Judy

ına Wren and her husband buy a rambling farmhouse in Wales with three ıer couples, intending to grow old with the support of trusted friends. But the relationships that have shaped her life start to crumble, Anna is forced confront the changing nature of her own desire and the consequences of ·ing in…

ISBN – 1870206703 EAN – 9781870206709

About Honno

Honno Welsh Women's Press was set up in 1986 by a group of wome who felt strongly that women in Wales needed wider opportuniti to see their writing in print and to become involved in the publishin process. Our aim is to develop the writing talents of women in Wale give them new and exciting opportunities to see their work publishe and often to give them their first 'break' as a writer.

Honno is registered as a community co-operative. Any profit th Honno makes goes towards the cost of future publications. Since it w established over 450 women from Wales and around the world ha expressed their support for its work by buying shares at £5 each in t co-operative. We hope that many more women will be able to help in this way. Shareholders' liability is limited to the amount investe and each shareholder, regardless of the number of shares held, can ha her say in the company and a vote at the Annual General Meeting.

To buy shares or to receive further information about forthcomi publications, please write to Honno at the address below, or visit o website: **www.honno.co.uk**.

Honno
'Ailsa Craig'
Heol y Cawl
Dinas Powys
Bro Morgannwg
CF64 4AH